# DEATH OF A GOOD SAMARITAN

## WILLIAM SAVAGE

Ridge & Bourne

# ACKNOWLEDGMENTS

My particular thanks go to my wife, Jenn, who produced the "Map of Millgate, Aylsham (1794)" and has supported me in endless ways through all my writing.

# FOREWORD

As in my previous books, I have combined real places with imaginary ones to provide the background to this story. The Bure Navigation is real enough and survived until 1912. The Anchor Inn survives as private house. What was once the maltings also survives as a row of cottages. The brewery is a product of my imagination, as is Millgate Manor and the surgeon's house, from which he set out to meet with his death. Even the great mill, which still spans the river, has become luxury apartments. The gap between Millgate and Aylsham itself has long been filled in, so that it seems more obviously a part of Aylsham that it would have done in 1794.

*William Savage*

# MILLGATE MAP

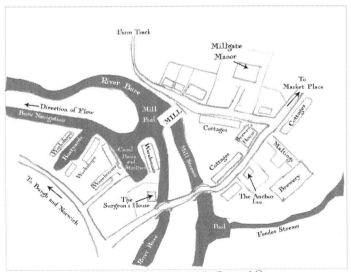

Millgate, Aylsham and The Bure Navigation
(circa 1794)

In any conspiracy, every decision leads to another, driven by the characters of the people involved and whatever seems best to them at the time. Event succeeds event. Choice follows upon choice. In that manner, step by step, the group proceeds towards a destination ultimately determined as much by chance as design. Thus, as it was in the small Norfolk market town of Aylsham in April, 1794 — only this time all the steps were leading inexorably to murder.

In that month, an observer standing at the edge of a small wood on the brow of a hill running down to the River Bure would have seen two men making their way through the trees. They were an odd pair. The one in front was tall and wore good leather boots, moleskin breeches and a coat suitable for a day's shooting. He also held a fine gun under his left arm. It was hard to tell his age with precision, for he looked neither young nor old. A man of middle years then, still in his prime, most likely with a face weathered by the vagaries of the English climate. It was impossible to be sure, since his hat was set at an angle. Whether this was to protect his face from the wind or conceal his identity was unclear. To all outward appearances, he was a country squire, walking the lands of his estate in the hope of bagging a hare or a brace of partridges for the pot. If that image was not exactly correct, it would be close enough to the truth to deceive any casual observer — had one been present. He certainly liked to be seen as a squire, though his small estate was recently purchased and his status as a gentleman entirely of his own creation. It was he who had insisted on meeting in this lonely spot, far from prying eyes.

The second man was completely out of place in such a rural setting. He was a short fellow, with sallow, pock-marked skin, a large paunch and was on the wrong side of middle age. He was also unused to walking far. Even his pallid, smooth complexion showed him to be the kind who kept himself indoors as much as he could. The clothes he wore were strikingly unsuitable for the countryside, for he was dressed in a dark frock-coat of conventional cut with matching breeches, both decorated with embroidery in gold and silver threads. On his head was an old-fashioned periwig and a somewhat shabby tricorn hat. He had been struggling to keep up with his companion for some time, and not helped by continually looking at his feet, unhappy about the amount of mud which had fouled his shoes. He had no gun and would not have known what to do with it if he had. In his experience, rabbits, hares and other kinds of meat were best obtained, neatly prepared, from a butcher.

Everything about the fellow said he spent all his time with paper and ink. In this case, unlike his companion's, appearance was in no way deceptive. The scowl on his face spoke eloquently of his deep dislike of being dragged away from his natural, indoor surroundings and plunged into a place as remote to him as the jungles of Africa or the plains of North America.

The two men had met some fifteen minutes earlier on the driveway to the tall man's house. The shorter one hoped this was simply a matter of convenience and they would retire inside, hopefully to sit in a warm room and lubricate their discussion with several glasses of sack or canary. When it became clear that was not to be, and his companion insisted on going somewhere where they could not be overheard, he expected to retire to an outhouse or barn. Somewhere warm and dry and out of sight of the house and the road. Instead, the tall fellow plunged aside into a shrubbery, then led him up increasingly muddy paths at what felt to be breakneck speed, until he arrived, quite out of breath, at this place on a slope above the river.

'Keep up, damn you!' the tall man said as they came out from amongst the trees. 'If you took some healthy exercise each day, as I do, you wouldn't puff and blow like that. It wouldn't do you any harm to eat a good deal less as well. Look at you! And those clothes! I told you we would have to walk a little way to find a place where we could be secret. And what do you do? You come dressed for a day spent in the town. You look ridiculous!'

'If you're so ashamed of how I look,' the short man said, punctuating his words with more gasps for air, 'we should have stayed back there among the trees. No one would see us there, would they? I have no clothes like yours, since I never submit myself to the dangers of these damp, squalid fields. Dear God! How this wind cuts into my very flesh. Let's find somewhere more sheltered, where the trees are thickest and offer most protection. If we stand here much longer, I shall doubtless be struck down by a violent ague.'

'Idiot!' the tall one snapped back. 'Two men skulking in a dense wood? Can you imagine anything more likely to excite suspicion? Besides, woods are full of hiding places for those who want to overhear what they should not. Out here, we can see anyone approaching long before they're near enough to be a danger. If you'll only bestir yourself to step further away from the trees, even someone hiding behind the nearest ones will be too distant to hear what we are saying.'

'Look at my shoes!' the other wailed. 'Covered in mud!'

His companion was fast losing patience. 'Shoes get covered in mud in the streets of the town after a rainstorm. It washes off. Stop complaining and let's get down to discussing what brought us here. If it were not for the crisis we are now facing, we would not be meeting at all. I have always made it a rule that we should not be seen together, if it can be avoided in any way. The safety of our little venture depends on it being invisible. Now I'm risking being seen talking to someone I have taken great care should be reckoned as no more than a remote acquaintance.'

'You could have written.'

'This is not something to be committed to paper, believe me.'

'Anyway, this isn't such a wonderful place to meet, is it?' The short one had not yet had his fill of complaints. 'The River Bure is navigable, you know. A wherry could pass by below us at any time.'

'Hardly. This may be the Bure, but it's only navigable downstream of the mill and staithes on the other side of the town. Here it's just a local river, where cattle drink and the occasional idiot tries to catch a few trout. I ought to know. I own the land from here to the river. Now, stop your whining and listen to me. We're facing a serious problem. One of our number — you can guess who it is — has gambled away his wealth to the point where he's found himself facing ruin on two counts. Firstly, by his inability to pay his debts; secondly, because he was caught trying to win his money back by cheating.'

'What has that to do with us and our enterprise?'

'Remember that sudden jump in the profits of late? I've learned that he's been making extra cash by sending little parcels of sealed documents and letters down to the coast along with the payments for our normal goods. By doing so, the wretch has condemned us all to the gallows, should we be caught.'

'Surely you're over-dramatising events? What's the harm in a few letters for the smugglers? It's probably orders for goods.'

'There are unusual passengers too.'

'Why not? Our boats often carry passengers. It's better than trusting yourself to the terrors and discomforts of the roads.'

'Most of these passengers are French and eager to leave our shores as secretly as they came.'

'Good! There are too many Frenchies in our country since they began their revolution, or whatever they call it. I think we should send 'em all back.'

The other man turned on him in a fury. 'You boneheaded fool! These letters aren't harmless. Our mutual friend needs large amounts of money, not a few pence for each item like a common carrier. They're letters to and from spies! The passengers are the spies themselves! Don't you realise handling letters for French spies is treason, let alone agreeing to smuggle them down to the coast where they can be picked up by a privateer and taken back to France? How can the rest of us prove we knew nothing of what's been going on until it was too late?

The whole country is in a state of near panic over the notion of an invasion by a French army, while here we are, helping the enemy.'

These words hit his listener like a boot driven into his belly. His face turned chalk-white and he staggered back, then rushed amongst the trees behind him. A moment later came the sounds of retching and vomiting. When he returned, after several minutes, he was barely able to stay on his feet.

'You've shit your breeches too,' the tall man said, his voice cold and laden with contempt. 'I might have guessed you'd prove to be a coward. Besides, I haven't explained the worst of it yet. Our mutual friend — this reckless, gambling fool turned traitor — is drinking more and more, just to prop himself up. No drunkard can be trusted to keep his mouth shut, especially when he's in his cups. Hold on there!' For his companion had begun to sway on his feet and his breathing sounded shallow and rapid.

'Sit down on this log for a moment.' The tall man managed to lead the tottering fellow a few feet to where a convenient tree stump protruded from the ground. 'Now, take some deep breaths and calm yourself.'

The other, held fast in the grip of panic, merely clutched at his throat and gasped. When he could speak again, his first words were that they were all going to die on the gallows.

'We're not done yet,' the tall man said, using the falsely cheerful tone people use with those who have given up all hope. 'All I'm saying is that the fellow can't be trusted to keep what we're doing secret. That being so, we have to shut his mouth for him. Provided we act quickly and resolutely, we can still save ourselves. It's plain to me the one who got us into this situation has to die. No other option is suitable. Only death will shut his mouth for good. Then he'll be unable to cause us any more trouble.'

'His death!' the short man gasped. The other one had to grab his shoulder to stop him falling off the tree stump.

'A necessary death, my friend, like disposing of a mad dog before it can bite you a second time. Unpleasant, but unavoidable under the circumstances.'

'I couldn't kill anyone!' His companion's fear had now become focussed on the idea that he would be expected to commit murder. 'Don't expect me to do it. I can't, I tell you! Just can't!'

The tall man's hand was still laid on the other man's shoulder, in a semblance of offering comfort, though his face expressed nothing but contempt. He was a cold-hearted person, ruled by logic and custom, unable to summon up any empathy for the other's feelings. They'd only invited him to join the enterprise for the money he could invest at the start and the benefits his official status could offer them, should it be needed. For the rest, he was a fool and a weakling. Fortunately, he was also extremely greedy. Whatever his fears, he would never give up so much lucrative income by some thoughtless act of betrayal. Not like the man whose fate he intended should to be sealed between them.

'Calm yourself. I never for a moment considered you capable of any more than fleecing unsuspecting people and eating large dinners. I haven't mentioned you committing murder, have I? I'd deal with the matter myself, only I must not be suspected of any involvement, just in case I'm needed in an official position — to smooth things over, you understand; to make certain there are no unpleasant consequences from the fellow's death. Besides, I have to protect my family's name—'

'Your family's name? Pig breeders — or sheep herders — weren't they? I don't quite recall.'

The tall man's gun swung up until it was pointing directly at the other's chest, while his face took on a dangerously mottled colouring.

'You can thank your lucky stars this gun isn't loaded,' he said harshly. 'If it was, you would probably just have suffered a most unfortunate — and fatal — accident. By all that's holy, I'd never suffer you a moment if it wasn't for your usefulness. Don't imagine there isn't a part for you to play in this business. Your job is to keep those events which must follow after the fellow's death from causing any stir. If you fail, and the problem gets to me, I'll know your usefulness is at an end. Then you may be sure I won't forget the slur you just laid on my family.'

The short man was silent. He had amassed a long list of occasions on which the man before him had treated him with contempt. One day, he told himself, I'll find a way to pay him back in full. He won't be so proud of his family then, believe me!

He returned from this pleasant daydream of revenge to find his companion was still talking.

'Listen to me! I must keep well clear of even the vaguest suspicion of involvement, if I'm to be able to deal with any mess you create. That rules us both out from doing what needs to be done. Now, as I see it, this problem was caused by a certain family. It's therefore up to them to provide the solution. Do you agree?'

The other nodded his head vigorously. He'd agree to anything which kept him away from involvement with a possible murder.

'Here's my suggestion. I need you to support me fully, just in case there's an objection from you know who. We aren't going to ask him nicely to do as we say, either. We're going to make it quite clear he has no choice. Agreed?'

More nodding of the head. So, it went on. The tall fellow set out what he intended and the short one agreed to every point. By the time the two parted, some ten minutes later, it was all finalised and the short one had recovered some of his confidence. It's a good way of dealing with the problem, he said to himself later that evening, when he was safely back in his own home. Best of all, my part in it is sufficiently far from the action to make sure I stay safe.

In fact, despite their expressed willingness to resort to coercion, neither man had any doubt the person they had selected to do the deed would play his part in full. They were correct. He not only agreed to do it, he took pleasure in doing so, for he'd secretly feared and hated the intended victim for most of his life. Now all he had to do was contrive a suitable plan and look for an opportunity to put it into practice.

Mr Robert Laven, merchant and carrier of Millgate Manor, Aylsham, killed himself almost exactly ten days later.

## 2

lmost three weeks after Robert Laven's death, Dr Adam
Bascom finally returned home. He hadn't planned to stay
away for more than a single night, but circumstances had
dictated otherwise. It began when his mother had paid him a brief
visit, accompanied — probably for the last time — by her companion,
Miss Sophia LaSalle. They were on their way to Mossterton Hall, the
home of Lady Alice Fouchard, where Miss LaSalle was due to marry
Lady Alice's nephew, Charles Scudamore, at the end of May. A large
number of Scudamore family guests had already indicated they wished
to attend, so it had been agreed Mossterton Hall would make a better
venue for the wedding breakfast than Mrs Bascom's modest house in
Norwich. Miss LaSalle's own family — what little there was — had
fallen on hard times and could not offer more than a token contribu-
tion to the festivities. The two women had therefore been invited to
stay at the hall for a few days to take part in planning the wedding
festivities. All that had been decided until then was that Charles, the
bridegroom, would spend the night before the wedding with Adam in
Aylsham. The pair of them would then travel together to Mossterton
Hall for the ceremonies. Charles himself was presently in London,
making various arrangements — mainly financial — with his father.

Sophia was no heiress, though descended from a good family now fallen on hard times, thanks to one profligate member. Indeed, she would have had no dowry whatsoever, had it not been for her maternal grandmother. Perhaps already expecting the worst, that lady had put enough money in trust for her only granddaughter to provide a modest, but still respectable dowry on her marriage. They say love conquers all, but Charles and his new bride were going to need a sufficient amount of capital to lease a suitable house, hire servants and allow time for Charles to establish himself as a lawyer. They had already settled on Holt, not far away from friends and family, as the place where they would live, and Charles had finally found a suitable property in Bull Street from where he could operate his legal practice.

Normally, Adam would have despatched his mother and Miss LaSalle on their way to Mosserton Hall in the care of William, the groom. This time, however, he had a very personal and private reason for wishing to be at Mossterton himself. That was why he had gone out of his way to stress the poor condition of the roads after the winter, before announcing that he would accompany his mother and Miss Sophia on their journey to Mossterton, stay there that night, and return to his home and practice the next morning. He had a standing invitation from Lady Alice to stay at her house whenever he wished. Her late husband, Sir Daniel, had charged Adam with looking after his widow's interests and well-being. It was a duty Adam took extremely seriously — not least because he had finally admitted to himself that he was hopelessly in love with her and desired nothing more than to make her his wife.

It had been a lovely spring morning when the three of them left Aylsham, and the roads — despite Adam's dire predictions — were mostly dry and firm. They had therefore bowled along at some speed and without too many diversions where the main part of the roadway had become mired in mud through the passage of heavy carts. These local roads would be broad, sandy trackways in the hot, dry days of summer. Dusty, it was true, and rough with flints, but firm enough to bear all the traffic without too much damage. But by the end of winter, most turned into a series of interlacing paths as successive vehicles twisted and turned to avoid the deepest areas of mud and the worst rutting. It could make for very slow going, always assuming the driver kept his wits about him and you didn't end up with the wheels on one side of the carriage trapped in a foot or more of glutinous mire.

All through the journey, Mrs Bascom and Miss LaSalle sat and chattered together, excited to see all the signs of fresh growth about the fields and hedgerows. Spring had come late that year, held back by cold northerly winds, but now the winds had swung around into the west, the temperature had risen, and everything seemed to be trying to make up for the time lost to winter. The plants called Alexanders, which grew along the sides of the road and in the base of the hedgerows, were nearly at their full height, all bearing flat umbels of bright green buds, which would very soon turn into dull, yellow flowers. The blackthorn bloom was at the full, covering the bushes with pure white stars. 'Blackthorn winter' some countryfolk called that time of year, for it was not unusual for the opening of the blackthorn blossom to be accompanied by late frosts and snows. Now, however, even the hawthorn bushes were swollen with leaves of freshest green. When the blackthorn had finished, it would be the turn of the hawthorn flowers to spangle the thickets and fill the air with their distinctive perfume. Now that so many of the former open commons had been enclosed by hawthorn hedges to make individual fields, the spring display promised to be even more lavish than usual. The prickly branches of hawthorn rooted easily and grew quickly, earning it the common name of 'quickset' and making it ideal for the hedging now needed to keep stock from roaming as they used to do.

Living in Norwich as they did, Mrs Bascom and Sophia were aware of the progress of spring in the gardens and pleasure grounds of the city, but had seen nothing on this scale for several years. The entire countryside seemed to be turning into one vast flower border. Everywhere you looked, there was fresh colour: the gold of gorse and the bright yellow of dandelions almost everywhere; in sheltered hollows, the paler yellow of early primroses; and on the banks, the deep purple and blue of violets.

Adam sat opposite the ladies, his back towards the direction of their progress. They looked about them constantly, now exclaiming at some fresh patch of flowers, now trying to identify a bird darting out of the bushes or flying up from the roadway ahead. Once they called out in delight as they saw an early swallow skim the ground beside them. Adam too stared at the countryside yet saw nothing — his mind was too full of hopes and fears to find space for such mundane matters as the beauties of nature on a fine day in Norfolk in mid-April. How could he find a private time with Lady Alice for what he had in mind? If he did, would his resolution be strong enough to speak? All the arguments against the action he planned sprang into his mind, one after the other, each appearing stronger and more obvious than the last. Would it not be better to stay silent, rather than make a fool of himself and spoil what he already had in seeking for more? Would things turn out as he had planned; or would all his hopes for future happiness be cast down into ruin?

Of course, nothing during that visit went as Adam had anticipated, so that one day stretched into two and then into three before he was able to set out for his home again.

The first cause of delay was occasioned by the total collapse of all Lady Alice's plans for renovating and extending her dower house of Irmingland Abbey, when Mossterton passed into the hands of Sir Daniel Fouchard's heir on Michaelmas Day of that year. As soon as Adam arrived with his mother and Miss LaSalle, he sensed something was seriously amiss. Lady Alice greeted her guests warmly enough, yet Adam detected an ominous change: a sense of dullness and weary disappointment; an absence of her usual bright manner and firmness of purpose. When she drew him aside and asked that he stay at Mossterton another day, so she might seek his advice on what she termed 'a major setback', his mood sank into near despair.

Of course, he agreed to stay. If he left that same day, as he had first planned, he would have no chance to talk with Lady Alice alone, for she was certain to be much engaged with his mother and Miss LaSalle on the day of their arrival. She must show them around the house and gardens, listen to their concerns on the subject of wedding arrangements, and generally act the part of the gracious hostess. There would be no chance for her to escape for a suitable period to speak with Adam in private until the next day — and perhaps precious little opportunity even then. Miss LaSalle might be left for a while to talk with the housekeeper and the cook about the menu for the wedding breakfast. As for Adam's mother, their best hope lay with Miss Ruth Scudamore, Charles's twin sister. She could probably be persuaded to entertain Mrs Bascom with discussions of how they would spend their time when she moved into Mrs Bascom's house in Norwich, replacing Miss LaSalle as Mrs Bascom's companion. Not a paid position this time, naturally. Merely a happy arrangement that would allow Ruth to pursue her artistic and botanical studies more easily, while providing continued companionship to the older woman.

The remainder of that first day was torment to Adam. His mind constructed ever more fantastic and terrifying notions of what the 'major setback' Lady Alice had mentioned would prove to be. As a result, he ate and spoke little, sat through dinner in such a silent mood as to obstruct everyone else's conversation, then retired to his room, pleading an indisposition. Even his mother's angry glances could not jolt him into acting as he knew she expected of him.

Adam almost decided not to take breakfast next morning, but his growling stomach persuaded him some food was necessary, however much he would prefer to be on his own. As he feared, he found his mother waiting for him, demanding to know why his behaviour the previous day had been so peculiar.

'Are you unwell? Or are you involving yourself in another investigation, or whatever you call them?' she demanded. 'Leave such matters to those whose proper business it is: the magistrates and judges. Whenever you begin taxing your brain with some mystery, there is always trouble.'

'I am not investigating anything, Mother,' Adam said. 'I am also perfectly well, thank you.'

'It's no use trying to lie to me, Adam. I can always see through your silly evasions and limp excuses. A mother knows, believe me! Indeed, your problem has been obvious to me for a long time now.'

'And what problem is that?'

'Your lack of a wife. You are almost thirty years of age, well established in your profession and more than rich enough, if I am any judge. It's high time you got married. I have explained several times that I am willing to find you a suitable partner. Indeed, only the other day I was talking to Mrs—'

'Do not proceed down that path again, I implore you, Mother. I have told you a hundred times that I will find my own wife — if and when I do decide marriage is what I want. Now, if you will excuse me, I need some fresh air. Lady Alice has asked for my advice on a matter of business and I need to have my wits about me.'

In speaking with such confidence to his mother, Adam knew he was mostly attempting to shore up his own belief. Early this morning, one of the servants had brought Adam a message, saying that Lady Alice would be walking on the terrace at half-past nine and would be grateful if he could join her there. It seemed an odd place to meet, but Adam quickly realised that she must be concerned to make sure they could not be overheard, even by the servants. That sounded ominous enough. His own mood served only to intensify his fears.

For months he had been trying to pluck up the courage to propose to Lady Alice. Her period of formal mourning for her late husband, Sir Daniel, would end in two months. She would then be free to think of her future. Any man with an ounce of common sense would have foreseen the outcome of such a proposal, but Adam had managed to work himself into such a state of anxiety that he was certain he would be rejected.

He found her ladyship pacing up and down waiting for him. The moment he came up to where she was, she placed her finger on her lips to enjoin silence, then led him to a stone seat screened from the house by a thick planting of shrubs of some kind. Here she sat down, motioned to him to sit beside her, and launched into her tale.

The setback — to Adam's huge relief — concerned her plans for her new home at Irmingland Abbey. The architect she had engaged had now examined the current building and reached a most unwelcome conclusion: the ideas she had for alterations would not be possible without a considerable amount of demolition and rebuilding, leading to a cost far in excess of the sums she had discussed with him. He had found that the major part of the existing building had been constructed around the great dining hall of the former abbey. It appeared more modern from the outside — dating to the reign of Good Queen Bess — only because what was within was mostly hidden by brick walls and stucco. The actual fabric consisted mostly of stone-faced walls some three feet thick, the spaces between the dressed stones being filled with a rough mixture of stones, flints and building rubbish, and all held together by nothing more thaexclaimedn mortar poured in from above. To cut new ways through the walls to allow for the extra wing she had in mind — or even to provide adequate doorways to new passages or rooms — risked causing large areas of the building to collapse.

Even worse, he had found the main roof of the house, though it seemed to be fine pottery pantiles of the type common in the county, in truth rested on the original mediaeval joists and battens. These, in turn, were held up by stone vaulting, once exposed to those dining below, but now hidden by two added levels of flooring. Indeed, from side to side, Irmingland Abbey, stripped of later additions, would resemble nothing more than the lofty nave of a great church.

'I confessed to you before how rash I had been in agreeing to give up my right to live here at Mossterton without proper thought — and without consulting you first. Now I am soundly punished. I promised to leave by Michaelmas,' Lady Alice wailed. 'That means in barely six months I will have nowhere to live! Oh, I know I can rent somewhere, but I had set my heart on having my own property, laid out and deco-rated exactly as I wished it to be. What shall I do, doctor? I am heart-broken and more angry with myself than I can express. What shall I do?'

With that, she burst into tears.

The sight of Lady Alice, normally the most serene and resolute of people, reduced to sobs of anguish swept away the last vestiges of Adam's resistance. It wasn't the most elegant or romantic of proposals on his part, but it served the purpose.

'What you must do is come and live with me,' Adam said.

At once, the lady's tears ceased, to be replaced by a look on her face that Adam was quite unable to interpret. Was it amazement? Surprise? Shock? Horror, perhaps? Whatever it meant, there was no going back now.

'Marry me,' Adam blurted out, wishing the ground might open and swallow him. 'Then you can come to live with me in Aylsham for the time being, while I find us a proper home. I know my home is far below the standard you are used to — as am I myself. I have no noble kin, no title and —'

But by now, Lady Alice was staring at him with such a degree of intensity that he found himself bereft of speech.

'Did I hear aright? Did you just propose marriage?' she asked.

'Oh, my dear, dear Alice!' Adam said, his voice trembling with emotion. 'It all came out wrongly. I hadn't meant to say anything at all. Well, I did, I suppose, but not like that and not right now. Only I couldn't stand you crying as you did, and it was the only solution my mind could come up with. Please forgive my presumption. Forget I ever—'

'Forget? Forget you just said what I have longed to hear from your lips for more months than I can recall? You did ask me to marry you, didn't you?'

'I did — only I didn't mean to insult you, Lady Alice. Anything but that.'

'Stop! Stop!' She leaned forward and put her finger to his lips now. 'Of course I will marry you, doctor — I mean Adam — my dearest, most foolish Adam. Nothing could please me more. No, I am wrong about that. There is something I desire even more than that this moment. Kiss me!'

Adam, temporarily incapable of speech or rational thought, did as she asked, surprising himself by the passion he managed to infuse into the process. For a moment, he feared he had gone too far, then felt an answering passion at least as great as his own. Only as he wrapped his arms fiercely around her did he recall how small and fragile she appeared. He would have pulled back then, but in a moment, he was reminded that, though she might be little more than five feet tall, and surprisingly slender, it was quite evident she was made of steel in every part of her body. The fierce hug she gave him, before breaking away, drove all the air from his lungs and left him gasping.

'It is as well I chose this seat, my dearest,' she said, her own breathing a little ragged, but far steadier than his. 'It would never do to risk such unseemly behaviour being witnessed by anyone, let alone your mother. Now, Adam, I must have your solemn promise on an important matter. We agreed once before — or, rather, I laid an injunction on you — that our relationship must seem to the world no closer than it has been, until the complete period of mourning for Sir Daniel has ended. I know neither of us would wish in the slightest to sully our genuine regard for a kind, wise and dear man — even though I know he wanted nothing more than to see me happy after his death, and would have regarded you as the most suitable man to become my second husband. Nothing must be said of what has happened here this morning. Nothing! Not for the next — what is it? — two months. Only then can we make our situation public. Do I have your promise?'

Adam would, at that moment, have promised to walk barefoot to the North Pole, or dip his toes in boiling lava, had Lady Alice required it of him. The promise she required troubled him not at all. That, however, was before he had realised that he must spend the next two months in a fog of joyous euphoria, while appearing to everyone — especially his mother — to be entirely unchanged.

After that, it took them barely a few moments to agree that Irmingland Abbey and its lands should be rented out. The house was in good condition and would make an excellent home for a tenant farmer. It was only the changes Lady Alice had planned that had produced the problem. Once they were married, Lady Alice would move in with Adam in his present home while he sought a finer property more suited to her status and his hopes for their future.

'Let us stay here a few moments longer,' Lady Alice said, 'and compose ourselves, so that we give no hint of what has taken place between us, when we return to the house. I doubt Sophia would notice if you had grown a second head, but your mother strikes me as a difficult person to mislead, especially when it comes to her favourite son. No, don't bother to deny it. I am sure she loves your brother well enough, but you are the apple of her eye. I am genuinely concerned that I might fail to come up to the standards she will set for any wife of yours.'

'Never! Believe me, dearest Alice, she will be transported with joy, as I am.'

'She will sense some change. I am sure of that. What story can we concoct to draw her away from the truth?'

'She accused me over breakfast of being unsociable and distant, with my mind filled with some new mystery. Indeed, she complained that I was never so happy as when I was on the track of some malefactor involved in wrongdoing. That's it. I will tell her I have received a message from Aylsham that there is a new mystery for me to enquire into.'

In the event, it proved easier than they expected to convince his mother that Adam was indeed turning over some new mystery in his mind and not involved in keeping something from her — which, of course, he most certainly was. Then he almost spoiled it all by letting slip he would be staying another day at Mossterton Hall. Lady Alice saved him by inventing still more pressing business that he must transact on her behalf; something so important that, despite his eagerness to be on his way home, he had agreed with every reluctance to undertake. It must, she said, involve spending time with her land agent, who was unfortunately absent until late that evening. The reality, of course, was that he could not bear to leave Mossterton so soon.

For her part, Lady Alice made a far better job than Adam did of keeping up a pretence of normality. She was simply even more assiduous in her duties as hostess than she would have been otherwise. As a result, she and Adam had almost no chance to be alone again and out of sight and hearing of others. On the rare occasions it could be managed, they flew into each other's arms. Even then, Lady Alice would not allow too many kisses on her lips, fearing Adam's ardour would leave traces obvious to all. Adam had to be content with placing the gentlest of kisses on her neck and throat and burying his face in her hair. It was torment, but torment of the most delicious kind.

$\mathbf{3}$

'Here you are then. Back at last, damn your eyes!' Peter Lassimer, the local apothecary in Aylsham, almost thrust himself into Adam's study within a few minutes of its owner's return. The moment Hannah, the maid, had opened the door in response to her master's call of 'Come!', Peter pushed past her and snapped out what sounded much more like an accusation than a greeting.

It wasn't the best of welcomes, nor the politest. Perhaps, Adam thought, it was all he deserved for trying to deceive his mother by claiming there was an important mystery waiting for him when he returned home. What was about to make his old friend's rough greeting worse was finding his fiction was true. There was a mystery waiting, and a complex one to boot.

Adam's response to Peter's words, not surprisingly, was distinctly chilly. He ignored his visitor, held up a hand for silence, and turned to Hannah.

'Thank you, Hannah,' he said. 'Please show Mr Lassimer in. Oh, I see he is here already. Very well, you may leave us.'

Adam's irony was wasted on his old friend. 'This is no time to be bothered with politeness and niceties,' Peter said. 'While you've been dallying with Lady Alice Fouchard, over at Mossterton Hall, the rest of us have been doing your job for you.'

'In what way? My assistant, Dr Harrison Henshaw, has been here. He is quite capable of looking after any patients who needed assistance or treatment. I admit I stayed away longer than I had intended, but there were . . . particular circumstances which made it essential.'

'Ha! I know what — or rather, who — those "particular circumstances" were! Yes, poor young Henshaw was here, but did you expect him to be pressed into carrying out an autopsy, when you were required and could not be found? Was he capable of that, in your opinion?'

'I feel sure he was,' Adam said mildly. 'Such a request would be extremely unusual anyway. Mr Sleeth, the local coroner, is known to favour others for that kind of work. There is one elderly physician in particular who seems to suit his purposes, despite being, as I have heard, almost stone deaf and nearly blind as well. Why couldn't he do the job?'

'He died two months ago.'

'That might tell against him. Even so, I have no idea why this Sleeth fellow should suddenly wish to summon my services instead. So far as I know, we have never encountered one another. I probably would have declined his invitation anyway and suggested Dr Henshaw in my place. If that didn't suit, he could always have asked you.'

'Never!' Peter said. 'He would rather have all his teeth drawn out, one by one, then ask me for anything. I know Sleeth to be a confounded fool, and he knows that I am right. Indeed, I have told him as much on several occasions.'

'Knowing you, I imagined you must have shared that opinion with him somewhat forcibly.' Adam said. 'Well, as I said, I know nothing of the man save his name — and his reputation for being dogmatic — so I would probably agree with you.'

'I tell you, Bascom. The man's not only a fool. He's also pompous, arrogant, opinionated and argumentative. I also have good reason to believe him to be sly, devious and generally untrustworthy in all matters, save his own welfare. But then, he is some kind of lawyer. I believe such character traits are sadly common in that profession. The fact that he is our local coroner is regrettable, but one we must live with.'

'Let us not go any further along that track. Clearly, this matter of the autopsy has upset you in some way. Hadn't you better tell me the reason?'

Peter sat himself in one of the chairs, giving all the signs of being about to embark on a long and detailed explanation.

'As I said,' he began, 'while you were wasting your time dallying with Lady Alice—'

'Now who's wasting time. I was not dallying with Lady Alice, as you very well know.' The lie slipped out easily enough. 'I went to Mossterton Hall to escort my mother and Miss Sophia LaSalle. They have both been invited to stay by Lady Alice, to finalise the necessary arrangements for Miss LaSalle's coming wedding to Charles Scudamore, Lady Alice's nephew. My mother also wishes to speak with Miss Ruth Scudamore about her move to Norwich to take up residence in my mother's house.'

'So how did either of those matters involve you?'

'If you must know, Lassimer,' Adam continued, worried in case his falsehoods had been detected, 'Lady Alice kindly invited me to stay for a short while, because she had some matters of a financial nature that she wished to discuss with me. I have been away but two nights. It is hardly my fault if some person managed to die during my absence in such a manner as to require an autopsy. Moreover, you have yet to explain why our esteemed coroner, wishing to avoid asking you and finding me away, did not go to one of the other medical practitioners in the town to carry out the autopsy. What about the man down in Millgate? Mr Hawley, I believe. A most capable surgeon. Why couldn't he have served.'

'For a very simple reason,' Peter replied. 'Mr Matthew Hawley was the corpse.'

He expected this news to jolt Adam out of his calmness at once, yet his friend merely nodded and continued to stare out of the window, as he had been doing for the last few minutes.

'Did you hear what I said? Mr Hawley is dead.'

'Most certainly,' Adam said, still displaying the same maddening indifference to Peter's news. 'I agree he could hardly be called to undertake an autopsy on himself. Dr Henson did a fine job in my place, I'm sure.'

'He did, but that isn't the point. Dr Henshaw asked me to advise him on the procedure, since he had never done such work before and wished to be certain he missed nothing.'

'Very sensible.'

'Indeed so, especially in this case. He and I quickly came to the conclusion Mr Hawley was most foully murdered.'

'Really? How strange. Who would want to kill the poor man? I always thought he was a popular figure.'

'Don't you want to know how he died? His body was found floating in the water near one of the staithes belonging to the Bure Navigation.'

'Probably drowned then.'

'For God's sake, Bascom! What in heaven's name is the matter with you? Here I am, telling you of a murder almost on your doorstep and you aren't showing the slightest sign of interest. Yes, Hawley was drowned, but someone had knocked him unconscious first by striking him on the back of his head. That makes it murder.'

'Possibly. Assuming he didn't hit his head on anything when he fell in. Maybe he simply couldn't swim.'

'I am going to hit you on the head, I swear, if you continue in this vein! Listen — and use your brain! I declare something at Mossterton Hall has robbed you of what little wit you possessed before! Has Lady Alice so bewitched you that your mind is filled with nothing but thoughts of her? At least I hope they are indelicate ones.'

'Lady Alice has nothing to do with my state of mind,' Adam lied. *Really, it's becoming a habit already!* 'Nor would I ever entertain any thoughts of her that were less than entirely respectable.' *There I go again!* 'If you barge into my home, the moment I return from several days away and after a somewhat uncomfortable journey—' *Perhaps it was. I can't say I even remember, my mind was so filled with such shameful, wonderful imaginings about how I propose to spend my first few nights with sweetest Alice.* '—you can hardly complain if I find it hard to work myself up into the state of agitation you appear to require of me. Tell me why it is so silly to ask whether the man could swim?'

'Because the water in that part of the Navigation is nowhere more than three or four foot deep. Had he been conscious when he went in, he could have stood up and *walked* to the bank to get out. He had no need to swim. The fact that he did not must prove he was unconscious. Nor did he hit his head when he fell. There was no wherry moored at the staithe at the time, and there was nothing in the water on which he could have hit his head. Taking all that into account, it's plain he was struck down either before he went into the water or as he tried to climb out again. Being unconscious and probably lying face down — that was how his body was found — he then drowned. And before you make some silly remark about him being intoxicated, your colleague found no trace of alcohol in his stomach contents. He was also well known to be a total abstainer.'

'So, he was murdered. I imagine Dr Henshaw gave these details in his evidence to the jury at the inquest and they returned their verdict according to his evidence. I still cannot see what it has to do with me.'

Peter's expression was eloquent of exactly what he would like to do to his friend at this point. Summoning all his scanty reserves of patience, he continued with his narrative.

'Dr Henshaw tried to explain but had a hard time of it. Mr Sleeth, for some reason known only to himself, had already decided Mr Hawley's death was accidental. That being the case, he did everything he could to prevent any evidence being given that might point in another direction. First, he tried to rule a good part of Dr Henshaw's testimony irrelevant to the case. When Henshaw persisted, as he was duty bound to do, Sleeth could scarcely contain his anger. He then told Henshaw to sit down and directed the jury to bring in a verdict in accordance with his own views. He even went so far as to warn them against what he called, ". . . imaginative and theoretical notions advanced by a young and inexperienced physician, more attracted to drama than to truth." That was when I stood up and protested. He had me removed from the court, damn him!'

'Hardly surprising . . .' Adam counted to smile happily at some internal recollection. It took him a few moments to grasp what a public exhibition of rudeness his young colleague had been subjected to. Even when he did, his response was still a long way short of Peter's expectations.

'I agree it was most impolite of Mr Sleeth to speak to Dr Henshaw in such a way,' he continued. 'I shall write to him, I think, and express my gravest displeasure. I'll talk to Dr Henshaw too. It's regrettable that he had to be subjected to such an experience on his first occasion of giving evidence at an inquest. However, from what you tell me, he behaved exactly as I would have done. You wanted to take a horse-whip to Sleeth, I suppose.'

'I did, but, being a lawyer, he would probably bring a charge of assault against me.'

'How did Dr Henshaw react?'

'I don't know. If you can recall what I said, through whatever fog has taken possession of your brain, I had been ejected from the court by this time.'

'I'm sure his response was less impulsive than your own. Did Mr Sleeth get his way as regards the verdict?'

'He did not, which must have reduced him to complete fury. When they returned from their deliberations, the jury gave their verdict as "unlawfully killed by person or persons unknown." I'm only sad Sleeth didn't succumb to an apoplexy on the spot. The jury didn't dare use the actual word "murder" — they were too afraid of Sleeth to do that. Still, they went as far as they could in saying Hawley's death had been some kind of unlawful killing, and thus accepting Henshaw's evidence about the cause of death.'

'I appreciate you telling me all this, Lassimer, especially about Mr Sleeth's uncommon rudeness to Dr Henshaw. However, the circum-stances surrounding the death of poor Mr Hawley are no concern of mine, even if it was murder. I do not need to investigate every unlawful death in this part of Norfolk, as you well know. Now, if there's no more, I need to look over the correspondence that has arrived here during my absence. There are also certain business matters to be attended to.'

'Don't worry, I'm leaving. If I stay, there will be *another* murder in Aylsham for Mr Sleeth to try to turn into an accidental death! I cannot imagine what sickness of the brain has struck you down, but its effects are plain enough. Good day to you, Bascom. I hope you recover soon — I think.'

After Peter left, Adam sat in silence, trying to recover his composure after what must surely have been the most tumultuous few days of his life. What had begun in fear, and the determination that comes only when all alternatives have been abandoned, had ended in a confusion of joy, accompanied by trepidation for what the future would hold. What he needed now, more than anything, was time to adjust himself, his expectations and his activities to meet his new life. Thanks to Peter and Mr Sleeth, he seemed unlikely to be able to find it — unless, of course, he was as good as his word and stayed well away from any involvement in investigating the murder of poor Surgeon Hawley.

That presented him with a fresh dilemma. Peter was already suspicious of some change in his friend — his irritation was proof of that. If Adam kept away from anything connected with this suspicious death, he would be doubly and trebly alert to find out what was truly afoot. Peter had long been convinced Lady Alice was trying to inveigle Adam into matrimony. Worse, in all the years he and Peter had known one another, Adam had never walked away from any mystery. He was notorious amongst his friends and family for his curiosity and his determination to satisfy it, come what may. Now, his mind befuddled with thoughts of Lady Alice, he had just said he saw no reason to become involved in considering the circumstances surrounding the death of Matthew Hawley! The reality was, he had no choice but to get involved. To do otherwise would not only force him to give Peter some reason for such strange behaviour, it would leave his own curiosity so far unsatisfied as to turn the immediate future into a period of continual torture.

For a while, Adam was at a loss over how he could retract his earlier statement, without drawing even closer scrutiny to his reasons. Then it came to him. He would claim it had all been a joke, aimed at punishing Peter for the abruptness of his entry into Adam's library. It wasn't perfect, but it would do. Adam knew he had no reputation for humour or practical jokes, so any clumsiness about the matter would be put down to his incompetence. All he had to do after that was agree that the death of the surgeon was most certainly odd and merited careful analysis. Best of all, once embarked on his investigation, any periods of distraction over his forthcoming nuptials and the search for permanent accommodation could be explained as being due to puzzling over this new mystery. It would also, of course, wipe out the blatant lies he had told his mother. She would be bound to sniff out how he was spending his days. If she found he was not doing what he had claimed, she would not only berate him severely; she would give herself — and him — no peace until she had flushed out the truth.

First, he would need to make his peace with Lassimer, of course, although that could be set aside for at least a day. It was going to take that long for the apothecary's temper to have cooled. No, on second thoughts he had best go the next morning. His explanation would be thin enough, without giving Lassimer any longer to brood on the reasons for Adam's odd behaviour. The fact of the matter was Adam didn't want to do anything nowadays, save enjoy the wonderful thought that very soon he would be married to Lady Alice.

Of course, Adam knew this was foolish thinking. To do anything so far out of his usual mode of living would have unacceptable consequences. If it led people to suspect what was afoot, he would be forced either to lie or risk breaking his promise to keep all hidden for another two months. The odd saying he'd heard as a child came to him: 'He's a bigger liar than Tom Pepper, and he was thrown out of hell for telling lies.' He was coming perilously close to that being true of him already.

The more he thought about it the more he realised that this sad affair of the surgeon's death might offer him what he needed: something to help make the time before his engagement to Lady Alice pass more quickly, and at the same time provide a good excuse for any periods of solitary introspection. Besides, what little he knew of Surgeon Hawley suggested he had been both good at his profession and genuinely concerned for his patients. Nothing about him so far suggested he was the type of person who would bring about his own death through involvement in criminal or dishonest enterprise. Not only was this murder an affront to any civilised society, it had actually taken place in Aylsham — right under Adam's nose, had he only been there at the time. That was a personal affront he was not minded to overlook.

'No,' Adam told himself. 'I cannot tolerate such a thing taking place almost on my doorstep. Nor can I accept what amounts to a slur on the practice of medicine. Until the killer has been brought to justice, there is no way I can rest easy in my mind.'

Others might rather have pointed to his insatiable curiosity, but there was a streak of romanticism in Adam that had now come to the fore. The brave knight, having at last won his fair lady, must set out again to do battle with the forces of evil and chaos — beginning by eating humble pie before his friend, the apothecary, and listening to his story properly this time.

## ❦ 4 ❧

The next morning, Adam did as he had determined and went at once to Peter's shop to make his peace with his friend. He found the apothecary in his compounding room behind the shop, grinding spices for his various mixtures and medicines. Their greetings were somewhat formal, for it would have been hard to decide which of them was more embarrassed about their parting the day before.

Adam decided it would be best to plunge ahead and get things out in the open. 'I must apologise for my manner yesterday, Lassimer,' he said. 'I realise I was quite absent in mind when you told me about the death of Mr Hawley. Please do not think I was uninterested in what you had to say, or in poor Hawley's death. To tell you the truth, my mind was taken up with other matters. Lady Alice has been consulting me on certain problems relating to her place of residence after she leaves Mossterton Hall. I spent most of the journey home trying to find some way to set her mind at rest. I was also extremely tired and so unprepared to think about anything difficult or demanding.'

It wasn't a complete lie this time. More a matter of ignoring the real reason for his distraction and substituting a minor, yet plausible, difficulty in way of explanation. Fortunately for Adam, his friend was as eager as he was to set things right between them.

'I too was gravely at fault, Bascom,' Peter said. 'As usual, I let my emotions run ahead of my good sense. You had only just returned home, so I can see now how my sudden visit and startling news must have left you somewhat mystified. Let us say no more about it. Matthew Hawley was a good man, you see. A man whose friendship I cherished. Not only did I know him as someone from whom I often obtained supplies of dried herbs, his reputation was such as to convince me of his skill in dealing with the sick and his generosity towards those in need.'

'That much I knew also,' Adam said. 'Unfortunately, I barely had any acquaintance with the man himself.'

'I am not so surprised I knew him better than you,' Peter replied. 'There's quite a gulf between physicians and mere surgeons; while Millgate, where he lived and practised, is almost a separate place from Aylsham, even though it lies scarcely half a mile out of the town. Nearly all who live there make their livelihood from the trade which flows up and down the Bure Navigation between here and Great Yarmouth. In many ways, it's more like a port than part of our inland market town. Those who live there have much more in common with the folk who live on the coast. They're insular and wary of strangers.'

'I don't believe I've ever been there,' Adam said. 'I know about the Bure Navigation, of course, but that's about all.'

'Few of the people in that neighbourhood could afford the services of a rich physician like you,' Peter said laughing. 'Your fee for one consultation would be more than a good many of them earn in a year.'

'Yet Mr Hawley made his livelihood amongst them?'

'Whether he made enough from his work to keep him I don't know. Perhaps he had some private means. I cannot see how he could have afforded to keep a housekeeper otherwise. Still, the nub of the matter is he was a good man and didn't deserve to die in the way he did. You need to talk with his housekeeper, if you ask me. She'll probably be able to tell you more.'

'This housekeeper isn't yet another of your amorous widows, is she?' Adam said.

'No, she's not. She isn't a widow either, so far as I know. Just a pleasant young woman trying to make her way in the world by honest work.'

'Some time you must tell me about her,' Adam said, 'but that can wait. For the moment, what bothers me most is what must be seen as a blatant attempt on the part of the coroner to mislead his jury into returning a false verdict. Tell me again what you and Henshaw found during the autopsy.'

'To our minds, clear evidence of murder. He died by drowning, true enough, but that was only because he had been struck with a heavy blow to the head, which must have rendered him unconscious. The water where his body was discovered is so shallow that he could have saved himself merely by getting to his feet. There was nothing obvious — or even not so obvious — on which he could have struck his head on falling in. Indeed, the staithe at that point stands barely a foot above the level of the water. To strike his head with sufficient force to account for his injury, he would have needed to throw himself head first at some suitable object.'

'Do you know the circumstances of the man's death? Tell me what happened. If no one else will take this poor man's murder seriously, I will.'

'For a start,' Peter began, 'it all took place at night, sometime around 9:30. I say that with confidence, because, as you shall hear, the murder was discovered within minutes of it taking place. A wherryman was leaving the inn there, The Anchor, when he heard a loud splash from the area of one of the staithes beside the road. Fearing some fellow had fallen in while the worse for drink, he ran over and peered about him, expecting to discover someone struggling and shouting in the water. Yet all was quiet again. Indeed, he had almost decided to forget the matter and continue on his way when he noticed a man's foot and leg sticking up out of the water, close to the edge of the staithe. A rope was left tied there between two of the mooring posts and the man's foot had somehow become entangled in it. The wherryman pulled him out, but it was too late.'

'He had not struggled when he went into the water?'

'It does not seem so. Of course, thanks to Henshaw we now know why. He must have fallen face down and unconscious. He'd probably have drifted out of sight into the darkness and drowned anyway had it not been for his foot getting trapped.'

'So, there was a witness who heard him go into the water and could testify that he had neither called out nor struggled?'

'Exactly so.'

'How did the coroner account for that testimony?'

'As proving his belief that Mr Hawley had struck his head when he fell in. But let us take things in order, Bascom. I have not yet finished with the matter of what happened that night. You will soon see what I mean by calling the events a disgrace and those who took part no better than poltroons.

'You'll recall that it was dark. The wherryman, as I told you, pulled the surgeon's body out of the water, but it was clear he was dead. By this time, several other people, alerted by the noise, had come up and one of them went to summon the constable.'

'A local man?'

'Indeed, and not the quickest of fellows either physically or mentally. It took him quite a few minutes to arrive and still longer to grasp what had happened. The surgeon's housekeeper had arrived by then and it was she who took charge of matters. Indeed, she seems to have kept her head best out of all of them that night. The constable had never encountered murder before and was at a loss for what action he should take. He dithered around until, in desperation, the house-keeper told him to go and inform the magistrate of what had happened. He obeyed her without question. Isn't it funny how, in a crisis, there are people like that who will obey a firm order, regardless of who gives it?'

'Not really. Confused and frightened people cling to anything which offers them some certainty. Besides, it was the obvious thing to do. What time was it when the constable finally got around to telling someone in authority?'

'It seems it was around 10:45. The magistrate was in bed, of course. His servant went to rouse him, but he declined to become involved, declaring it was a matter for the coroner. He then told the constable, again via this servant, to go to the coroner's house and report the matter there.'

'And he went back to sleep?'

'So far as I know, yes.'

'A suspicious death is reported, and he takes no action, save to go back to sleep? Who is this magistrate?'

'I can't recall his name for the moment. I suppose you would call him a local gentleman. I gather his father yearned to see the family counted amongst the gentry and therefore used his wealth to purchase a small estate near Burgh. That's where his son now lives, doubtless maintaining himself on the income and any other investments. He certainly does no other work that I know of.'

'What of the coroner?'

'This is the best part of the tale. From what I heard, the constable arrived at the coroner's house shortly after eleven. He was told Mr Sleeth had retired for the night and was unwilling to be roused. The constable, stout fellow, insisted, saying the magistrate had sent him expressly to report what had happened and receive his orders.'

'Did Sleeth appear?'

'Eventually. He came downstairs at around half-past eleven. Did I mention all this took place on a Saturday? I should have done. You see, when he did put in an appearance, Mr Sleeth declared it would be improper to undertake his legal duties on what would soon be the Sabbath — and went back to bed! He didn't summon a jury until the Monday morning. Only then, it seems, did he realise the man he intended to ask to carry out the post mortem was himself the victim. The whole inquest was a farce! A disgrace! Consider the manner in which Mr Hawley's death was dealt with on the night it happened. That too was more worthy of a stage pantomime than the actions of serious men charged with upholding the rule of law in our town.'

'I'm totally amazed at Sleeth's actions,' Adam said. 'Either he's incompetent or there's something very wrong there. Either way, I owe it to the people of Aylsham to find out. From all you've told me, it's obvious there are those who would wish the matter either ignored or forgotten as swiftly as possible. I wonder why that should be?'

'I knew you couldn't resist!' Peter cried. 'All that nonsense about it being none of your concern. As the locals say in these parts, "that's nought but a load of ol' squit!" Surgeon Hawley was a benefactor to many, and his death has accorded less consideration than might be bestowed on a beggar found dead upon the highway. It surely cannot be allowed to go unchallenged!'

'No,' Adam said, his face having grown dark with anger. 'It cannot.'

THERE WAS PLENTY OF TIME BEFORE DINNER FOR ADAM TO SEEK OUT Dr Henshaw at his lodgings in Hungate. It wasn't far from his own house, but the abundance of mud and horse manure everywhere made even such a short walk an uncomfortable experience. The weather was to blame. The last few days had seen a constant mix of showers and short intervals of sun. It had left the ground soaked yet failed to wash away the filth that was only to be expected, given the number of horses using the road. It was usual for Dr Henshaw to come to Adam. Indeed, he could not recall whether he had ever been to Henshaw's lodgings before that day. Still, under the circumstances, he felt that to summon his assistant to see him would set the wrong tone from the start.

He found Henshaw at ease, having not long returned from visiting his patients. He'd removed his coat and waistcoat and was now dressed in what was plainly an old, but much loved, day gown, frayed at the ends of the sleeves and none too clean either. When he realised who his visitor was, the poor man was all for changing into more suitable attire, but Adam wouldn't hear of it. He waved him back to the chair he'd been sprawled in, gratefully accepted an offer of tea from the lodging-keeper, who clearly did duty for cook and maid as well, and settled himself in the only other chair. The fire in the grate had clearly not been lit long yet was already giving out just enough heat to make the room seem cosy.

'My dear Henshaw,' Adam began. 'You must first let me apologise for two things: for coming upon you unannounced in this way and for staying away longer than I had anticipated. It is a mark of my trust in you that I felt able to do so. Even so, had I not been so distracted by unexpected events myself, I should at least have sent word to warn you I could not return when I said I would.'

'It is of no consequence, sir,' Henshaw said. 'There was nothing regarding our patients which demanded your presence, or I should have asked if you could return. We all knew you were not far away.'

'Nothing regarding our usual patients perhaps,' Adam replied. 'However, I know there was something which I would not have left you to deal with alone, had I known it would arise. I refer, of course, to the death of Surgeon Hawley and the autopsy you were asked to perform in my place.'

'I believe Mr Sleeth, the coroner, only asked me because he could find no one else to do it. He could have sought a replacement from Saxthorpe or Roughton, but that would have occasioned too much delay. You weren't here, so he couldn't approach you. I believe it was a member of the jury who suggested he should ask me to do it. That's why I didn't get to see the body until nearly noon that day. Unfortunately, I had never conducted a post mortem before, so you can imagine I was quite uncertain whether to take the task upon me or not. In the end, I agreed, but only because Mr Lassimer undertook to assist me and provide his advice. He even had to do so without the coroner knowing, since I gather he and Mr Sleeth are on the poorest of terms.'

'So I believe. I also believe it is much to your credit that you stood your ground at the inquest and insisted the full facts should be put before the jury. Lassimer has told me you are certain poor Mr Hawley was struck on the head with some heavy object, before being pushed or thrown into the water. Is that correct?'

'Completely. He died by drowning. His lungs were full of water. However, the water was too shallow for that to have come about, had he not been unconscious at the time and unable to save himself by the simple expedient of standing up. He was struck on the head hard enough to crack his skull, then put into the water face down.'

'Would the blow have been sufficient to kill him anyway?'

'Very possibly. However, I could only speculate on that point. The proven cause of death was drowning, and since it could not have happened in the normal course of events, even through falling into the water accidentally, it had to be murder.'

'He wasn't too drunk at the time to save himself?'

'I could smell no alcohol in the stomach contents. Had he been that drunk, I surely would have done. Don't you agree?'

'I do. What about some drug?'

'I found no sign to indicate he had been drugged or poisoned. Besides, why hit a man over the head, if you have already given him enough of some narcotic to cause him to drown anyway? No, Dr Bascom. You may imagine all kinds of alternatives, but the plain facts point to only one answer: he was knocked unconscious and pushed into the water to drown.'

'I agree with you entirely, Henshaw. I was only exploring alternatives in the way any sceptical lawyer might. You did an excellent job and I commend you for it. What's more, I fully intend to get to the bottom of this strange behaviour on the part of Mr Sleeth. When I have done so, I am certain that your evidence at the inquest will be vindicated in full.'

BACK IN HIS OWN HOUSE, ADAM MULLED OVER ALL THAT HE HAD learned so far about the death of Matthew Hawley, the surgeon. The poor man's drowning was strange enough. The response of those in authority, both coroner and magistrate, was unworthy of the most remote village in the kingdom. The case cried out for someone to make a proper investigation. However, as his emotions cooled, he began to see formidable obstacles in his path. He could expect no help from those who had already shown themselves indifferent to the claims of justice. Nor could he go about himself, asking questions and seeking out the truth. Everyone agreed the people of Millgate were insular and wary of all outsiders. Most were wherrymen, labourers on the staithes or workers in the great mill which stood over one branch of the River Bure at that point. The appearance in their midst of someone they would see as a rich gentleman, as well as a person from up the hill in Aylsham, would produce nought but suspicion and silence. Somehow, he had to find ways of collecting the facts he needed. How he would do that, he had no idea.

After more than half an hour of intense thought, Adam could still see no way forward. He had never, to his recollection, had any personal contact with Mr Hawley, and no idea of his acquaintances or the circles in which he moved. Did he leave a widow or any family? Where did he live? Who were his patients?

It was time to set those problems aside until the morning and turn to more pleasant matters. He would turn his mind away from murder and think instead of his plans for his future life with Lady Alice.

It came as a severe jolt to him that he had not spared her a single thought for most of the day. How could he be so heartless? How could he forget so easily the woman upon whom all his hopes of future happiness depended? What must she be thinking of his silence since he had left her side?

He gobbled down his dinner, scarcely tasting what he ate, and hastened back to his desk, where he took up pen and paper, determined to send his beloved the kind of letter that would convince her she was foremost in his mind.

He couldn't do it. All his attempts to express his love and desire in suitable language sounded like the effusions of some third-rate writer of novels. Sheet after sheet of paper was torn up and discarded. Disheartened, he wrote instead of his surprise at finding himself at once drawn into a new mystery on his return, giving an outline of the situation and hoping he might be forgiven for giving over any part of his mind to matters unconnected with their future together. Then he ended the letter with a simple declaration of love and the hope that she might find the time to write to him and help keep his spirits up, for he anticipated a good deal of frustration and disappointment ahead.

He knew if he left the letter on his desk, he would soon tear it up and begin again the whole process of agonising over what to write. Instead, he folded and sealed the paper and rang the bell for Hannah, instructing her to give the missive to William, his groom, with instructions to deliver it to Mossterton Hall first thing the next morning.

At once, his mind reverted to the problem of Matthew Hawley's death and how best to conduct an investigation. Now, however, at least two courses of action presented themselves. First, he would visit his Quaker friend, Mr Jempson. He had lived in Aylsham for many years and would at least be able to give him some information about those who lived and worked near the Bure Navigation, in the area known as Millgate. That done, he would take a walk himself down to the Mill-gate area as soon as he could. To the best of his recollection, he had never even seen the wharves and staithes on the Navigation, let alone considered how a wherry — a sailing vessel — could make its way so far inland and along what was, in all truth, no more than a typical river of these parts. An inconsequential, slow-flowing stream which rose somewhere near Melton Constable and finally lost itself in the Broads near Wroxham. Maybe twenty or twenty-one miles long in total and most of it too shallow and narrow for any kind of craft, besides being encumbered by many watermills. If it proved a waste of time as regards the killing of Mr Hawley, his day might prove educational in other ways. At least he could see for himself where the murder happened.

## 5

Adam rose early the next day, eager to shake off any temptation to waste his time in daydreaming and idleness. They had been with him since he returned from Mosserton Hall. Now it was time to make a proper start on investigating the death of the surgeon, Matthew Hawley. Since he had already sent William on his errand, he therefore told Hannah to walk the short distance to Mr Jempson's house and enquire whether a visit from her master would be acceptable that morning. Fortunately, Mr Jempson proved to be both at home and at leisure. He would, he said, be delighted to welcome the doctor at any time before noon.

Adam presented himself at ten, judging that to be an acceptable hour to call on someone; late enough to be sure not to interrupt breakfast, yet early enough to leave sufficient time before noon to ask the questions he had in mind.

As usual, Mr Jempson's welcome was a genuine one. They had helped one another on several previous occasions and the bond between them was a deep one. The first half hour or so was therefore taken up with the kind of topics you would expect to hear when two friends meet again after a modest time apart. Only when each had expressed delight at seeing the other again, followed by assurances they would not allow such a lengthy interruption of their contact to arise in the future, could Adam pose the questions he had come to ask.

'I fear I can tell thee little of Mr Hawley beyond what is common knowledge,' Jempson replied. 'By all accounts, he was a good surgeon and a good man besides. His death has, I fear, robbed this world of one who helped many, both rich and poor. To take another man's life is, as thou knowest, an affront to God's holy law as well as the laws of men. It must surely put whoever does such a foul deed in peril of giving over his immortal soul to the forces of evil. Aye, and that for all eternity too.'

'Did you ever meet Surgeon Hawley?' Adam asked.

'Not so far as I can recollect,' Jempson said. 'He lived in Millgate and found the vast majority of his patients from those who did the same. Whether he was a religious man, I know not. He was not a member of our Society for certain, for I would have been told at once if any such member had met their death in such a violent fashion.'

'And you know nothing more about him?'

'I fear I must disappoint thee, my friend, for I do not.' There was a pause, then Jempson seemed to recall something more.

'Listen, my friend. I may not be able to assist thee myself, but I think I may be able to set thee on the right path even so. Mr Hawley had a housekeeper. A lady perhaps in her mid-twenties and one possessed of both a keen mind and a greater level of learning than you would expect from someone in her position. If thou hast not yet spoken with her, I recommend most strongly that thou should'st do so, for she must know more of her master and the comings and goings in his life than anyone else. Her name is Rose ... Rose ... Yes, that's it: Rose Thoday. Besides being his housekeeper, she is, so I have been told, most skilled in growing and preparing all kinds of medicinal herbs. So skilled indeed that she is the supplier of herbs to several apothecaries and other medical practitioners hereabout. I am surprised thou dost not know of her thyself.'

'I rarely purchase items of that kind,' Adam said. 'If I need any drug or preparation, I turn to my friend Mr Lassimer.'

'Of course. Ask him about Miss Thoday then.'

'I will. Still, I would be glad to hear anything you know of her as well. If I must rely on her for nearly all detailed information about her former master, it would be most helpful to have an objective view of the person I will be dealing with.'

'Very well. Rose Thoday's father was a minister of the established church. Do not assume that means he had wealth or position in society. The Reverend Mr Thoday was one of the many ordained men who exist by carrying out the parish duties of wealthier parsons in return for a meagre annual stipend. Nor was he ever likely to gain a parish of his own, since he had no patron to exert the necessary influence on his behalf. It was not an especially comfortable life, but it was, at least, a respectable one. Then, so I was told, he lost his faith, and with it both status and income. Shortly afterwards, he took his own life.

'I know not how his poor wife and daughter managed after that. The daughter, Miss Rose then appeared again in the employ of Surgeon Hawley. I believe each found the other suited them admirably and they settled down into what must have seemed a stable and comfortable existence. I presume her mother either died or married again, but which I do not know.'

'What sort of a person is Miss Thoday, if you are prepared to venture an opinion?'

'To be honest, I do not know enough of her character to do so. What I do know is that she is well-educated. I imagine, being an only child, her father must have schooled her himself. The folk of Millgate look up to her as a person to be consulted on all manner of problems, not just medical ones. I have heard my friend, Mr Bale, describe her as a source of wise counsel to many, especially the poor. If that is so — and he would not say it otherwise — she must be well-respected, just as her master was.'

'Thank you. I still cannot quite grasp how this area, Millgate, can be so close to the town and yet so little known — at least to me. I do not recall ever having been there.'

'It is not a place likely to afford thee many patients, doctor. The people who live there are mostly artisans and poor labourers. For the rest, I suppose they must be termed sailors, though their boats go only upon the river as far as Coltishall, or sometimes Great Yarmouth.'

'The Bure Navigation is yet another topic on which my ignorance is profound, I regret to tell you.'

'If thou needest to know more about the business of the Navigation and the people of Millgate, go and talk with my friend Mr Bale. He is a member of the Society of Friends, as I am, and a most pleasant and honest gentleman. Best of all, he lives in Millgate and has done so for many a year, for he owns both a maltings and a brewery there. I will write him a note this very morning, asking him to welcome thee and tell thee all thou may wish to know. Not that he would have done otherwise, for he is most hospitable, but it will do no harm to have an introduction.'

Adam thanked his friend heartily. He knew Jempson was seen as an important person amongst the Quakers, locally and in the county as a whole. A request from him would be tantamount to a command to Mr Bale to tell all he knew.

EAGER TO FIND OUT YET MORE ABOUT THE SURGEON AND HIS household, Adam hurried back along the street and turned into the doorway to the apothecary's shop. If his luck was in, he should find Peter Lassimer present and sufficiently free from business to talk with him. That turned out to be the case. The apothecary was not out on his rounds, but standing behind the counter. On that day of the week, many shopkeepers closed their shops at noon or soon after, allowing themselves time to undertake necessary tasks, such as casting their accounts and sending out invoices. Meanwhile, their employees either had a little free time to make up for the long hours they were expected to work every other day of the week save for Sunday, or were given the task of cleaning and sweeping the premises.

That day, Adam found Peter with his eye on the clock and his mind already on closing for the day. The weather had kept most people inside and sales scarcely sufficient to justify waiting to see if any late-comers might yet put in an appearance. He at once took Adam's arrival as a sign to shut up the shop and call on his housekeeper to bring them something warming to drink.

The two were soon settled in Peter's parlour with glasses of warm punch before them. Not surprisingly, the apothecary was eager to know everything that Adam had been doing since they talked last.

'It feels little enough,' Adam said. 'I've been to visit Mr Jempson. He says the person I need to talk with is Surgeon Hawley's housekeeper. She should have the closest knowledge of his state of mind and activities in the days before his death. Mr Jempson's personal knowledge of her was rather limited, and he seemed sure you would know her better than he did.' Adam smiled. 'I didn't ask him why he thought you would know her.'

Peter frowned. 'I do not make a habit of bedding every woman in this town,' he said.

'Only a large proportion of them, perhaps?'

'Not even that. As you well know, I keep my distance from married women.'

'So, this housekeeper is married?'

'Not at all. Some call her Mrs Thoday, but that is only the convention by which all housekeepers bear the title of Mrs. I understand she prefers Miss.'

'Was Surgeon Hawley married? No, you would have told me. A widower perhaps?'

'He certainly had no wife that I knew of. Whether he ever had been married, I can't say, but there's never been any sign of a wife while he's been here. No children either. Just him on his own, at first, until about three years ago, when he somehow came into contact with Rose Thoday and took her on to keep house for him.'

'Is she a lady of mature years? A widow, perhaps?' Adam couldn't stop himself.

'I know you think I do nothing but chase every widow within miles,' Peter said, his voice betraying some uncharacteristic irritation. 'It's very far from true. Before you manage to build up some fantasy to connect me with Rose Thoday, let me tell you what I know of her. I would judge her age to be between twenty-five and thirty. She's comely without being beautiful, tall for a woman and has a good figure.'

'Surgeon Hawley was what? In his early fifties? And they lived together?'

'Now you're off in another direction, aren't you? Listen! I've only dealt with Miss Rose to buy dried herbs from her garden. Normally, I would admit she's very much the kind of woman I would be interested in. However, I've never made the smallest move to deal with her in other than the most polite and formal way. That's the truth.'

'I believe you, but why?'

'Hard to say. Hawley was very protective of her, but not for the reason you think. If I had to describe what I saw of their relationship, I would say she was more his pupil and assistant than anything else.'

'Pupil? But a woman can't be a surgeon.'

'Let me finish. Most of what he was teaching her seemed to be concerned with the growing and preparing of medicinal herbs. There's a large garden attached to Hawley's house and, between them, they kept it in excellent order. It's full of herbs, including a good few I've never seen before. Maybe he brought them back from foreign parts as a result of his service in the navy. I wouldn't know. What I do know is that she has become a skilled herbalist. I buy dried herbs from her myself, from time to time, and their quality is far above those supplied by anyone else. I know she also makes up various potions and salves, using some of the exotic plants she grows. People go to her for cures as much, perhaps more, than they did to her master.'

'He didn't mind?'

'Not at all. He always gave the impression of being proud of her. A little like a father with a favourite daughter.'

'And nothing else?'

'Nothing. He was universally revered for the way he extended help to all who needed it. For example, I know he was assisting several local lads with learning to write and reckon up figures. The minister at the dissenting chapel in Millgate runs a Sunday school, I believe, at which he teaches basic reading. Hawley took the more promising students and taught them to write more than their names and do basic accounts, so they could find better-paid work as clerks or bookkeepers. That's the kind of man he was. As a doctor, he readily accepted whatever people could pay for his services, whether in cash or kind. The very poorest he would treat gratis.'

'A veritable Good Samaritan! What else can you tell me about his housekeeper, Miss Thoday? Is there some way I could approach her?'

'I said I never even considered trying to tempt her into my bed. I didn't tell you why. The trouble is, I'm not sure I can explain in any sensible way. Yes, she's good looking and pleasant to converse with, but there's something different about her. The best I can do is say that she's uncommonly self-sufficient and confident. She knows her own mind and isn't afraid to say what she wants — or doesn't want. She's also much better educated than other women of her class. She strikes you at once as sharp-witted, even gifted in some way. If she wanted you to make love to her, she'd tell you openly. If she didn't — and I don't think she's interested in me — she'd say nothing unless you provoked her. What she'd say or do in that case I have no idea, but I'm convinced it wouldn't be pleasant.'

'You sound as if you're a little afraid of her?'

'Yes, I am, and not ashamed to admit it. Wait until you meet her, Bascom. You may be the gentleman and the learned physician, but you'll find that counts for little with her. When Rose Thoday looks at you, you'll feel like that King of Babylon in the bible. What does it say of him? "Weighed in the balance and found wanting." That's exactly how I feel she looks at me.'

'A strong character?'

'Definitely. You asked if you could approach her to answer your questions. I see no reason why not, so long as you do so openly and honestly. Tell her what you want and why you want it. She'll most likely see through any tricks you come up with and mark you down as a fool and a liar. Then she'll not even give you a good-day. Be open, honest and forthright. It's the only way. If she wants to help you, she'll be the best of informants. If she does not, she'll tell you nothing.'

'Now you're making me feel nervous.'

'Good. Arrogance will get you shown the door in a moment. There's one other thing too. The local people both love her dearly and fear her too. Many say she's a Wise Woman, though I've never heard that she claims as much. It's true she's somehow related to Old Goody Otley, who was notorious in these parts for having the Second Sight, casting spells and generally terrifying anyone who crossed her. She died years ago, but her memory is still a powerful force in Millgate. If you get on the wrong side of Miss Thoday, you can say goodbye to any chance of a single person around there telling you anything. In fact, you'd be lucky to get away without some good kicks in the backside to send you on your way. Be warned!'

Adam knew Peter wasn't the kind of person to over-dramatise or concoct stories in a situation like this. What he said had to be taken seriously. Still, what it amounted to was little more than the suggestion Miss Thoday was not a typical housekeeper. Nor was Adam so surprised by that. Mr Jempson's explanation of her background suggested she had been brought up in better circumstances than had been open to her after her father's suicide. If Miss Rose Thoday was willing to help him, he would be more than pleased. If not ... well, he would have to take his chances. He was certainly not about to give up before he'd started, just because the credulous natives of Millgate might take against him if he upset her.

## 6

Next morning, while Adam was barely awake, Rose Thoday stepped out from the kitchen of what had been the surgeon's house and came to a halt, irresolute, in the middle of the parlour. The house had only three rooms on the ground floor, besides the kitchen with scullery and pantry attached. There was a dining room, simply furnished with a good table and four chairs, together with a sideboard to hold crockery and cutlery. There was also a room, maybe once used as a withdrawing room, which Mr Hawley had turned into a consulting room. This was the third room and the smallest. The place where Mr Hawley had sat of an evening after dinner, smoking his pipe and trying to read some book by the uncertain light of one or two candles.

She was here now because it was the only room which possessed a mirror, hung above a cupboard on the wall opposite the window. It wasn't a very good mirror — at least, in the sense of allowing her to look at herself properly. It was too old for that, its glass now somewhat dulled by age and the silvering behind showing through in irregular spots and patches. Of course, it wasn't there to allow people to admire themselves. Its purpose was to reflect daylight back from the window into the room. This it did well enough, she supposed. The trouble was you had to stand with your back to the window to look at yourself, so that your body seemed ringed by a nimbus of light, while your face and features were in shadow.

Rose rarely considered what she looked like, so long as she was clean and her clothes respectable. She'd never had money enough to buy fine cloth or have it made up into some fashionable style which would fade long before the fabric was even half worn out. Not that there had been any need for that. As the daughter of an impoverished curate, she was under no illusion that any potential husband would see her as more than a sturdy helpmeet, able to bear his children and keep his house as frugally as possible. She was well used to the second of these. Of the first, she knew little save that it held few attractions for a woman who liked to use her brains whenever she could.

Rose had been raised in a household which lacked servants, save for a series of half-starved maids-of-all-work — the only kind willing to come for the pittance her father could offer. Most of these had been supplied by the Overseers of the Poor and few lasted more than a year or so, before some local lad managed to get them with child. Then it was off to the workhouse, while another of the same type took their place. Her mother had done the cooking on her own, until Rose was old enough to help in the kitchen. While her father had fretted over his lack of opportunities for promotion in the church, his wife and daughter had scrimped and saved to keep a respectable roof over their heads. There had been no point in complaining. What was true of them was equally true of the majority of families in Millgate.

It had not been a very comfortable upbringing, but it had, on the whole, been a happy one. Her father treated her more like a son than a daughter, seeing she learned how to read and write and encouraging her to make full use of the only luxury he allowed himself — his small library. Perhaps he hoped she might be able to attract a better husband that way. If he did, it showed his unworldliness when it came to matrimonial choices. The one or two young ministers — copies of her father — who had shown some interest when she reached sixteen, had swiftly made a retreat when they realised she had no dowry and was at least their equal in learning. Her attempts to engage them in serious conversation proved a most effective way of pouring ice-cold water over their already tepid ardour.

She would have settled down to spinsterhood in her parents' home had not a bitter fate intervened. Finding himself caught between loneliness and loss of faith, the Reverend Elias Thoday had resolved his dilemma by hanging himself in the vestry of the church where he had just celebrated Evensong, leaving the churchwardens baffled and his wife and daughter facing a life of poverty and dependency on others.

Mrs Grace Thoday, always fragile in mind as well as body, took her child to live with a cousin. There, she swiftly gave up the struggle to survive what she felt was an insupportable disgrace, visited on her by a husband she had long since dismissed as a failure in every sense. Within six months, she had lost her mind; in seven, she had taken a malignant fever; and before the eighth was out, she lay in her grave. The cousin, who had taken the two of them in only from a sense of duty, decided young Rose would best be accommodated as an unpaid servant. After all, no man would be fool enough to marry a woman both of whose parents had ended their lives so badly. At the age of thirteen, Rose had become an orphan with nowhere to live save in conditions of near slavery.

Rose turned back to the mirror, staring at her face and trying to understand what Mr Hawley had seen that made him treat her as he had the day she came to ask for work. Whatever it was, he had revealed himself as the greatest benefactor she could have imagined. He took her request seriously — far more seriously than her background deserved. Then, by gentle questions, he drew out that the two things she liked best in the world were reading and the study of plants. To her mind at the time, neither were going to help her survive, but he proved her wrong. Within barely an hour on that first day, he had offered her the post of his housekeeper with a modest salary. He also promised he would teach her what little he knew about the growing and use of medicinal plants. She could also have free run of his garden and a sturdy, dry building, once a carriage house, in which to hang up the bunches of herbs after harvesting. For the rest, she would have to draw upon her memory of what her great-aunt, Goody Otley, had taught her, supplemented by the two precious books the old woman had bequeathed to her when she died. Now, six years later, she knew herself to be a more-than-competent medical herbalist and dispenser. She had also watched her master when he set broken bones and dealt with dislocations, so that she could do the job almost as well as him. For a time, life had been good. Officially his housekeeper, Rose had become Matthew Hawley's star pupil and assistant — until some wicked man came behind Hawley in the dark and struck him down.

It should have been the end of everything good in her life. That it was not was once again due to the surgeon's kindness and generosity. They had never talked of marriage, his or hers. Indeed, they had talked of little save the cases he was treating, the properties of herbs and drugs, and the times she could help him by counselling the despairing and comforting those whose lives had been wrecked by loss or disappointment. It was assumed between them that she would stand alongside him in providing what help they could to the sick and unfortunate. Everyone locally knew of her family connection with Old Goody Otley, of course. Many, privately, called Rose a Wise Woman, and wondered what unknown powers of divination or spell-casting she might possess. She never encouraged such ideas. So far as she knew, she had no supernatural ability whatsoever. What help she could give was based on her knowledge of herbs, her capacity to take pains, and a more than normal amount of sound common sense. On the other hand, she knew better than to ignore the healing powers of harmless superstition. Once, when she was young and Goody Otley was nearing ninety years of age, she had plucked up the courage to ask the old woman whether she truly believed in the rituals and incarnations she often used over her patients.

'Don't matter squit whether I does or no,' the old woman had said with a laugh. 'All as matters is whether they does. If I gives someone a jar of ointment for a bad case of ringworms, they'll use it once or twice and, like as not, get impatient and decide it ain't working. 'Course, you and I knows they ain't given it time, but they won't want to wait. But if I gives 'em the same stuff an' tells 'em it has to be rubbed on nine times — no more an' no less — when the moon is waxin', they'll do it and be cured. What cured 'em? The ointment, or the superstition that made sure they used it aright? I've lived a powerful long time, young Rose, and there's stories I could tell 'ee that you'd scarce believe when it come to the power of belief to cure on its own. I seen men lie down and die 'cos they thought someone 'ad cursed them; and all the time they was fit as fleas. I seen many ignore good advice, then do th'exact same thing when one o' the Cunning Folk said they'd read it in the cards. Don't you ignore my kind o' flummery, when you comes to have your own patients, my girl. 'Appen you'll find it makes them 'erbs o' yours work even better.'

Well, if you wanted possible proof of Goody Otley's power of fore-telling, there you had it. Those words had been spoken more than ten years ago, when there was not the slightest suggestion Rose would spend her time trying to heal the sick. How had she known? Had she guessed? Rose shook her head in wonderment and set the matter aside.

Back to what mattered now. How would she make her way in the world? She had lost her master and with him her position as his house-keeper. She had lain awake a good part of the last three nights, going over and over the possibilities in her mind. Each time she came back to the same impossible desire: to set herself up in some way in the business of healing the sick. She had loved working as she had until now: growing herbs, making up medicines and helping the surgeon treat the sick. She would rather die than give that up. She also felt, somewhere in the depth of her heart, she had a duty to Mr Hawley she must discharge. She had to try to find his killer. If she failed, so be it. If she didn't even try, she'd live for the rest of her life feeling wretched and disgraced. She must do all she could to bring his killer to justice, whatever it cost her.

If what she had to do was clear, how to do it was utterly uncertain. Then an idea came to her. Only yesterday, she had been walking in the market place and noticed a man passing on the other side of the street. Not just any man either, but the unmistakable figure of Dr Adam Bascom. She'd known who he was because she'd caught sight of him once when she'd been delivering herbs to the apothecary, Mr Lassimer. She'd asked out of idle curiosity who the young man was. Mr Lassimer had laughed and told her it was his good friend, Dr Bascom. He'd gone on to describe him as a fine physician, who was now rich and famous, thanks to his exploits in bringing criminals to justice. Her way forward was therefore clear. She would call on this Dr Bascom and seek to persuade him to help her find out who had killed Mr Hawley.

Yet again, she looked in the mirror. She was definitely no beauty, but she supposed her face was pleasant enough, if somewhat longer than it should be. Her dress, however, had to be changed before she ventured to speak with a gentleman.

'I'm a little too tall to be a woman of fashion,' she told herself. 'Too thin as well. Still, I have a passable figure, even if no one would class it as voluptuous. If I put on my best dress, with my green cloak and best bonnet, I imagine I will pass well enough to call on Dr Bascom. After all, for all his wealth and renown, he cannot be more than a few years older than I am. Still unmarried as well, so there will be no disdainful wife to pass comment on me after I have left.'

In Rose's mind, there was no chance Adam would seek her out, so she would have to go to him. She'd even considered pretending to be ill, but if he was as good a doctor as people said, he'd see through that in a few moments. People often said that honesty was the best policy. In her case, it was all she had.

The trouble would come in trying to convince him to get involved. She had no experience of dealing with gentlemen. No experience of winning over any man, if she were honest with herself. She knew roughly what flirting meant, but she'd never tried it. The same was true of seduction or the use of so-called womanly wiles. If anything was needed beyond rational argument, she would be in the dark. Nevertheless, she was determined to do whatever it took.

She peered in the mirror while she lifted one side of her skirt and twisted her ankle from side to side. Was that a comely ankle? She had no idea, save that it was the only right ankle she had. She pulled the skirt a little higher and stared glumly at her calf. Like the rest of her, her legs were slim, but was that enough?

The only thing Rose Thoday thought she understood about wealthy young men — especially the younger members of the gentry — was that, when it came to women, they were only interested in one thing. She had therefore convinced herself that, if it would take letting Dr Bascom have his way with her to persuade him to help her find Mr Hawley's killer, she would submit without a murmur.

$$\text{❧} \quad 7 \quad \text{❧}$$

'It's hopeless,' Adam said. 'I cannot even find where to start my investigation. If there was only some clue — some indication of what might be worth exploring further. But there's nothing. From every account I've had so far, the man was some sort of Good Samaritan, living a blameless life and liked by everyone. How does someone like that come to be murdered?'

They were sitting in Peter's compounding room; Adam hunched over, with his head in his hands, Peter busy rolling out pills.

'An angry husband or brother?'

'I have no evidence that Mr Hawley was like you in the least, my friend. I could well imagine you being done to death by someone angry at your lascivious ways.'

'Not a husband at any rate. No married women! You know I never stray from that particular rule, however tempted I may be.'

'A brother then, or a son who's infuriated by seeing his mother fawn all over you.'

'It hasn't happened yet,' Peter said. 'Most of my lady friends would probably give any such murderer a good hiding and tell them not to interfere. Still, we aren't talking about my peccadilloes, are we?'

'Peccadilloes? I believe sins is the word. However, the surgeon seems to have sought out neither women nor boys nor anyone else for bedtime games — at least, so far as I can discover.'

'You may yet find someone.'

'I may. To be honest, it would be a relief if I did. At least I would be able to start on something tangible. No. So far as I can see, sexual misdeeds are not the answer.'

'An angry patient?'

'No one has mentioned that either. Besides, the patient would need to have a most substantial grudge to resort to killing his doctor.'

'Of course, if he was being treated by a physician, like you, the size of the account he would receive would be more than enough justification for assassination.'

'Very droll. I wondered how long it would be before you started to make fun of me.'

'All I'm trying to do is cheer you up. At the moment, you look like some poor fellow on the eve of his execution.'

'I feel like one. Don't imagine I haven't already considered all these possibilities. I have, and there's not the slightest evidence for any of them.'

'Perhaps he knew something dangerous; something that might send another person to the gallows. They had to silence him or risk him informing on them. What about smugglers? No one lasts long if those banditti believe he or she is a potential informer.'

'Smugglers? Around here, everyone knows all about the smugglers. I could name twenty at least — probably more if I really thought about it. It's a way of life for perhaps half the population. The other half profit to the tune of cheap brandy, tobacco and heaven knows what else. Who's going to turn informer? If anybody was going to be done to death because of knowing about smuggling, it would be one of the Riding Officers or other Revenue men. If the smugglers set out to eliminate every potential informer, the streets would be running with blood.'

'Despite your mockery, I still think the idea that Mr Hawley knew something he shouldn't is the best idea so far.'

Adam thought about it. What Lassimer said was true. Unfortunately, even if it proved to be the answer, it didn't get him much further forward.

'Even if you're right,' he said grudgingly, 'until we know the nature of this dreadful secret it was worth killing a man to protect, we're no further forward, are we?'

'A secret birth in a respectable family?'

'The man was a surgeon, not a midwife!'

'The identity of a murderer?'

'His own, perhaps? How many unsolved murders have there been in this area in the past year? None. In the past two years? None.'

'Maybe it was longer ago.'

'During the Civil War, perhaps? That's barely a hundred and fifty years back. Be serious, Lassimer. If knowing the identity of someone who committed a serious crime were enough to get you killed, wouldn't that crime be something well known?'

'A crime we don't know was a crime—'

'Done by someone we don't know is a criminal for reasons we don't know either. Very helpful!'

'Then we're back to a random, purposeless killing by someone who was simply passing by. No, we've forgotten robbery gone wrong.'

'Nothing was stolen, so far as we know. Look, my friend, no robber knocks someone on the head and throws him into a river before checking through his pockets and taking anything of value. Barely two or three minutes passed between people hearing the sounds of the killing, then the splash and the first person arriving on the scene. It was pitch black too. No one mentioned observing any light. Let's say our imaginary person banged poor Mr Hawley on the head. Then what. If the evidence of the sounds is accepted, he heaved the body into the river almost at once. That's an assassination, not a robbery. Unless the witnesses are all mistaken — or lying — there was no time for any theft to have taken place.'

Adam sat back, then banged his hand on the counter in front of him in frustration.

'Stop that,' Peter said angrily. 'You've just made all my pills jump out of place and ruined half-an-hour's work. If you want to hit something, go home and hit your own furniture.'

'Sorry,' Adam mumbled. 'It's just so maddening. Whatever you say, I'm convinced this was a cold-blooded killing, carried out for a definite purpose. But why? If I knew that, I'd at least be on my way to finding out the identity of the killer.'

'Why not take a walk to Millgate yourself?' Peter said. 'At least you can see where it happened. That might give you some ideas. You could also talk to some of those who live and work in that area and find out if they know anything helpful. If nothing else, the walk might help you work off some of your spleen.'

'I think I will,' Adam replied. 'While I'm there, I could also take a look at this Bure Navigation. It probably has nothing to do with the murder, but people keep mentioning it and I feel somewhat foolish being ignorant of it myself. If the weather is fine, I'll go tomorrow.'

⚜

WHEN HE RETURNED TO HIS HOME, ADAM WAS DELIGHTED TO FIND a letter for him from Lady Alice. In it, along with some heart-warming expressions of devotion, she made her views plain on the subject of investigating the death of the surgeon. Far from apologising for deciding to look into the murder, she wrote, he should give it whatever time and attention it required. She would be deeply disappointed in him if he did not. She had known nothing of Mr Hawley, but some superficial questioning of her land agent and the senior servants had confirmed what Adam had written in his previous letter. The surgeon had been a good man, well known for many miles around for his charitable deeds and likeable manner. Her only regret was that there did not seem to be much assistance she could offer, except to serve as a sounding board for his ideas. What he needed, she continued, was someone who could act as his local 'champion'; a person known and trusted in the area who could vouch for him. Was the surgeon married? If he was, his wife would certainly be well worth talking to.

The remainder of the letter was taken up with a report on another conversation with her agent about Irmingland Abbey. Although it was not suitable as the basis for the home she had planned, he assured her it was in good repair and should make an excellent home for a tenant, should she decide to let the land she had been holding back. What did Adam think? Should she do as her agent suggested?

Unfortunately, Adam had scarcely given the question of their future home any thought at all, between his excitement at the prospect of marriage and the sudden plunge into the mystery of Matthew Hawley's death. He therefore determined to set all else aside that evening, after completing his dinner, and consider what advice he could offer.

It was a well-meant decision, but one that was bound to be doomed to failure. His mind kept returning to Matthew Hawley and running over what little he had learned so far. If all he had been told were true, it was hard to believe the man could have any enemies — let alone one ready to strike him down and push him into the water to drown. What could he have done to bring such an attack about? So far as Adam knew, his life had been blameless ...

So far as he knew. There was the first requirement: to speak to the one who had been first on the scene, if he could. The constable for certain, as well as the wherryman who first heard the splash and tried to give help. He might be more difficult to approach, but an attempt would have to be made. Mrs Brigstone, his housekeeper, had asked him for permission to go to see her sister the next day. She had also told him her sister lived in Millgate. If he asked her, he was sure she would do her best to discover the names of these people and where they might be found.

It wasn't much, but it was a kind of start. What about Lady Alice's suggestion of seeking out Hawley's wife? He didn't have one, but he did have a housekeeper. Mr Jempson had suggested it would be well worth Adam talking to her. Peter's description of her was a little off-putting, but the apothecary was given to exaggeration in describing women. His ideal in womanhood tended towards the voluptuous and passionate. Strong, capable women probably frightened him. If Miss Thoday was one of these, he was more than likely to see her as someone to avoid. Whatever her nature, there was no doubt she had to be seen and questioned. Servants usually knew far more about their master's business than their employer expected. Whether she would be willing to share what she knew was another matter.

At this point, the uncertainty and frustration which had held Adam back finally passed. Other ideas came to him.

The attack had taken place after dark, about half-past nine. Not too late for people to be brought running by the sound of Hawley falling, or being pushed, into the water.

What time was it now?

Adan peered at the dial of the splendid, long-case clock which stood near the door of his parlour, trying to make out the positions of the hands in the dim, flickering light of the candles beside him. It looked like ten minutes past eight. He wouldn't be thinking of going to his bed for another two hours or so. Poor people retired early, of course, since candles were expensive. However, the speed with which a crowd had assembled that night argued that few were asleep, even if they were in their beds.

What had taken Hawley outside at that time? He had been struck down not far from his own door, if his house was in the position Adam thought it was. An odd distance. Not close enough to suggest a brief walk outside to take the air; not far enough to prove he was on his way somewhere else. After all, the most likely explanation for any medical man being out in the dark was a sudden call from a patient. Was that what had taken place that night? Had some message come, asking the surgeon to make an urgent call? If it had, who had sent it? Had it been expected? Was it even genuine? The housekeeper might know, though there was no reason why Hawley should have informed her of his actions. Still, if he, Adam, was called out at night, he usually told someone he was going out. Hannah, perhaps. William, if he needed a horse or the carriage. Maybe his own housekeeper, Mrs Brigstone, if she had been roused. He wasn't systematic about it, but he couldn't imagine leaving without letting anyone know.

Of course, Hawley had only one person to tell: his housekeeper. Yet was that true? She was the only member of his household he knew about. That didn't mean there were no others. Housekeepers didn't usually do everything themselves. There should be at least one maid, probably two. One for the house and one to help the cook in the kitchen. Hawley probably had a horse for riding or pulling a carriage. That would demand a groom. The more Adam thought about it, the less he realised he knew of even the most obvious details of Hawley's household.

If Hawley had been called out suddenly, how would his assailant know of it? Had he brought the message? Had he been prowling around, simply hoping to come upon his victim? Unless it really had been a chance attack by some vagrant — an answer Adam strongly doubted — the murderer must have known he stood a good chance of finding Hawley where he could launch his attack safely.

That brought Adam back to the reason why the surgeon had been killed. He felt sure he could set aside a cuckolded husband or a jealous lover, unless he had specific evidence pointing to either. It wasn't a robbery either. That left two main possibilities. Either the surgeon had disturbed someone, and thus posed the threat of discovery; or he knew something and was expected to speak out. In the first case, the only credible reason for killing him would be that he had recognised those engaged in illegal activity. In the second, he must have found out about some serious wrongdoing and be about to tell the authorities.

What could it be? The answer wasn't simple smuggling. Of that Adam felt sure, for all the reasons he had given Peter. What else then …

Adam came to with a jolt. The excitement of the past few days must have tired him out, and he'd fallen asleep in the midst of trying to work things out. Slept for some time too. The candles had burned down a good way since he had looked at them last.

He got up, stretched to expel the cricks from his neck and moved closer to the clock. A quarter past nine. He crossed to the window. The shutters were in place, so someone, probably Hannah or Mrs Brigstone, had come in while he was sleeping and tidied up. He unlatched the shutters on one window and pushed them back far enough to look outside. As far as he could judge, it was fully dark. He could see virtually nothing. There had been thick cloud all day, so any moon would be completely hidden. What had the weather been like on the day the surgeon was killed? When had the moon risen and how close had it been to the full? More important questions to be answered. How easy would it have been for the mysterious assailant to hide himself, then dart out to strike with sufficient accuracy? Could he even be certain he was attacking the right man?

Disgusted with himself for spending a whole day in conversation without tackling any of the most obvious matters to be resolved, Adam took up the small candle someone had left beside his hand, lit it from the stump of one in the candle-holder on the table, blew out the rest, and made his way to his bed.

## 8

A dam's thoughts as he began to walk down the hill towards Millgate and away from the areas of Aylsham most familiar to him, combined trepidation and curiosity. The River Bure approached Aylsham from the north-west, then swept around the central part of the town, which clustered around the parish church, set on a modest hill well above the river. Whichever way you chose to approach the Bure, your path must be downwards and away from the part of the town where most of the better houses and buildings could be found. Millgate itself lay at the end of a road which led down from the church and marketplace towards the great mill, which straddled part of the River Bure. After that, the road crossed the river on a bridge and wandered off towards Ingworth and North Walsham.

Until some fifteen years before the time of this story, there would have been little more to say. Then, in 1779, the building of the Navigation — a process of straightening the river and constructing locks to render it navigable by small cargo vessels — opened the way from Aylsham to Coltishall, the Broads, Great Yarmouth and the sea. Adam knew little of the Navigation, save that it had made the river navigable by small boats driven by towering sails. Several times, while travelling to visit patients, he had been startled by the sight of such a sail moving slowly amongst the green fields and hedgerows.

With these ships came a new population: not just the sailors who handled them, but shipbuilders, blacksmiths, those who loaded and unloaded the cargoes, warehousemen and a host of associated trades-people, attracted by the prospect of a growth in trade between the agricultural heartland of the county and the vessels which sailed constantly along its coast. There were some merchants living in Mill-gate, but the vast majority of its population were working men and artisans. Many of those who worked at the staithes, or in the boat building and repairing yards, chose to live close by, as did a good number of the wherrymen and others who worked on the maintenance of the Navigation itself. They formed a community quite distinct from the people who lived in the rest of the town; one looking to the river and the sea, rather than the rich fields which spread on all sides. They had their own inns, their own society, and their own way of doing things. It would be difficult indeed for any 'outsider', especially a gentleman like Adam, to move amongst them, let alone persuade them to speak freely. Such people could ill afford the services of a physician, even if they wanted to, so there had not, until that day, been the slightest reason for Adam to venture amongst them.

Millgate was *terra incognita* — unexplored territory surrounding the canal basin, Aylsham Staithe, and the various smaller basins, quays and warehouses around them. Goods were unloaded there as they arrived or loaded ready for shipment to the coast. There were the warehouses, filled with goods awaiting transport and even one or two shipbuilders, who specialised in building and repairing the smaller wherries used on the Navigation itself. A poor, rough district, Adam expected, much like those encountered in fishing villages along the coast.

Adam's attitudes towards the majority of the population who earned their bread by manual labour were typical enough. Like most of the gentry and middling sort, he found little problem in dealing with them as individuals. However, taken *en masse*, they became 'the mob': an amorphous underclass, prone to riots and harbouring criminals of all sorts amongst them. That was why he felt uneasy about venturing into an area where such people must predominate. Most of the inhabitants were, doubtless, honest enough, but it was always possible one or two might see an opportunity for robbery in the appearance of a gentleman of means amongst them.

A flamboyant style of dress did not become a physician. People liked to see their doctor as a staid, sober fellow, more given to medical study than concern with the latest fashions. Even so, Adam took care next morning to choose clothing that was unlikely to draw too much attention. He did not feel quite secure while it was daylight. He would never dream of venturing into such an area after dark.

In fact, Adam's idea of Millgate, like his view of those who lived there, proved entirely untrue. As he reached the bottom of the hill and the land levelled out, he noticed a fine house to his right. It was set back amidst trees and shrubberies, somewhat hidden from the road, but still visible enough to show it had been built of good brick in a modern style. Not a grand mansion by any means, but definitely a house suitable for a gentleman to call his own.

Next, he passed a row of neat cottages, built of good brick and flint. Workers' homes, to be sure, but well made, suggesting those who lived in them earned sufficient from their labour to provide properly for a wife and family. Next came an inn, The Anchor, also built of good brick, with Dutch gables and a fine pantiled roof. This was no low beer house or grog-shop, but an inn such as might have graced the market place itself. And what was that behind the inn, set at right-angles to the road and main flow of the river? It must be a maltings and a brewery, both newly constructed by the look of them. Across the river stood yards where wherries were clearly being repaired or built. Beyond and to the right stood the great mill, now modernised and extended to cope with the increased business the river traffic had brought. Norfolk's superb barley made some of the country's best malt for brewing. Large quantities of both barley and malt were sent to London every year, while equally substantial amounts were shipped across the German Ocean to the Low Countries, Germany and the Baltic states. Taking such heavy goods along the roads to the coast had been slow and expensive. The ability to sail sixteen tons at a time down the Navigation to the sea added greatly to the prosperity of the town. Millgate might be insular and wary of outsiders, but it was definitely prosperous. There was no doubt about that.

Adam stood for a while on a stone bridge over the river, looking from the inn and maltings behind him, round past a line of staithes, busy with wherries loading and unloading, and up to the mill itself. On all sides, the influence of the Low Countries was striking, from the prevalence of red brick in the buildings to the use of clay pantiles on the roofs, rather than thatch. Some two hundred years before, protestant families had been driven from the Spanish Netherlands and adjacent areas of France by a wave of religious persecution. A good many had come to England, welcomed for the skills they brought in weaving and dying cloth. The majority had settled in London, in the area called Smithfield, but others had moved further north into Norfolk, which already had a flourishing trade in the export of raw wool. Thanks to their expertise, and that of others who followed them over the years, Norwich had developed a highly-successful trade in using that wool to manufacture richly coloured and patterned cloth: the so-called "Norwich stuffs" so sought after in Britain and overseas. By Adam's time, many a household, both in the city and its surrounding towns and villages, resounded with the constant clacking of weavers at work.

Now, where Adam had imagined a poor area of dilapidated cottages and wooden shacks for storage, he saw all the signs of a successful and flourishing centre of commerce. If this was where Matthew Hawley had set up his business, Adam could well imagine he would find patients more than able to afford the modest fees most surgeons charged.

Adam must have remained on the bridge for almost a quarter of an hour, wrapped in thought, when a voice from behind startled him into realising others had been passing him all that time.

'Good morrow, sir,' the voice said. 'From your dress, I suspect thou art a physician. Few such ever venture into this area, so I trust thou wilt pardon my curiosity in addressing thee and asking if thou art one Dr Bascom, a friend of Mr Joseph Jempson?'

The style of speech, so familiar to Adam from his Quaker friend, instantly identified the speaker as another member of the Society of Friends, which was able to assemble a goodly number at its Sunday meetings in the town.

'My name is Bale, sir,' the voice continued. 'Ethan Bale, maltster and brewer, at your service. My business premises lie there, behind the inn.'

Adam turned and saw before him a sturdy man of late middle age, dressed in the sober clothing and broad hat that must identify him to anyone as a Quaker.

'Adam Bascom, physician, as you guessed.'

'I thought thou must be he. I am delighted to make thy acquaintance, doctor. I am a member of the same meeting of the Society of Friends as Mr Jempson. He has written to me and asked that I give you such help as I can. From what he writes, I gather thou art engaged in seeking to discover who killed poor Matthew Hawley. A most worthy endeavour, sir. Surgeon Hawley is sorely missed in these parts and, to date, those in positions of authority seem remarkably dilatory in seeking out his killer. It is, doctor, an honour to be able to greet thee and offer my poor assistance to one who has so distinguished himself in bringing criminals to justice. Brother Jempson writes of you in the warmest terms.'

For a moment, Adam was caught totally unprepared. He had not expected to meet Mr Bale in such a manner; nor to find him so well-informed about his previous investigations.

Bale laughed at the expression on Adam's face. 'Do not look so surprised, doctor. I daresay almost everyone in these parts knows thou hadst a hand in thwarting the seditious riot at Baconsthorpe, then unmasking that treacherous quack, Professor Panacea, and his henchman.'

'Yet I told no one, aside from my immediate circle, sir. How has word got out?'

'Aylsham is a small town, doctor, and Millgate but a smaller part of it. The great affairs of state may pass us by, but people take great delight in local affairs and gossip. I know from Brother Jempson that thou are a modest man, but it would take far more than modesty to keep such brave deeds from becoming public knowledge. Aye, and being added to and embroidered in the telling, I have no doubt. But let us turn for a moment to more immediate matters. If there is ought I can do in this new endeavour on thy part, thou needst only ask. I will also pray for thee, Dr Bascom, and ask the Lord to direct thy feet into the right paths.'

Adam was unsure how best to reply to these offers, so he simply smiled and nodded. Then an idea came to him.

'There is one way in which you may be able to assist me right away, Mr Bale,' he said. 'I do not know this part of Aylsham. I also have to admit that it is not at all as I expected it to be. For example, as I came down from the marketplace, I passed what seemed to a be house suitable for a gentleman to one side. Do you know who lives there?'

'Indeed, sir. That is Millgate Manor, the current home of the Laven family. A fine property indeed, built by the grandfather of the present owner. But I am in haste now and should not have spent even as much time talking with you as I have. My business takes me first to King's Lynn, then to Wisbech, Ely and Cambridge. In all, I must be absent six days. I pray thee, doctor, if it be convenient, visit me on this day next week, about noon. At that time, I will happily share with thee all I know of this place — for I have lived here nigh on fifty years. My house lies over there, behind the malt house. Thou canst just see the chimney stacks over the roof. If thou art unsure, ask any of those who work hereabouts. I am well-known to all. Now I must, with great regret I assure thee, hasten on my way. I shall look for thee next week.'

'A day full of surprises,' Adam thought, after Mr Bale had hastened on his way. 'This place is far more prosperous and busier than I expected. I must remember to ask my new friend about these boats. I assume they're wherries. Don't boats of that kind use large sails? See, this one has a great mast laid down its full length and more. How can such a vessel move along a narrow river like the Bure? What if the wind blows in the wrong direction?'

The vessel he was looking at was around fourteen or fifteen feet in length and perhaps three or four broad at its widest. From his vantage-point on the bridge, he could see the boat was open for almost its full length, providing a hold for goods — in this case, large sacks, which, from the dirt which clung to them, contained coal. Several men were manhandling the sacks to a point underneath a simple winch, while three others were lifting one sack at a time and placing it into a wagon drawn up on the staithe. All this under the stern eye of a weather-beaten man of at least sixty years, his hair and beard almost white, save where it was stained about his mouth. The source of this staining was obvious, for he had a short, clay pipe clamped between his lips and was puffing on it vigorously.

Adam waited until the old sailor looked in his direction then called to him.

'You there, standing in the stern. Can you tell me what type of boat it is that you are standing in?'

The man stared at Adam for a long moment, almost as if the question was impertinent. Then he took his pipe from his mouth, coughed and hawked loudly, and spat the result over the side into the water. That performance over, he squinted up to Adam and deigned to reply.

'This be what they calls a wherry, mister. One special built for the Navigation. Can't get a normal keel along it, see? Locks be too narrow and channel twists too much, despite all that so-called straightenin' they done. They be three times as long and wide as this 'un and carries thirty ton. All we can manage is ten or a dozen ton of coal per load. Aye, only ten ton it were on this sailin', but it still be heavy work, for the wind were either flat calm or agin us, so we had to quant most o' the way.'

The man's accent was so strong Adam struggled to understand his words. 'Keel' he understood. That was a kind of barge. Coal from Great Yarmouth was plain enough, but what in heaven's name did 'quant' mean?'

'Quant?' he said. 'Did you say quant?'

'Aye, that I did. Quant — push the boat forwards with the quant-pole on the bottom. This 'un, here,' and he lifted one end of a pole from beside the mast. The pole was the thickness of a man's wrist and at least eighteen long, but he lifted it one-handed. 'You push with 'un, see? Ram the bottom into the mud and heave the boat forrard. 'Tis rare hard work, I tell 'ee, mister. Got to do it, though. Ain't many spots along Navigation where you can sail — not till you gets to Coltishall an' into the Broads. Then 'tis like being on a smooth lake, almost all the way to Yarmouth. We don't often sail beyond Coltishall though in these boats. They brings great, sixty-foot wherries up that far and we puts our loads into 'em, see?'

'Surely you don't do it all by yourself?'

'Nah! I bain't that strong, bless 'ee. I got Arnie to help me. That's Arnie helpin' to work the winch. One as looks a mite shanny!' With those words, the man burst into what started as laughter, then quickly turned into a wracking cough that doubled him over. Adam had heard such coughs many times before. They never presaged good. Taken with the man's bulbous nose and the blue-veined skin on his face, it was obvious a lifetime of hard drinking and heavy smoking was not far off from ending his time on the river.

'Shanny?' Adam queried, when the coughing had subsided. 'What's shanny mean?'

'Bloody furriner!' the man muttered, before calling out, 'Weak in the 'ead. Silly — bit like you,' he added in a lower voice, yet still loud enough to hear.

Adam decided to ignore it. 'Is that your mast laid down along the boat?' he asked instead.

'Course it be! Gotta go under bridges and low trees, ain't we? Can't do that wi' a bloody great mast stuck up in th'air. Lays 'ee down, we does, then puts 'ee up again — allus supposin' there be enough wind. Otherwise we bloody quants, like I said! Now, 'as you finished wi' your questions, mister? I ain't got all day to stand 'ere an' mardle. I got things to do.'

Since the man had done nothing since Adam first saw him but stand in the stern of the boat and puff on his pipe, it was hard to imagine what those things might be. However, the dismissal was obvious, and Adam didn't want to risk a mouthful of coarse abuse by continuing. It was clear the fellow was in no way intimidated by speaking to a gentleman. Why should he be? Here, he was the expert and Adam the ignorant bystander.

ADAM RETURNED HOME IN QUITE A DIFFERENT STATE OF MIND FROM the one with which he had started. Although he was encouraged by Mr Bale's ready offer of help, at least in understanding something of the area and its history, there was the disappointment of needing to wait at least a week to obtain it. It seemed that every move forward was swiftly followed by something that set him back almost as far. He could not ever recall an investigation which had moved so slowly.

Mr Bale's need to leave for King's Lynn wasn't to be Adam's only setback that day either. As Hannah was taking his coat and hat, she informed him that a Miss Rose Thoday had called while he was out, asking to speak with him.

'She didn't leave a card, master,' the maid said. 'Didn't seem to have any. But she was most insistent that she had to speak with you as soon as possible. Quite put out that you weren't here, because she'd made a special journey.'

'Damn!' Adam said. 'I want to talk with her too. Did she say when I might call on her?'

'No, master. She wouldn't leave a message or anything. Said it was a private matter, not a medical one, and she'd call again when she was next in this part of the town.' The girl frowned as she said this. It was obvious she'd not taken a liking to Miss Thoday.

'I'm guessing that you didn't much like her, Hannah,' Adam said. 'Is that the case?'

'It's not my place to like or dislike your visitors, sir, but I has to say I thought her manners were not quite what I would expect from a well-brought-up lady. Too abrupt by a long way, if you ask me.'

Adam was intrigued. 'She is a lady, then? I mean, a person of quality.'

'Maybe, is all I can say. I'm sure she'd like to be thought of in that way, but there was something about her that didn't ring true, for my money. Almost like a superior servant trying to copy her mistress's ways, if you know what I mean. Nothing I could put my finger on, but ...'

She trailed off, clearly unable to put her feelings into words. Adam decided to move onto more solid ground.

'I was told Miss Thoday is quite young,' he said. 'Is that so? Can you describe her person? Did she appear to you attractive and well-dressed?'

'I suppose men would find her comely enough,' the maid said. 'She's rather tall, though a bit on the skinny side in my view. I suppose her clothes were good enough — just — but you wouldn't call her well turned-out or elegant. Not like a real lady. Young? Probably around twenty-five or six, I reckon.'

Since Hannah herself was no beauty, being both short and inclined to plumpness, these observations came with a distinct edge of jealousy. Adam ignored all that. What was clear enough was that Miss Thoday was trying hard to fit into society's expectations of an independent young woman, not a servant, even a superior one. Something had changed with the death of her former master.

Hannah was still speaking. 'That's the thing, you see, master. There was something odd about her, wherever you looked. As if she didn't quite fit anywhere. Not a servant or a tradeswoman, but not quite a lady either. Not someone a man would rush to marry, but not one of them as is spinsters from the day they was born.'

Despite the difficulty Hannah felt with expressing herself clearly, Adam had by this time gained a detailed image of his disappointed visitor. A woman on the boundary between youth and maturity; comely without being beautiful; someone who knew how to behave in polite society but hadn't had to practise those skills in a long time. Most of all, a woman used to fending for herself in a hostile world. No wonder Lassimer felt daunted by her and had shied away from trying to include her in his harem. The poor woman's history had stamped itself on her plainly enough: brought up in a good, middle-class home, then suddenly thrown into the role of a servant and expected to fetch and carry and endure all the slights that went with subservience. Then, just as suddenly, she was transformed by Mr Hawley into something between an assistant and a superior servant, but still most used to dealing with the artisans and tradespeople who made up the bulk of his patients.

And now? What would she do now? What was behind this urge to talk with him? He'd thought of her only as a useful source of information. Was it possible she saw him as a source of new employment?

With the surgeon dead, her employment had been taken from her. Since she had probably been able to absorb a good deal of medical and nursing understanding over the years that she had lived under Mr Hawley's roof, wouldn't it be likely she'd try to use that knowledge to find a position with another medical man?

# 9

Thanks to all his suppressed excitement over Lady Alice's willingness to become his wife, coupled with his frustrations at trying to make some kind of start on exploring the reason for the surgeon's death and the likely perpetrator, Adam knew very well how he had been neglecting his own medical practice. Harrison Henshaw was an extremely capable assistant and handled the bulk of the daily demands for medical help. Nonetheless, there were still patients who expected — nay, demanded — to deal with Adam in person. It was high time he set all these other activities aside and spent a few days dealing with them.

It was while he was bleeding one of these patients, Sir Luke Farley, in the hope of alleviating the severe headaches which had been bothering him of late, that the name of Jacob Sleeth came up in their conversation.

Sir Luke was a man in his early sixties, who had once been notable in a wide range of outdoor pursuits. He had ridden to hounds, played a notable game of cricket, and plagued his tenants by walking his estate and finding fault with many of their farming decisions. Now, however, a combination of gout and arthritis in his joints was turning him into a peevish old man, trapped in what was still an elegant mansion, despite years of neglect in favour of the open air. Since he could no longer annoy his tenants directly, he had turned to the practice of urging on his land-agent to do so by letter, and, when that did not suffice, by raising obscure matters connected with their leases.

Like many a physically active man prevented, in later life, from straying far from a chair in his house, Sir Luke was also running to fat. Many times, Adam had urged him to lessen his habit of consuming the same gargantuan meals that had once sustained him during hours in the saddle. It was to no avail. Sir Luke ate too much, drank far too much, and was able to take little or no exercise. All of this was more than enough to explain his headaches and the increasing pain he suffered from gout, but he refused even to consider such a diagnosis. Instead, he paid Adam handsomely to bleed him on a regular basis, while obliging him to listen to a never-ending tirade of complaints against everyone the aging knight had to deal with.

On that day, Sir Luke's special hate was attorneys. One of his more prosperous tenants, doubtless tired of dealing with Sir Luke in person, had gone to the length of employing an attorney to respond to his letters and joust with him over the terms of the tenancy agreement.

'Terrible fellow!' Sir Luke said. 'Plays with words like a cat plays with a mouse. I write to him plainly and he responds with a mass of ambiguities and platitudes enough to drive any sensible man off his head.'

Adam grunted. He was not usually expected to do more than signal from time to time that he was still awake and — supposedly — listening.

'Got a silly name too. Sleeth. Sounds like teeth. Never met the fellow, but always imagine him being like a weasel; all slithering about and sinking little, sharp teeth into your leg. Have you ever come across him, Bascom?'

'I've never met him,' Adam replied, giving a truthful answer, if not an entirely accurate one.

'Lucky man! Sleeth! Typical bloody attorney. A mass of deceit wrapped up in a cloak of sham respectability. You know, he even managed somehow to get himself appointed coroner. Can you believe it? Bribed someone, I expect. No one in their right mind would give him the job otherwise.'

'Is that so?'

'Bugger me if it ain't! I'll tell you about Sleeth the coroner, Bascom. Damned incompetent, for a start, as well as dictatorial. Did you hear about that Laven fellow who committed suicide a couple of months or so ago? You didn't? Let me tell you and you'll see the kind of coroner Sleeth makes.

'There's a family lives in Aylsham, somewhere down by the Navigation. Name of Laven. I believe they used to be gentry, before one of them got himself mixed up in the Jacobite Rebellion of 1745 and lost all his lands. Now they're merchants of a kind. They run boats on the Navigation to take goods and people to and fro between Aylsham, Coltishall and Great Yarmouth. There were two brothers, neither of them married. Richard — that's the younger one — is a steady sort of fellow. His brother, Robert, was always wild and foolish. A drunkard, you understand, and a gambler as well. His brother was always having to pay off his gambling debts. Anyhow, a little while ago, as I said, this Robert shot himself. There had to be an inquest and Sleeth was the coroner. It was clear from the start, as I heard, that Sleeth had decided this was a simple, straightforward suicide, which could be dismissed in an hour or less. The man was shot with his own pistol and the body was behind a locked door in his house. The pistol was even found by his hand. The butler gave evidence that people in the house heard the shot and broke down the door within a few minutes. What else could it have been but suicide?

'The trouble was, some medical fellow who'd examined the body tried to say that things weren't right. We'll never know what it was he thought he found, because Sleeth wouldn't let him speak beyond giving evidence along the lines I've just mentioned. More or less shouted him down. Naturally, on the basis of what they'd heard, the jury brought in a verdict of suicide. They were probably right, but, even so, they ought to have been given the chance to hear what it was that had bothered that doctor.'

'That seems rather odd to me,' Adam said. 'Most families will go to great lengths to avoid a verdict of suicide on a family member.'

'I think this family were only too happy to be rid of their black sheep,' Sir Luke replied. 'They'd lost their lands and fortune once. I doubt they'd want to see it disappear again across the gaming tables. There was the normal nonsense of saying that he'd taken his own life in a fit of madness. That let his body be buried in consecrated ground.'

'Are you saying that verdicts reached at inquests presided over by Mr Sleeth are not to be trusted?'

'That's exactly what I am saying, doctor. The man always has to be right. I imagine that most of the time it makes little difference. As I'm sure you know, we don't get many suspicious deaths in these parts. Still, there are times I'm sure when he's browbeaten the jury to bring in the wrong verdict, just because he couldn't be bothered to take the time to find out what really happened.'

⚜

As WILLIAM DROVE HIM BACK HOME, ADAM TRIED TO MAKE SENSE of what Sir Luke had told him. If Mr Sleeth's handling of inquests was always so arbitrary, was the way that he had treated Dr Henshaw as suspicious as it had first appeared? Since he had been given all the facts by his assistant, Adam knew that Henshaw was right and Sleeth's eagerness to bring in a verdict of accidental death would have been a serious miscarriage of justice. However, if his behaviour was due mostly to laziness and incompetence, would it be best for Adam simply to ignore him and get on with finding out what had really happened? Might the apparent unwillingness of the authorities to set up a proper investigation into Mr Hawley's death have an innocent explanation? If they had come to suspect any of the verdicts reached by inquests where Sleeth was coroner, he could well imagine them treating this one in the same way.

On the other hand, if there was some unknown reason why Sleeth was so keen to record a verdict of suicide in the earlier case, might that not reinforce the suspicion that he had tried to do the same thing in coming to a verdict on Matthew Hawley? This case had been confusing enough before. Now, thanks to Sir Luke Farley, it seemed even more problematic.

Still further complications raised their heads when Adam reached home and looked through the letters that had arrived for him that day. He immediately recognised the handwriting on one of them as being that of Sir Percival Wicken, Permanent Secretary at the Home Department. Wicken was the man in charge of the major part of the government's domestic network of spies and informers. Now that the country was at war, the seeking out of French spies had been added to his existing targets of Irish rebels and radicals involved in domestic sedition. Since he never wrote to Adam without there being a pressing reason, the arrival of such a letter was more a reason for trepidation than pleasure.

As usual, his letter came straight to the point.

*My Dear Bascom,*

*I thought that we had finally blocked any route for spies, seditious persons and their correspondence to travel to and from the continent by the smugglers who use the coasts in your vicinity. I have been proved wrong. It seems that, once again, those who wish harm to this realm have found a means of evading our scrutiny. Information has reached me suggesting that regular messages are being passed between those engaged in espionage on behalf of the French and their masters in the Low Countries. For a while, this correspondence was sent via disaffected persons using the packet route from Harwich. When they were detected and arrested, a new route was found. It is this new route that we believe passes between the small market towns in the northern part of Norfolk and thence to the coast.*

*We were recently able to arrest one of those seeking to foment rebellion on the island of Ireland and subject him to close questioning. As a result, we learnt that he had crossed into France from Falmouth some months ago. His mission was to try to persuade the French government to supply arms and money to groups of Irish dissidents, who would then rise in rebellion in concert with the French invasion. He has admitted that he was only partially successful, having obtained promises of small deliveries of arms and money only. When we intercepted him, he was on his way back to his fellow-conspirators in Ireland. The significant point is that he had been advised not to attempt to land anywhere along the south coast of England, since the chances of capture were said to be too great.*

*Instead, he told us that he had travelled to Amsterdam and been taken from there down to the coast, where he was put aboard a vessel carrying a large consignment of brandy and gin bound for the English coast. He would not – or could not — tell us exactly where he came ashore, save that it was by rowing boat and somewhere close to Great Yarmouth. After that, he said he travelled inland 'by river' to a place where he was able to hire a carriage to take him to Cambridge.*

*Thanks to the vigilance of one of our informers in that place, he was detected offering a large sum of money to a known group of radicals to help him travel in secret to Bristol.*

*I know that I can rely on you to make your best efforts to discover the route this person took between Great Yarmouth and Cambridge and the person or persons who helped him upon his way.*

*I am, as always, your most appreciative and obedient servant,*
*Percival Wicken,*
*Home Department.*

'IT REALLY IS TOO MUCH!' ADAM COMPLAINED TO PETER THE NEXT day. 'After all that trouble over Professor Panacea and his followers, I was looking forward to a period of peace and quiet. Time to attend to my practice and to various matters of a personal nature.' That was as close as he felt he could go in alluding to finding somewhere for Lady Alice and himself to live after their marriage. 'Instead, here I am trying to investigate the suspicious death of the local surgeon, the strange behaviour of the coroner, and now yet another case of spies using secret routes to and from the continent. I swear Wicken sometimes believes he employs me in his service.'

'You know you love this kind of thing,' Peter replied mildly. 'You're never happier than when you have your teeth into a good mystery. Besides, Henshaw does the vast bulk of the work in your practice; mostly so that you can spend your time trotting backwards and forwards between here and Mossterton Hall on some spurious pretext.'

'I do not go to Mossterton Hall on spurious pretexts, I'll have you know!' Adam said, growing quite red in the face. 'As you are very well aware, Sir Daniel charged me on his deathbed with helping his widow cope with life on her own. I promised I would do so, and that is a promise I take most seriously.'

'Of course, you do,' Peter said. 'Especially since the widow in question is both young and beautiful.'

'Just because you can see nothing in any woman, other than her appearance and the opportunities she offers you for dalliance—'

'Calm yourself! If you go on like this, you'll give yourself an apoplexy, and then you'll be no use whatsoever to the lady. I have never pretended to be other than what I am; nor do I deny that the approach I take to comforting widows in their solitude is as much carnal as charitable. You really should try it yourself, Bascom. I can assure you that I have more willing takers for my assistance than I can possibly cope with.'

'Bah!' Adam said. 'Don't try to involve me in your dubious lifestyle. Some of us take our obligations to others more seriously.'

'I assure you I take my obligations in this respect very seriously,' Peter replied. 'But all that is of little consequence. Can't you see that I am merely trying to deflect you from yet another tirade of complaints? All you've done of late when you come to see me is whine and moan. What ails you, man? You are in good health, your practice is flourishing, you are disgustingly wealthy, and you have friends in high places. Yet still you complain! For goodness sake, pull yourself together and get on with life. I swear that if you devoted the same effort to solving these mysteries as you are doing to complain about them, they would all have been cleared up long ago. Take yourself out of my compounding room and my shop and set about it right away. If I hear any more complaints, I shall be forced to make you up a nice mixture of arsenic and prussic acid, which will cure all your problems forever.'

## 10

For two days now, Rose had been wondering whether she should return to Dr Bascom's house in the hope of finding him at home. In many ways, she now regretted being impetuous enough to seek him out so quickly. If she'd thought about it more carefully, she could have saved herself what had proved to be an unpleasant experience. That supercilious maid had made it perfectly obvious Rose wasn't, in her view, the right class of person to be knocking at the front door. Although she hadn't actually told her to go to the tradesman's entrance, her expression had been quite sufficient for Rose to understand that was what was going through her mind. Well, if Dr Bascom was too grand to be bothered with her, she would have to do the best she could on her own. What if the doctor had asked for a fee for helping her? She had very little money. She didn't even know how long she'd be able to stay in the surgeon's house, nor grow herbs in the garden she had attended to so lovingly until now. She had no idea whether her master had made a Will. If he had, to whom had he left his house and other possessions? She had no idea. He scarcely ever talked about his life before coming to Aylsham. She didn't even know whether he had a family somewhere. The house and land might well be sold and she might be forced once again to fend for herself.

It was thoughts such as these which at last persuaded Rose to give up any idea of returning to Adam's house, or asking him to undertake any kind of investigation into her master's death. Instead, she made herself busy with preparations in case she was forced to leave the house and garden in the near future. She harvested all the herbs she could and hung them to dry in the shed. Those she found already dry enough, she put into jars and bottles that she could take with her. It might be a long time before she could find another piece of land where she could establish a garden and produce fresh supplies.

She was tempted to give up and seek another post as housekeeper, even if it meant moving away from Aylsham. Then her stubbornness took over and she began to visit as many as she could of the surgeon's regular patients — especially those whom she knew had not required his surgical skills. These she told of her hopes to set herself up eventually as a herbalist and healer, staying in the neighbourhood if that proved possible. Then she asked them if they would be willing to let her continue to help them in this new capacity. To her great pleasure, the vast majority of them agreed at once. It would mean nothing if she was not able to survive on her own long enough to find somewhere to live, but it was a start. For the moment, no one had come to tell her that she must leave the surgeon's house. With luck, if they continued to delay, and perhaps agreed to give her a little time to find somewhere else to live, she could establish a modest practice that might yield just enough to live on.

Although these preparations for a new life left her little time for anything else, Rose found that she could not quite give up her determination to find out who had killed Mr Hawley. Her plan had been to hand over all of that to Dr Bascom to deal with, since he had done it before and knew how to go about things. Neither of those applied to her. Now she would either have to let the whole matter drop, or do what she could on her own in the hope of coming upon the right approach by chance.

For the whole of one sleepless night, she went over and over these two options trying to work out which one would be for the best. Then, just as dawn was showing itself, she reached a decision. She would make a start and see what information she could collect over the next few days. If that failed and she could find no other way forward, the only sensible course of action would be to set any hope of finding Mr Hawley's murderer aside and get on with her life.

ROSE HAD NEVER BEEN ONE TO SIT QUIETLY AND WAIT WHILE OTHERS decided what was best for her, so she began by trying to track down and question the wherryman who had been first on the scene of Matthew Hawley's murder. She had a shrewd idea that the best place to find him would be in the Anchor Inn. Naturally, it would not be proper for her to go inside to find him. When she noticed a young lad hanging around the door of the inn, hoping to earn a few pennies for holding people's horses, she therefore sent him inside in her place.

As she waited to find out whether the man she sought was there and would speak to her, Rose realised she had seen that young lad before. Wasn't he the one who she had caught a few days before in the surgeon's garden?

He must have come in through a gap in the hedge, for she had been harvesting herbs that day and had not seen him enter. At first, she was alarmed, assuming he had come to steal, since his clothes were patched and his skin had certainly not felt water in many days. But all he did was stand and stare at the plants, moving slowly between then, sometimes bending to sniff at a bloom, touching nothing. When he discovered he had been seen, he would have dashed off if he could, but Rose was close enough by then to seize his arm. He had seemed fascinated by what he saw. Indeed, his behaviour was so unusual Rose was determined to find out the reason for it.

Seen from close up, his appearance was far from appealing, thanks to layers of grime and marks from an encounter with smallpox. Rose longed to take him inside, give him a good wash and use her own compounding of herbs on his face to start the process of minimising the pock-marks. Instead, she kept a firm hold on his arm, telling herself to hold him far enough away to stop his fleas jumping onto her, and proceeded to question him.

'What's your name and what are you doing in this garden,' she said.

'Speak up now! I won't hurt you.' The boy was cringing from her in anticipation of a beating. 'Even so, I won't let people wander in and out of here as they please — at least not as long as I am in charge of the house.'

'Jack,' he said.

'Jack what?'

'Jack Nugent, missus.'

'Where do you live, Jack Nugent?'

'Behind the mill. I weren't doing no harm, honest! We ain't got any kind of garden, see. Me mam's too poor and too busy with the little 'uns and we ain't seen me dad in three years or more. I loves plants and flowers, see? I goes about when I can and seeks out wild 'uns, only I doesn't know any of their names, beyond daisies and dandelions and the like. But these in your garden are so ....' He was lost for words for a moment. 'I don't know. They smells so wonderful too. Why d'you grow so many of 'em and all different kinds?'

'They're herbs,' Rose said. 'Do you know what that means? It means plants I can use to help sick people get well.'

The boy's eyes grew round with wonder and excitement. He was probably about twelve years of age she guessed, though as thin as a rail. She wondered when was the last time he'd had anything to eat.

'Are you hungry, Jack Nugent?' she asked.

'I'm allus hungry, missus. Me mam says I got worms.'

You probably have, Rose thought. Those I can drive out of your poor stomach, though it will take a little time. I can feed you right away.

'If I let you go, you won't run, will you? Only I need to go inside to fetch you something to eat. Do you like bread and butter?'

'Real butter, missus? I ain't never tried real butter.'

'Sit here and wait for me then.'

She returned with three thick slices of bread, liberally covered in butter. Jack consumed all three in less than two minutes, so she went back for more. When he finally pronounced himself full, six slices had disappeared.

THANKS TO THE BOY'S HELP, ROSE DISCOVERED THE WHERRYMAN SHE wanted had just returned from the three-day journey along the Navigation to and from Coltishall. Progress was never especially swift on the Bure, what with the locks and the need to stop at several villages along the way to pick up extra cargo, and then going and dropping off coal and similar items on his return. According to what Jack told her, the landlord of the inn even knew where he lived. He would show her the way, if she wanted him to do so. Rose hurriedly accepted his offer, though she told the lad firmly he must leave the two of them alone when she got there. She needed no eavesdroppers present.

When they came to the man's house, Rose found the wherryman sitting on the doorstep, smoking a pipe. Inside, his wife was doubtless preparing him a meal before he left for yet another trip along the Navigation. At first, he was unwilling to say much, until she had invested a whole shilling to help him change his mind. Then he was eager enough to tell his tale, though it proved a poor return for her limited supply of money, since what he told her was little different from his evidence before the coroner. The moon had been a long way from full, so had provided little natural illumination on the scene. Some of those who ran up to join the swelling crowd of onlookers carried lanterns. Even then, it was impossible to see much beyond the edge of the staithe itself. If the surgeon's leg had not been caught, and his body had drifted out further, no one would have been able to see it before morning — if it was still afloat. He had noticed two largish pieces of wood in the water but paid them little attention. Part of that staithe was occupied by a tradesman who built and repaired wherries, so there were always odd pieces of timber lying about. When they were bored, the local children would heave one into the water and pretend it was a galleon, pushing it along with sticks until their clumsy efforts drove it too far from the bank. Drove the wherry-builder wild, it did, since the pieces they liked best were those already planed smooth, ready for use.

'Was that what you saw?' Rose asked.

'Could 'ave been. It were too dark to see aright, as I told 'ee.' The man paused and scratched himself liberally, causing Rose to draw back somewhat in case the fleas he disturbed sought better quarters elsewhere. 'Nah! Come to think on it, they was just rough bits of wood.

The kind they uses there to prop up the wherries when they be out o' the water.'

'Large? Small?'

'Good size. Mebbe three feet long and three or four inches across.'

'How many were there?'

'I only saw two, 'cos they was close to the edge. Might 'ave been more further out. Too dark to see, as I told you. Don't know no more. Why be you so interested in them ol' bits o' wood? Why d'you ask 'ow big they was?'

'One of them might have been used as the weapon which knocked poor Mr Hawley into the water.'

'Thass right enough, that is! Gar, missus, ain't you quick! I'd never 'ave thought o' that.'

Rose smiled at the compliment. In truth, it wasn't much of an achievement to link pieces of wood with the attack on Mr Hawley. The killer had to have used something, and the most obvious place to dispose of it afterwards was in the water. Of course, those particular pieces of wood might be irrelevant. The weapon might have been a hammer or a piece of iron. In which case, it was probably lost in the mud on the bottom of the pool beyond the staithe. Still, this wherryman said he'd seen pieces of wood in the water at the time Surgeon Hawley had been killed. Two certainly, maybe more. Yet only one would have been needed to commit the murder, so why throw others in as well?

Later that evening, Rose turned the problem over in her mind once again. If the murderer had come unarmed, relying on using a piece of wood from the shipbuilder's yard, the killing must have been done on the spur of the moment. Either that, or undertaken by someone who knew the area well enough to be sure of finding what he wanted. The first point argued for the convenient assumption of some vagrant as the killer; a robbery gone wrong when the surgeon's body pitched into the water and put itself out of reach. The second pointed to a premeditated act by someone local. Someone who either didn't have anything to use as a bludgeon or didn't want to risk being seen carrying such a thing.

Which was it? How could she find out? If only she could go to see

Dr Bascom and talk it through with him. Not for the first time in her life, Rose retired to her bed that night frustrated at the limitations society placed on women, especially those whose station in life rendered them less than respectable. It was almost enough to make you want to become a whore. At least they were free to do much as they wished, without considering what polite society might think.

A sudden vision of her father's face made her laugh aloud. What would he, a most sober minister of religion, have thought of his daughter considering the benefits of prostitution as a way of life? Would he have been shocked and scolded her unmercifully? No, she knew the answer. He would have sat her down and argued the matter through, logically and rationally. If he'd quoted scripture, it would only have been to illustrate a point. A good man and a father in a million, like the surgeon would have been, had he ever had a family. It was her wretched fate to have lost both. Once again, that night Rose Thoday cried herself to sleep.

THOUGH ROSE COULD NOT HAVE KNOWN IT, THAT NIGHT WAS TO represent the lowest point in her fortunes. Next morning, a young man came to her door bearing a message from one of the lawyers whose offices clustered round the marketplace. Would she please call at her earliest convenience? There were matters in Mr Matthew Hawley's Will which concerned her.

Rose was terrified. She'd been stealing herself against the day when she was told to leave this house. Now it had come, it seemed too great a misfortune for her to bear. Nevertheless, she squared her shoulders, managed to hold the tears in check, and told the young man that, if he would come inside and wait for a short time, she would accompany him on his return. Bad news it might be, but delay would not make it any better. It had always been Rose's way to face up to disasters quickly.

If the lawyer was surprised to see her so quickly, he gave no sign of it. Instead, he asked her to take a seat in his office, offered her refreshment — which she refused — and told the young man who had accompanied Rose to bring him the deed box containing the papers relating to Mr Matthew Hawley.

While they were waiting, the lawyer even did his best to set Rose's mind at rest over the reason why he had called her to see him. He was a kindly man, now a little past middle age but still willing enough to take pleasure in having a comely young woman in his office, rather than the sour-faced tradesmen and merchants who normally sat on the other side of his desk.

'Please set your mind at rest,' he said. 'Nothing in what I have to tell you should give you any cause for concern. There are certain procedures which I have to follow, both as Mr Hawley's lawyer and the executor of his Will. Ah, Johnson. Thank you. You may leave the box on the desk. When we have finished, I will call you to escort Miss Thoday back home.'

The lawyer — his name was Jenkins — extracted a single document from the box and spread it out before him.

'Properly speaking,' he said, 'I should read this through to you in full. However, the legal language in which it has been written is both dull and confusing. I will therefore simply confirm that this is the Last Will and Testament of Matthew Hawley, Surgeon, and tell you that it was made some two years ago. The provisions of his Will are extremely simple. Mr Hawley has bequeathed his house and land, the contents of said property, his wealth in the form of certain bonds, loans and cash, and all else he possessed at the time of his death to you, Miss Rose Thoday, to hold absolutely and in your own name — once I, as executor, have discharged any outstanding debts. It's all yours, Miss Thoday; house, land, money, everything. Mr Hawley was not a rich man, but he was not a poor one either. By my estimate, the value of his cash and investments alone will come close to eight hundred pounds.'

Had Rose been the kind of frail and shrinking creature many men at that time imagined all women to be, she would surely have fainted. As it was, she took a few moments to calm her breathing, shook her head once or twice, squared her shoulders, and asked Mr Jenkins to repeat what he had just said.

'I said that it is all yours, Miss Thoday. Mr Matthew Hawley left everything to you. Once probate has been cleared, which should not take too long, you will find yourself a wealthy young woman. Please be aware that that may be a place of some danger, since there are a good many feckless men eager to find an easy source of income by marrying an heiress. I will not press you further at this stage, but please be aware that I am more than ready to help you in any way that I can. Now that you are a woman of property, you will need a lawyer. I was pleased to be able to serve Mr Hawley from the time when he first came to Aylsham until his untimely death. I would be more than happy to act for you, should you wish it.'

All the way home, Rose thought over this new mark of Surgeon Hawley's kindness towards her. Thanks to him, she was to be restored to something like her proper position in local society. While not making her quite a lady of leisure, those eight hundred pounds would, if properly invested, earn her perhaps twenty-five or thirty pounds a year. That was enough to live on, if not much more than that. Still, she had never been someone who liked to spend her time solely in so-called genteel pursuits, like sewing or playing the spinet. What this new-found wealth would do, she decided, was give her a solid base on which to build. Thanks to the surgeon, she had a good roof over her head and — best of all — would not have to leave the garden where she had already established so many of her herbs.

As always with Rose, her thoughts went first to her beloved garden. Then she remembered again the boy whom she had found there not so long ago. If she was to have sufficient time to work as a healer, she would need others to do the work about the house and help tend her — yes, *her* — garden. What about Jack Nugent? He looked a likely enough lad. Given proper feeding, he'd soon be strong enough to do at least some of the heavy garden work. Most important of all, he loved plants. She'd need to trust anyone she employed in the garden not to cause havoc by digging up the wrong plants, or letting the stronger, more rampant ones crowd out the timid growers. Yes, he might very well do. He'd shown her he was interested in plants when she'd caught him trespassing. All she had to do now was find out where he lived.

It proved easy enough. The second person she asked directed her to a row of mean cottages beyond the mill. In fact, she found him wandering in the road before she got there.

'Would you like to work for me and help in my garden, Jack?' she said to him. 'I'll teach you the names of all the plants and how to grow and harvest them. It'll be hard work at times mind, and I'll expect you to be reliable. I'll be away seeing my patients, so I won't be able to keep an eye on you most of the time. There's a clean, warm place behind the building where I dry my plants. I could put you a bed in there, unless you want to go home each night. I'll provide you with your food, some clean clothes and pay you ...' She had no idea what she should offer, so she guessed, '... two shillings each week. How would that be?'

She was never in any doubt the boy would accept and he did so immediately. Still, she still wondered what his mother would say. He probably made himself useful around the house, as well as earning — or 'finding' — a few pennies to add to her meagre income from whatever it was she did. Took in washing and mending, probably. Many near-destitute women did that, if they didn't sell their bodies to the next drunk with sixpence in his pocket.

Jack took Rose to the hovel where his family lived and she spoke with his mother about employing Jack to help her in the garden and run general errands. Since the poor woman had four younger children to raise on such meagre earnings as she could make from taking in cleaning, she was delighted to accept. It was swiftly agreed between them that Jack would move to Rose's house, where she would provide him with his meals, a place to sleep in the outhouse behind the room where she dried and prepared her herbs, and the princely sum of two shillings each week as wages.

As earnest of her good faith, Rose gave Mrs Nugent two shillings and took young Jack along with her when she left. She asked him if he needed to pick up spare clothes, but he shook his head.

'All I got in the way o' clothes is on me back, missus, and they be bits and pieces some kind folk give to me mother. Ain't got no more.'

'Then I must get you some. The ones you are wearing are quite filthy and you'll need something while those are in the wash, won't you?'

However, the first step, Rose decided, was to strip him naked and give him the best wash he'd probably ever had in his young life. After that, she would dose him for his worms, cut his hair, and find him some better clothes. Despite his poor diet, he was more or less as tall as a twelve-year old ought to be. Perhaps some of Mr Hawley's old clothes might be made to fit.

Since Jack had no idea of the ordeal which awaited him, he went along happily enough, his mind on what seemed to him a future beyond his wildest dreams.

With the most important matter settled, how to keep her garden in proper order, Rose now had to think about the rest. The notion of employing a housekeeper and a cook did not appeal. Rose knew she was not much of a cook, but she and her master had both been used to living off plain food. Since he never entertained guests either, she had been able to cope by arranging with a poor girl from the neighbourhood to spend her mornings cleaning the kitchen and washing the tableware and cutlery. Besides, unless she became an overnight success as a herbalist and found a clutch of wealthy patients, her income would not run to employing a housekeeper. Most disdained doing menial work and would expect to have a cook, a full-time kitchen-maid and probably a housemaid to supervise. Was there an alternative? Rose enjoyed looking after the house and even a certain amount of cooking. Two women in the same kitchen was often a recipe for disaster! Still, her medical work must come first. If she continued to cook for herself, she could probably manage with a maid-of-all-work and a garden boy. When her income allowed, she might be able to find a cook who would not wish to live in.

## ❧ 11 ❧

In the days that followed, Rose set aside the problem of Surgeon Hawley's murder as she worked to organise her little household for her future as an independent woman. She'd never felt she needed — or wanted — a husband to rule her life. It was not that she disliked men — some she had liked very much. It was the way marriage made you into a mere appendage to your husband; while she liked some children, she had no wish to spend her life facing the dangers of childbirth again and again. Mr Hawley had given her a truly priceless gift; not just money and property, but the freedom to choose her own path in life. She was not about to throw it away at the dictates of convention. She would continue to build up her skills and knowledge as a herbalist. If that meant remaining a spinster all her life, it seemed to her a sound deal.

A few words with the cleaning girl the surgeon had employed quickly transformed her from part-time help into a full-time kitchen and scullery maid. The woman who came in to do the heavy work of cleaning the house agreed to continue as before, so Rose decided instead to look for a proper housemaid. This job she gave to a young woman who had worked at Millgate Manor, but was now seeking fresh employment, due to suffering the unwelcome attentions of both of the

Laven brothers. Rose had known the young woman since childhood, so her former master's refusal to give her a character was of no importance.

Having accomplished these arrangements shortly after noon on the first day, Rose turned her mind to her need for companionship, as well as household help. Overnight, an idea had come to her which might also remove the need for employing some haughty housekeeper. Putting on her best hat and coat, she therefore set out to walk the two miles to where her Aunt Matilda lived near Burgh. Persuading her aunt to leave the cousin and his wife with whom she lived and move in with her, at least on a trial basis, proved surprisingly easy. Matilda Thoday had never married, so when the mother to whom she had devoted her life died, she found herself without a home or income enough to live on. Much as she hated the idea, she had no option but to seek the charity of some member of the Thoday family. Rose's father couldn't help, even though she was his favourite sister. He had scarcely enough income to keep himself and his daughter. In the end, Matilda was forced to move in with a distant cousin and his shrewish wife. The six years she had spent within their household — where she was made to act as an unpaid housekeeper, berated continually by the wife for her multiple shortcomings in that role — had left the poor woman dreaming of escape at almost any price. Rose's proposal met with instant acceptance and an embarrassing level of gratitude. Matilda would come as soon as she could get her few things together. She was already gloating over the likely fury of her cousin and his wife at losing their unpaid help.

NOW HER DOMESTIC ARRANGEMENTS WERE SETTLED, AT LEAST IN part, Rose decided the next day should be devoted to beginning in her business as an independent herbalist and healer. She rose early and left Jack with strict instructions to carry water to only the beds of plants she had indicated. Then she set out to visit Surgeon Hawley's patients once more, this time assuring them she would be able to continue treating them right away as he had done — provided, of course, that was what they wished. Much to her satisfaction, all expressed themselves pleased with the arrangement.

It was while she was leaving the house of one of the carpenters who worked at the shipbuilder's that Jack caught up with her. A messenger had come from the maltings, he told her. One of the workers there had fallen and hurt his ankle badly. Might she be able to help?

Help she could, so she hurried over at once. The man was in considerable pain, but she didn't think any bones were broken. The joint was swollen and hot to the touch, but she felt sure it was nothing more than a severe sprain. Fumbling in the surgeon's bag — she had taken it to indicate her new status — she found the balm she had made up herself for just such a case as this. With that smeared on liberally and the ankle strapped, the man could be carried home by his workmates. She also gave him a tiny bottle of laudanum, with strict instructions to add no more than five drops to something like a glass of ale, three times a day to ease his pain. She would visit him the next day to see how he was faring.

Mr Bale, the maltster, had been informed of the accident and had arrived to see what was being done. He might have been surprised to see Rose dealing with the problem, but if he was, he took care not to show it. Indeed, when she had finished, he asked her to send her account to him. The workers at his maltings and brewery all paid into a club account to provide assistance in case of accidents or inability to work. Mr Bale held the money on their behalf, and he would honour her account from the club funds. By the time she returned to her home, just after noon, Rose was starting to feel well suited to her new role.

Even so, there would be no good in being a herbalist if she had no herbs ready for use. She therefore put on her oldest pinafore and went into the garden to work until the light should fail. It was also time Jack started on his education about which plants were important and which were weeds. She had visions of coming back one day and finding her precious garden wrecked by an over-enthusiastic garden boy.

Young Jack proved a hard worker and a quick learner. He also proved to be a chatterbox, seemingly unable to stay silent for more than a few moments. Rose considered telling him firmly to stop talking, but relented, deciding instead to learn how to shut her ears to his babbling. He never seemed to expect a response, so she soon found herself able to concentrate in her chosen tasks and treat his jabbering as she would treat the constant twittering of the birds.

It was fortunate that this ability to shut her ears was, as yet, poorly established. If it had been better, she would have missed something important. In the midst of some rambling tale of a quarrel with one of his brothers, Jack shifted direction and began to relate how large his wider family was and how many lived and worked in Millgate.

'My uncle Sam works at the place where they builds them wherries,' the lad said. 'Sleeps there sometimes too. He says they pays him extra to act as a night watchman, but we all thinks 'e does it to get away from 'is wife. Right misery guts, that 'un is. Nags 'im all the time.'

'Was he there the night poor Mr Hawley died?' Rose asked. 'Do you know if he saw or heard anything?'

'Dunno,' Jack said. ''E might 'ave been there. D'you want me to ask 'im? I could run over to the yard.'

'Do that, please,' Rose replied. 'Ask if he was there that night. If he was, see if he'll be willing to call on me here on his way home today.'

Uncle Sam was there that night, it seemed, and was agreeable to stopping at Rose's house on his way home.

He arrived as Rose and Jack were finishing their simple meal. At least, Jack was finishing it; having consumed what was set before him, he had begun staring at Rose's plate while she tried to ignore him. In the end, he'd so put her off her food she slid the half-finished plate across the table and pronounced herself full. She could always get herself more food after he'd retired to his bed in the outbuilding.

Uncle Sam Nugent proved to be a tall, thick-set man, with the weather-beaten look of those who work outdoors in all weathers. He also showed the diffidence nearly all the poorer people showed on being asked to step inside what they saw as the house of a person of superior class. Rose took him into her parlour where he perched unhappily on the edge of one of the chairs, obviously dreadfully conscious of his dirty working clothes and battered boots.

'Young Jack said as 'ow you wants to talk to me 'bout summat,' he said, his Norfolk accent strong enough to make it hard even for Rose to make out every word. 'Dunno what it could be, mind. I ain't done nothin', so far as I knows.'

'Don't worry, Mr Nugent,' Rose said. 'Jack simply happened to mention you worked at the yard where they build the wherries and sometimes acted as watchman there too.'

'Aye, that I does. Bin there nigh on twenty year.'

'And you were there the night the surgeon was killed?'

This was going too fast. Nugent's eyes narrowed at the question, obviously worried that this young woman was about to accuse him of playing some part in what happened. Fool! Rose said to herself. He's got to work out whether to trust you or not. If you push him, he'll either deny everything or give you a pack of lies. Talk about something else first.

"Appen I was, mebbe. What of it?'

'Nothing in particular. You know I'm planning to continue his business, so far as I can.'

She saw Nugent relax.

'I 'eard that. Good thing, I reckons, and so do most around 'ere. Needs someone local, not them rich b—, I means people, up around the market place. They doctors and 'pothecaries wants too much money, they does. Ordinary folk can't afford 'em. Old surgeon suited us down to the ground. If you does as good as 'e done, you'll be right enough.'

'I'll try. I can't do surgery, of course, but I can set bones and I know how to use herbs to deal with all kinds of illnesses.'

'Weren't old Goody Otley part o' your family, then?'

'My grandmother's sister.'

'Goes in families, it does. The Sight. People do say that's come to you now. That makes some on 'em afeared. Thinks you be a witch. You doesn't look much like a witch to me, mind.'

'I'm not a witch, Mr Nugent. That I can assure you. Just an ordinary woman who's going to do her best to help people around here.'

Nugent's expression made clear he didn't believe a word of this. To his mind, any female relative of Goody Otley should be regarded with suspicion, let alone one who lived on her own and dabbled in potions and the like.

'So what d'you want to know?' he asked. 'You didn't bring me 'ere to tell me what I knows already.'

Trust breeds trust, Rose's father used to tell her. If you want someone to trust you, try trusting them first.

'Mr Hawley was a good friend to me, Mr Nugent, as he was to many people in this neighbourhood. He didn't deserve to die. I'm not willing to leave it to people up in the town to find out who killed him. If I can, I'll do that for myself.'

Nugent regarded her solemnly for several moments.

'Aye, reckon as you might an' all. Them rich folk up in the town don't care a dog's turd about us. More'n 'alf on 'em be more'n half shanny too. We could all be murdered down 'ere an' they'd do nothin' about it. That's right about surgeon, that is. 'E were a good man and good friend to folk 'round 'ere. 'Asn't gone down well, 'is murder. Folks be mad as a 'ive o' bees what someone 'as poked wi' a stick. I'll tell 'em what you just said an' they'll be all on your side. That as 'as killed Surgeon 'Awley needs to be 'anging by the neck, that do. Now, you asked if I was at the yard that night.'

'Were you?'

'That I was. Master knows I gets me 'ead down for a few 'ours, but that don't matter. Light sleeper, see? Wakes at the slightest noise. That's 'ow I 'heard 'em.'

'Heard who?'

Nugent settled a little more. This was his tale and he would tell it in his own way.

'Must 'ave been early, just after it got proper dark, y'see. I'd only just dropped off, so I was awake right off. Someone in the yard, moving' things. Not a lot o' noise, mind you. That were tryin' 'ard to be quiet, that were. But I 'eard 'un. I gets up and creeps outside, 'spectin' to see a light, but there were none. Then I 'ears a funny noise. Bit like a cat mewin', it were. Cat or a baby. Then a splash — not loud. Like someone 'ad chucked summat into the water. I stands still and tries to work out where it's comin' from, but it goes quiet again.'

Rose opened her mouth to ask a question, then thought better of it. Let him finish first.

'Then I 'ears an odd kind o' sound, summat between a grunt and a thud, followed by a real loud splash. So, I goes towards the water quick as I could, seein' as 'ow 'tis dark as th'inside o' a bag. When I gets there, wherryman be pullin' surgeon out o' the water like.'

'Did you hear anything else?'

'Now you asks, I did. As I was goin' towards the water after the second splash, I thought I 'eard a third one. Not loud, mind, and real quick after the last one. Can't be sure, though. Might 'ave been summat o' nothin', but that's what I 'eard.'

'Three splashes?'

'Reckon so.'

'What do you think caused them?'

'The loud 'un was surely poor surgeon going into the water.'

'The others?'

'Them children, I reckons. Never known 'em to come at night afore, though. They throws our timber into the water to play games sailin' it about.'

'It was pieces of timber that caused the splashes?'

'Aye. 'Ad to be. Master and I found 'em next morning an' got 'em back using a boat. Two largish timbers as we'd bin usin' as props for hulls. Master said they was too big to have been taken by the children. They likes pieces about a foot or eighteen inches long and about two inches thick, y'see. Easier for small 'ands. Master said these bits 'ad probably bin thrown in by folk trying to use them to help get the body out. I says nothin', mind. Master don't like to be told 'e's wrong. But I knows what I 'eard and all they splashes 'appened afore anyone got there, even that wherryman.'

That was all. Rose thanked Nugent and sent him home to his evening meal with a shilling in his pocket for his trouble. What she'd learned was clearly another piece of the puzzle, but where it fitted, she had no idea.

The next two days were once again taken up almost entirely by domestic matters. Aunt Matilda arrived and had to be settled in. Rose gave her the bedroom she had used while the surgeon was alive, and she moved into the surgeon's room. Scarcely had Aunt Matilda finished putting her few things about in the room and arranging the place to her liking when the new housemaid also arrived. She was called Mary

Higget and her family came from Aylmerton. Rose took her up to the attic and showed her where she could share a room with Betsy Dix, the kitchen maid. She'd been given the name of someone who might be suitable as a cook, but she wouldn't need to live in. Her own cottage was scarcely a quarter of a mile away.

Helped by her aunt, and Mary and Betsy, Rose set about cleaning and sweeping the house from top to bottom. Mostly it was left as it had been when the surgeon was alive, but one or two pieces of furniture were moved to what Rose considered were better locations. She would have liked to move the surgeon's desk, but it proved too big and heavy, even for the combined strength of all the women.

'You'll not see this moved without emptying the drawers and cupboards first,' her aunt told Rose after their second futile attempt. 'What's in them, do you know?'

'I never pried into Mr Hawley's affairs, aunt,' Rose said. 'Papers, I expect.'

'Paper is dreadfully heavy, dear. You'll need to go through it all and throw out anything that isn't needed. You'll remember I did that with your dear father's desk after he died. Regular squirrel, my brother proved to be. He had papers and notebooks going back thirty years and more, as well as all his old sermons. Even letters from people who'd died decades ago. Some men are like that. You'll probably find your surgeon kept his desk filled with enough useless paper to start a thousand fires in the grate over there.'

'You're right,' Rose said. 'It's time I sorted out what to keep and what can be let go. Not now, though. Perhaps I'll make a start tomorrow on this desk. Mr Hawley liked it here, but it does take up so much room. Besides, people expect to see a professional man sitting at his desk. A mere herbalist — and a female one at that — sitting at a desk would look foolish and presumptuous. Even so, I'll need a room where I can talk with patients privately, so this will have to be the one. When people come to this house, I can't expect them to tell me their troubles outside in the garden or in my drying shed. What I need to do is turn this room into a consulting room that looks more appropriate to a woman.'

'Do you think people will accept you?' Matilda asked. 'You're not what most would expect, since you're young as well as female.'

'Time will tell,' Rose said. 'So far I've had no problems. You know, Aunt Matilda, I never thought I would be glad that people know Goody Otley was my great-aunt. I loved her dearly as a person, but I was always embarrassed by the tales that went around about her. All those love potions she was supposed to have handed out! The cursing too. But now, thinking about what they call my "lineage", I find they aren't surprised when I say I'm a healer. Probably think I'm a witch too. Perhaps I should get a black cat.'

To her surprise, her aunt seemed to take this suggestion seriously.

'I know I smelled mice in the larder just now,' she said, 'so getting a cat or two would be a sensible idea, regardless of colour. You shouldn't be ashamed of Bertha Otley, you know. She was a good woman and a skilled healer. I knew her for far longer than you did. By the time you encountered her, she was an old woman. I knew her in her prime. It's true people were afraid of her, but I never heard of her doing anyone any real harm. There were some she caused a good deal of trouble, but they usually deserved it. For a start, she had a tongue that could cut like a knife — and wasn't afraid to use it either. I saw strong men reduced to tears when she laid into them.'

'Did she really lay curses on people?'

'Some of them thought she had. Mostly, all that she'd done was curse them in words — gave them a lashing with her tongue and threatened to do worse if they didn't improve. All the rest was the work of their guilty consciences. If they did as she wanted, she always found a way to let them think they had been forgiven. I was amazed how many miraculous reformations she brought about in that way.'

'She told me you needed to work with people's minds as well as their bodies. According to her, most of her charms and rituals were only done to make people believe in the cures she gave them.'

'You need to remember that. More than half the time, people came to Goody Otley as much troubled in their minds as in their bodies. Sometimes the worries and anxiety had caused the pain and not the other way around. She'd give them something to take or rub on — they expected that — but often added some actions which they had to take as well. I believed the actions were what mattered, and the medicines were often not much more than sweetened water and perfumed fat. Have you ever thought that all the complex, Latin words the physicians use are more about creating an atmosphere of learning and mystery than necessary to understanding?'

'But they truly are learned and I'm not,' Rose protested.

'Don't belittle yourself, Rose. How many of those lordly physicians could grow their own herbs or mix up even a simple ointment? As for the apothecaries, the vast majority rely on a few basic ingredients, coupled with various patent medicines they buy from others. That Mr Lassimer in the town is unusual in buying herbs and the like from you and mixing up his own cures. Yet even he does a good trade in patent medicaments. Now, I think we've done enough for one day.'

Rose began sorting through the surgeon's papers the next day, as she had decided. Most were set aside as kindling, until she found a book containing the notes he had written on his patients. At least, that's what she thought it must contain. She could read Hawley's handwriting — just — but much of the book was written in a version of Latin like nothing her father had taught her. Were these the complex, Latin words physicians used to create an atmosphere of learning? If so, it was definitely going to take a person trained in proper medical terminology to understand them.

## 🐾 12 🐾

Despite some hours puzzling over what she now knew about the circumstances surrounding Surgeon Hawley's death, Rose felt she had not advanced far in seeking to discover who had killed her benefactor, let alone why. She was especially puzzled about two things: where the surgeon was going on the night he was killed, and what the splashes Sam Nugent had mentioned might indicate. Surely, in such a small community as Millgate, someone was bound to know something else of use in unravelling these questions. The trick would be to find out who it was and persuade them to tell all they knew. She also decided she must enlist her aunt fully in her investigation. That would mean bringing her up-to-date on all she had discovered so far.

Aunt Matilda proved to be a good listener, sitting quiet and attentive while Rose went over the whole story. She herself had only come on the scene about fifteen minutes after the surgeon had been pulled from the water. She'd always been a sound sleeper, so she hadn't heard Hawley leave the house. Even if she had, she'd have taken no notice, merely assuming someone had called to ask for him to go to an emergency. Once the sound of so many people outside had brought her awake, she'd still had to find something decent to cover up her nightgown and shoes for her feet, before she could venture out to see what was causing the hubbub.

Perhaps another woman would have had hysterics on discovering what had happened, but Rose Thoday was not that type. Instead, she told her aunt, she'd pushed her way through the mob and marshalled four men to carry the surgeon's body back to his house, then lay it down carefully on his bed. That done, she lit a candle-holder with three candles and used the extra light to examine the corpse. She'd seen the signs of a heavy blow to the head long before they were observed by Dr Henshaw during the autopsy. She knew he'd been murdered. But who would take the word of a woman? Not that fool of a coroner anyhow, with his stupid talk of accidents and tripping over something in the dark.

'Were you called to give evidence at the inquest?' Matilda asked quietly.

'Of course not! They used the evidence of the man from next door to establish identity. I was a nobody. A mere servant. What could I know?'

'But you went to the inquest?'

'Oh yes. I did, and heard the coroner doing his best to pretend Mr Hawley had died as the result of an accident.'

'I wonder why he did that?'

'Heaven knows! All I know is that the doctor who examined the surgeon's body insisted on giving his findings in full and saying it was murder. I could have kissed him! The jury believed him, of course, and ignored the coroner. That's why they brought in the verdict of "unlawfully killed by person or persons unknown." In other words, murder.'

'That must have caused a scandal! Do you recall the doctor's name?'

'It was Henshaw, I think. A young man, but a proper, trained physician all the same. There was no way the coroner could claim he'd been mistaken in his findings.'

'Henshaw. Isn't that Dr Bascom's assistant?'

'Don't talk to me about Dr Bascom, aunt. After the inquest, I plucked up enough courage to go to his house, hoping to ask him to look into the surgeon's death. He's done that before, you know —

investigated suspicious events and managed to bring the criminals behind them to justice.'

'Did he refuse to help you?'

'I never saw him. He was away somewhere when I called. A stuck-up maid answered the door and more or less told me her master wouldn't have the time or inclination to listen to the likes of me. The way she looked at me, you'd have thought I smelled of dung. She even had the nerve to imply that I should have gone to the servants' entrance, not the front door.'

'You don't have to believe maids like that, dear,' her aunt said. 'I've known a good many who gave themselves airs and graces they didn't deserve, and which their employers knew nothing about. If this Dr Bascom has investigated suspicious deaths before, he should know the best way of going about things. I know you're doing your best, but wouldn't it be useful to get some help?'

'Maybe,' Rose said, frowning at the prospect. 'But would he be interested? He must have heard about the death of Surgeon Hawley, but there's been no sign of him coming to ask questions of any of the people who helped to pull the surgeon's body out of the water. I assumed he would be concerned with it being the death of a fellow medical man, but it looks as if I was wrong.'

'What about going to talk to Dr Henshaw then? He carried out the examination of the body and gave evidence at the inquest. It was thanks to him, you say, that they brought in the right verdict. Surely he'd be interested in helping anyone who could find the culprit and prove that he had been right?'

'That's a very good idea, aunt. If he listens to me and thinks that what I am doing is right, he might be willing to speak to Dr Bascom on my behalf. Two things puzzled me especially: where was Mr Hawley going when he went out that night, and what the splashes in the water that Sam Nugent talked about might actually mean. I've racked my brains to think about other people to question but come up with nothing so far.'

'Perhaps it would be a good idea to sleep on it,' Matilda said. 'In the meantime, let's get on with all the other things we have to do.'

Rose sighed. 'You're right. I'm terribly behind with working on my medicines. When I thought I was going to have to leave this house, I took down most of my dried herbs, ground them up and put them into bottles and jars. There seemed to be no time to do anything else. Now I can stay here and go on with my work, I've realised that my supplies of medicines and salves have run very short. What I really need to do is spend several hours making up new ones, but there's all this work to do in the house as well.'

'I can't help you with your medicines, my dear,' Matilda said, 'but I can certainly do a good deal of the work in the house. For a start, I can sort through all this paper in Mr Hawley's desk. I imagine that most of it can be burned. If I'm not certain I'll put it aside and we can look at it together later. What's most important is to clear the desk, so we can move it out of the way. You go out to your shed and deal with the medicines and I'll get on with things in here.'

ROSE LIKED FEW THINGS BETTER THAN TO BE ABLE TO SPEND SOME time on her own working on her herbal remedies. She had sent young Jack out into the garden to clear the weeds from an empty patch of soil. That should take him most of the rest of the day. Tomorrow she would show him how to dig over the ground and get it ready for sowing a new crop.

Mr Hawley had arranged for a small hearth to be constructed at one end of her workshop, so that she could boil water and prepare those ingredients which needed prolonged cooking to draw out their virtues. The workshop was always full of the pungent smells of drying herbs and the various spices which she also used. Now there was an additional aroma as she began to heat almost a gallon of strong ale in the much-used cauldron she had set on a trivet over a hot charcoal fire. When her aunt came in, more than an hour after they had parted, the combined scents caused her to gasp and cover her nose with a handkerchief.

'What on earth are you doing?' she managed to say, between gulping in air and trying to prevent herself from coughing. 'I can scarcely breathe, yet you seem entirely unaffected.'

'I'm used to it,' Rose replied. 'You're like the surgeon. He said the smells I sometimes produced in making up my medicines either reminded him of the exotic markets of India, or the bilge water in his ship after three months at sea.'

'So, what are you making now?'

'This is a very old remedy, but one I would not be without. I had it from Goody Otley and she swore by it for almost any disease affecting the inward parts of the body. It's particularly good for dealing with coughs and shortness of breath.'

'It's managing to cause both in my case! What on earth is in it?'

'Many things. Sage, rosemary, thyme, hyssop, figs, aniseed, and liquorice for a start. You mix them all together and then you have to put them into boiling beer. That's what I have over there in my cauldron. After that, you let them boil until the liquid has reduced by half, then mix in a pound of best treacle and let them boil gently for several hours longer. If you drink a glass of that mixture in the morning before you take any food, and another in the evening when you go to bed, you'll be cured in no time.'

'Well, if you say so . . .'

'I do. I've proved its worth on many occasions. I've mixed up all the dry ingredients and I'm just about to put them in with the beer to boil. Then I'll need to leave them for about an hour.'

'Good,' her aunt said. 'I've decided to take a rest from what I was doing. If you come back into the house, we can drink some tea together. I've almost finished with the papers in that desk. Most of them turned out to be notebooks, so I put them all in a pile for us to look at together and decide what's worth keeping. To be honest, I found it extremely difficult to read most of the content. Everything is crammed together and written very small. A good deal of it is in some foreign language and his handwriting is terrible.'

'Latin, I expect. Doctors and other medical men seem to love writing things in Latin. Fortunately, my father taught me some of that language, so I may be able to make it out.' She laughed. 'I know exactly what you mean about the handwriting. It took me many months before I could make head or tail of even the simplest note. Mr Hawley could write beautifully when he took the time. When he thought he was the only person who would ever read it, he wrote quickly in that abominable scribble!'

'Are they diaries then?'

'Who knows? When I have a moment, I'll go through one or two and try to work it out. I know that he made notes on his cases, so it may be those. He encouraged me to do the same. Said it would help me remember what worked and what didn't. I've tried to follow his instruction, but I haven't always succeeded. Too busy with other things, I expect. He was meticulous.'

'From the number of notebooks, what's in them might even go back to his time in the Navy. Anyway, the desk is now empty, and we can get young Jack to help us push it into the corner. Thinking of that boy, why don't you send him to find Dr Henshaw's house? He could take a message explaining why you want to see the doctor and asking when would be a convenient time. That way, you can make sure the man is at home when you get there.'

'I'll do that right away,' Rose said. 'There. The mixture is boiling nicely now. If I move it to the side, I can be sure it won't boil over when I'm not here to watch it.'

The two women went through into the house and settled themselves comfortably in the parlour, while the maid was sent to boil a kettle and bring them all that was necessary to make tea. While they were waiting, Matilda had another idea.

'I've been wondering,' she said. 'Was the surgeon upset or worried in any way in the days before his death?'

'You're wondering whether he knew he had an enemy,' Rose replied. 'He certainly seemed rather distracted. Not worried exactly, more preoccupied with a problem. It all began when he had that summons to examine the body of the man who committed suicide. At least, that was the finding of the inquest. Mr Hawley didn't say much, but I was sure that he didn't agree with that verdict. However, the coroner overruled him and, since it was the first time he'd been asked to make such an examination, I think he wasn't confident enough to persist with his objections in open court. Mr Hawley rarely talked about his feelings or concerns, so I don't know for sure whether that was the reason or something completely different.'

'Some men are like that,' her aunt said. 'They feel they've got to be strong and deal with all their problems on their own. Your father had that trouble. If he'd only been willing to talk about his growing doubts on matters of faith, I'm sure he would never have reached the point where he killing himself became the only way out of his difficulties. He wasn't the first Christian minister to lose his faith, and he won't be the last.'

When Jack came back from Dr Henshaw's later that afternoon, the message that he brought was a discouraging one. Doctor Henshaw had said he would be happy to talk with Miss Thoday on any medical matter, but he was not the person to speak with about her concerns over the death of the surgeon. For that, she'd be best advised to go directly to Dr Bascom.

'Never mind, dear,' Matilda said, recognising the depth of Rose's disappointment at this response. 'You'll just have to get up your courage and face the man. He surely can't be that bad. Send Jack to make an appointment in advance, walk boldly up to the front door and remember that you aren't a servant any more. You're an independent woman with a substantial income, living in a property which you also own.'

'But I'll have to face that snobbish maid again,' Rose wailed. 'She's bound to remember me.'

'Who cares? You'll have a proper appointment this time. Just remember to dress like a lady and act like one. She is the servant, not you.'

'But I don't have any dresses like that. Only my best dress, I suppose. The one the surgeon had made for me one year for my birthday.'

'Wear that then. I'll lend you my best hat and my fine Norwich shawl. You'll certainly pass muster wearing those. We'll go to the dressmaker as soon we can and get you a proper wardrobe. The best of what you have will do to wear around the house and when you're working with your herbs. Everything else can be given to the poor. You also need to arrange a supply of proper visiting cards. There must be a printer in Aylsham who can produce them. Now, send Jack off right away, before you lose your courage and change your mind.'

'But it's getting dark,' Rose objected. 'I don't like to think of a young boy like that needing to walk into the town and back at this time of the evening.'

'Fiddlesticks! Didn't he spend nearly all his time on the streets and in the fields until you rescued him? He'll know how to look after himself a great deal better than you do. Still, if it upsets you, send him tomorrow morning. First thing, mind! There's to be no going back now.'

## ※ 13 ※

While Rose had been investigating what she could in Millgate, Adam had not been idle. Even so, he felt his progress was minimal. He had written to Captain Mimms in Holt and received a prompt reply, but it was not what he wished to hear. Mimms wrote that he didn't know anything about the surgeon directly, but would ask his sons and some of his contacts amongst the seafarers. He did know something of the Hawley family. The current head of the family was Luke Hawley, a prominent fish merchant and an important man in Great Yarmouth. He had, Mimms wrote, an excellent reputation amongst the fishermen for his honest dealing and fair prices.

All very well, Adam thought, but nothing to set him on a clear path to finding the killer. Of course, the king's navy employed many thousands of people and it had never been more than a faint hope that the captain might have encountered Hawley at some time during his service. It was foolish to feel disappointed as he did. At least Mimms had responded quickly.

During the business over the quack, Professor Panacea, Adam had realised he'd fallen into the habit of neglecting his pupil and assistant, Dr Harrison Henshaw. Since then, determined to set things right, he had made it his habit to meet with Henshaw at least once every week. They would talk over current cases, review the overall state of the practice, and often discuss some matter of special medical interest that one or the other of them had encountered.

Adam and Dr Henshaw were now due for one of these meetings. Since Adam had been away at Mossterton Hall a good deal lately, it began with some of the many routine matters to be covered. Henshaw then mentioned one or two urgent medical problems he wanted to discuss. The two had thus been talking for more than two hours before Adam decided they had done enough for one day. He rang the bell for Hannah and told her to bring them a jug of punch, intending to relax and spend perhaps another half hour in general conversation. Harrison Henshaw had a quick and lively mind and Adam greatly enjoyed the chance to discuss all matter of topics with him in this informal atmosphere.

It was inevitable that the subject of the surgeon's death should enter the conversation sooner or later.

'How goes your investigation, Dr Bascom?' Henshaw asked. 'Have you discovered anything important so far? Surgeon Hawley's former housekeeper asked to talk with me a day or so ago. I gather she has been trying to investigate the surgeon's death on her own. I replied saying she'd best speak with you directly on that topic.'

'Thank you,' Adam said. 'I knew I'd need to speak with her, but I simply haven't had the time. I've been busy enough with other matters, not just this unexplained death of the surgeon. Unfortunately, nothing I have done so far in my attempts to investigate has brought me much illumination. I had hoped to find out more about the surgeon from my friend, Captain Mimms, but the best he can do is enquire from others and promise to let me know if anything useful arises. I too had a message early this morning from Miss Thoday, Hawley's former house-keeper. She was asking for an appointment to talk about the surgeon's death, so she's taken your advice to heart. You know he has bequeathed her everything: house, land, money and household chattels?'

'I did not know that,' Henshaw said. 'He must have thought highly of her to do such a thing.'

'Indeed. Lassimer told me of her inheritance only last evening. His shop is the fountain-head of all the gossip in the town, so news like that was bound to reach him almost at once. It's odd, you know. Surgeon Hawley was a middle-aged man with a vigorous nature living in the same house with a young woman. I haven't met Miss Thoday. Though I believe she is no great beauty, she must surely have offered him some temptation. Have you met her? Is she comely enough to excite the passions of a man who sees her at close quarters every day?'

'I haven't met her either. Was she Hawley's mistress, do you think? Is that why he left her all he possessed? It seems the obvious explanation.'

'I cannot bring myself to believe it is true, for it would definitely have occasioned a good deal of gossip if it were. Lassimer would have heard it and passed the news on to me, I'm sure.'

'Of course! You fool!' Henshaw said loudly. Then he blushed and hastened to apologise. 'Not you, doctor. Please do not think I would ever be so rude as to call you a fool. It is myself I am berating. When I was telling you about my conclusions from the autopsy that I conducted on Surgeon Hawley, I told you only of those matters which pertained directly to his death. I believe at the time I did mention there were other findings of significance. I even promised to explain what those were, once we had dealt with the most important topics. Then, like the fool I am, I forgot. If you will allow me, sir, I believe I can explain how matters must have stood between Mr Hawley and Miss Thoday. Although Mr Lassiter advised me on conducting the autopsy, he was not able to be present during the process itself. He could not leave his shop unattended for so long. He will not, therefore, have known about those findings which did not relate directly to establishing how the poor man died.

'The surgeon's body bore the scars of several old wounds. Knowing he had served in our navy, I judged these scars to have been caused by wounds received in sea battles. They were most consistent with the kinds of gashes a man might receive from flying splinters. None were bullet wounds. Most were in the chest and abdomen. I could imagine our surgeon toiling over some wounded man, when the part of the ship where he was working was struck by an enemy cannonball. There would be a hail of vicious splinters from the shattered wood of the hull, decking and interior fittings. Anyone in the way must received multiple wounds, some superficial, but others deep enough to threaten life itself.

'I considered most of these old wounds, now well healed, had been in the former category: superficial wounds, though still painful enough, I imagine. However, there were clear signs that at some time poor Surgeon Hawley had received a more severe wound — or wounds — to his groin. Not to put too fine a point on it, he had been almost castrated by whatever hit him. Had Miss Thoday been both beautiful and wanton, doctor, the outcome would have been the same. Mr Hawley would have been no use to her in matters of the bedroom.'

'I wonder if she knew?' Adam said. 'It is not something I imagine Mr Hawley would have spoken of openly. Yet, if she did not, she must surely have wondered why he never made any attempt on her virtue.'

'You could ask her.'

'It is hardly something that would come up in idle conversation, and to pose the question directly would be most improper.'

'Of course. Forgive my stupidity.'

'More to the point, I wonder if others in that community knew? It seemed odd to me that nobody seemed to have objected to the arrangement between them. Had Miss Thoday been a close relative, I could have understood it. Many single men have a sister or a niece living with them to keep house. But there was, so far as I know, no family link between Mr Hawley and Miss Thoday. But if people knew he was a eunuch ...'

'Surely it cannot have any bearing on his death, other than ruling out the possibility of the murderer being an irate husband or brother?'

Adam thought for a moment. 'You're right, of course. Yet if Surgeon Hawley, well aware of his own state, had perhaps allowed the appearance of an untoward intimacy to arise between him and some lady ...'

Dr Henshaw laughed. 'If every cuckolded husband in this town resorted to killing his wife's lover, let alone every brother jealous of the family honour and his sister's virtue, the male population would be halved overnight. Our mutual friend Mr Lassimer would never survive!

I fear we are allowing our imaginations too much reign, sir. From all you have told me, Mr Hawley was uncommonly well liked and respected. That is hardly consistent with behaviour likely to produce an enraged husband, intent on murder.'

It was Adam's turn to grin. 'You see how desperate I am for anything which might suggest a reason for the surgeon's murder. Once again, you are correct. Yet no killing takes place without a cause, be that cause never so strange or trivial. So far, all we have is a man dead and nothing to even suggest why he was killed. I can't help feeling that, if I knew why the surgeon had to die, I would have a very good notion of who killed him.'

'I cannot argue with that. Why not ask Miss Thoday when you see her?'

'I will. I can only hope she knows no more than I do.'

'Perhaps she does not know that she knows.'

'What? Does not know that she knows? You'll have to explain that to me.'

'All I meant is that she may know of something in Mr Hawley's life — recent or not — which she has dismissed as irrelevant, but which might point to the cause of his death. A threatening letter, perhaps? A patient refusing to pay his account on the grounds that he received no benefit from Mr Hawley's treatment? Treatment given to some footpad or highwayman. We know Mr Hawley was a most conscientious man. I doubt he would have denied help to someone in need of his services, even if he knew that person to be in trouble with the law.'

'If every patient who got no benefit from his doctor's prescription resorted to murder, Dr Henshaw, you and I will soon be found dead in suspicious circumstances. Your other suggestion, however, is a good one. The surgeon worked a good deal amongst the artisans and labouring classes who gained their livelihood from the Bure Navigation. It would be a miracle if all were people of unblemished virtue.'

'Can you discover if Mr Hawley seemed especially worried about anything in the last days of his life? Had his manner changed? Was he markedly anxious? All of these behaviours could have simple explanations; all of them could indicate knowledge of some imminent threat. Miss Thoday would surely have noticed such a change. If she did, she might have put it down to overwork, financial worries, or an approaching illness. Until now, that is.'

'I am glad we had this discussion. I had not thought of that, even though it is an obvious question to ask her. Thank you, Dr Henshaw. You may be sure I shall question the lady closely. Now, before we part, is there anything else I have missed?'

Dr Henshaw said there was not, so the two men parted. Henshaw to return to his afternoon round of patients, Adam to sit and brood over his lack of method in seeking out Hawley's killer. It was not, he told himself, that he didn't know what he knew. In his case, he didn't even know what he didn't know — nor what he hadn't bothered to seek out. His mind was too full of other matters. That was the trouble. For example, he ought to have asked Miss Thoday to call on him tomorrow. Instead, he had postponed her visit until the day after that, only because he wished nothing more than to go to Mossterton to talk with Lady Alice. At least he could tell her about this investigation in proper detail. He knew any attempt to summarise things and set them down in a letter would be doomed to failure, not from complexity, but from the sheer vagueness of so much of it.

THE NEXT MORNING, THEREFORE, ADAM SET OUT EARLY FOR Mossterton Hall. Ever since the bad fall from his horse the previous year, he had become less and less willing to return to the saddle. He therefore went in his chaise with William driving. It was not a long journey, but several parts ran through areas of rough heathland and scrub, each of them an ideal lurking place for footpads or highwaymen. With times made harder by the war and opportunities for work on the land limited, more men than ever had turned to robbery to support themselves and their families. Nowadays, whenever he went more than a mile or so from his home, Adam made sure to carry two loaded pistols. He had them now, tucked under a cushion beside him.

Lady Alice was surprised and delighted to see Adam again so soon. However, by arriving so unexpectedly, Adam had ensured she would be able to spend little more than two hours with him. She had already agreed to visit Lord and Lady Baddiel at noon and her dressmaker was due to arrive at three. Neither appointment could now be postponed. They would have to try to make best use of what time was available.

After formal greetings, the two retired to her ladyship's dressing room, where they managed at last to snatch several warm kisses, hopefully away from prying eyes. Adam would have their whole time together in this delightful activity, but Lady Alice gently pushed him away, made him sit down at a little distance, and demanded an account of his activities since he had last written to her. He at once began to complain that his investigation into the death of the surgeon was taking up far too much of his time. To make matters worse, he had also received a letter from Wicken asking him to look into certain problems relating to smuggling and espionage. Then there was the question of Mr Sleeth's suitability to remain as coroner to be dealt with somehow—

'No more, my dearest,' Lady Alice interrupted. 'This is not like you. I have never before known you allow your personal concerns to get in the way of far more important matters. We have at least six weeks before we can tell the world that we are to be married. As for finding a house, I do not have to leave Mossterton for several months after that. Besides, I have already told you that I will happily live with you in your house in Aylsham, or rent a suitable property in Norwich, until we can find somewhere that will suit us permanently. Let us set these cares aside. Tell me, have you seen Mr Hawley's housekeeper yet? I recall that you were concerned that the locals in Millgate might not be willing to talk with you openly. Perhaps she could ask some questions on your behalf?'

'That young lady has made an appointment to visit me tomorrow,' Adam said, going on to tell her how, in his Will, Mr Hawley had disposed of his total estate in her favour, making her a woman of property and independent means. 'By her message, she is still determined to discover who killed her benefactor. Whether she knows I am already investigating his death, or does not know and means to ask me to do so, I cannot say.'

'Either way,' Lady Alice said, 'you must surely help her, as I know you will.' She paused for a moment. 'This might also discharge your obligation to your Mr Wicken — I mean Sir Percival Wicken. I believe Mr Hawley worked amongst the people whose livelihood comes from the Bure Navigation. Is it not likely that he came upon something which some smuggling gang hoped to keep secret? What better way to do so than to kill the man who had found them out?'

'A clear possibility, but a most unsatisfactory one,' Adam said. 'If the surgeon was killed by a smuggling gang, we will never bring the murderers to justice. Those gangs protect their members fiercely. However, I don't think that Mr Hawley was one of their victims.'

'Why not?'

'First of all, when a smuggling gang takes vengeance in that way, or seeks to prevent someone from giving away their secrets, they take good care to make their involvement public knowledge. By doing so, they frighten off anyone else who might be tempted to give them away in the future. In this case, no one has claimed responsibility for the surgeon's death. Indeed, the local people are said to be greatly angered at his murder. Many will, I'm sure, have connections with the smugglers in their locality. If they had killed the surgeon, would the locals not see his death in quite a different way?'

'A very good point,' Lady Alice said. 'Yet it is hardly conclusive.'

'Then I will give you another reason. We know that Mr Sleeth, the coroner, tried hard to have his jury find the surgeon's death to have been an accident. If a group of smugglers were responsible for the murder, that must mean that Sleeth is in league with them. Is that likely? In what way would they gain if he had succeeded? I am ready to believe many things of Mr Sleeth, but not that he is involved with common criminals and does their bidding.'

'Why has Sir Percival Wicken asked you to investigate the doings of the smugglers?' Lady Alice asked. 'Does he think that they are responsible in some way for the surgeon's death?'

'I was going to say that I doubted whether he even knew about it, but that would have been foolish. I am sometimes convinced that Wicken knows almost everything that happens, here and elsewhere. Still, if he does know, he has not mentioned it to me. What concerns him is that French spies might once again be using the smugglers to take messages in and out of the country.'

'But you live quite a long way from the coast. Why should you know anything about their dealings?'

'Given the threat of invasion, our coasts are watched more closely than ever. Wicken fears the smugglers have found a way past our defences by using the boats that move up and down the Bure Navigation.'

'Would that not increase the likelihood of the surgeon becoming involved with them in some way, probably unwittingly. Surgeons typically treat broken limbs, cuts, knocks, sprains and other accidental injuries. What if he were asked to treat someone who proved to be a Frenchman? As a doctor, he might have felt obliged to do so. As an Englishman, and one who had served in His Majesty's Navy, he would have been duty-bound to hand the man over to the authorities. Suppose he had been forced to continue his treatment in secret until such time as the Frenchman had escaped overseas. The smugglers could then have feared that his conscience would get the better of him and he would betray them.'

'What about Mr Sleeth? Might the surgeon somehow have discovered that the coroner was being controlled by the smuggling gang?'

'And they killed him to protect Sleeth? Certainly, I cannot see Sleeth committing murder on his own account. From all I hear, he seems something of a weakling in a physical sense. Still, he may well have been happy enough to see others act on his behalf. You make a most persuasive case, my lady. If I am honest, I must admit that the strongest reason for my reluctance to accept what you are saying is the first that I gave you: that if the surgeon was murdered by a gang of smugglers, we will never bring those who did it to justice.'

'Then I will not press the matter further. Since you tell me you cannot quite believe this simple explanation, I will trust you in this, as I do in all things. We will turn to other matters. Tell me more about Miss Thoday.'

'There is not much more that I know. My friend Lassimer knows her. She supplies him with many of his herbs and he has the highest opinion of her skills as a herbalist. It may also amuse you to hear that I believe him to be frightened of her.'

'How so? Have you not told me before that he is an unrepentant womaniser? I could not imagine any female causing him fear.'

'Then you would be wrong. Our apothecary likes women who are noted for their good looks and warm natures — and the looseness of their morals. By his own admission, Miss Thoday is well educated, highly intelligent, possessed of considerable self-confidence, and entirely respectable. Not his kind of woman at all. She is also a descendant of a woman called Goody Otley, who had a powerful reputation for miles around as a Wise Woman. People believe she had strange powers, both to heal and to harm. She was also said to be able to foretell the future. Whatever the truth of that, Miss Thoday's connection with her has convinced most of the local people that she herself has similar gifts. They do not only go to her for healing; they take their troubles to her, though many must be twice her age and more. According to Lassimer, they treat her with enormous respect for fear that she might place a curse upon them if they did not.'

'I long to meet your Miss Thoday,' Lady Alice said. 'She seems to me to be a most intelligent and competent young woman. It's now doubly obvious to me the two of you should cooperate. You each have access to sources of information the other lacks. You told me yourself that you could not see how to persuade the ordinary people of the area to tell you what they had seen or heard. Miss Thoday is, from what you have said, well-known and respected amongst just those people. She will have no difficulty tapping their memories and knowledge. You can deal with the better class of people, who would certainly not talk to anyone who had once been a servant. It is a perfect arrangement.'

'You do realise I will need to speak with her quite often,' Adam said, 'sometimes in private?'

'Of course, my dear,' Lady Alice replied, just managing to conceal her amusement at the expression on Adam's face. 'And it would never occur to me to doubt you will always conduct yourself with perfect propriety towards her, alone or in company. If I did not trust you in such circumstances, you may be assured I would never have agreed to marry you.'

Adam was about to interrupt, but she held up her hand to prevent it.

'Still, you are right to be concerned that other people might take a different view. All you need is always to meet in the presence of a suitable chaperone. You may also be able to stay in touch by letter. Do you know if she can write with some ease and facility?'

'I know she reads extensively. Lassimer said she told him that was how she gained much of her knowledge of medicinal herbs.'

'Then let us assume she can write well too. When you wish to communicate without meeting, simply send a servant with a written message. If she also has access to a servant or other trustworthy person to deliver replies to your house, I am certain many of your necessary exchanges of information can be done in that way. When talking with her in person is essential, use your calling as a physician and let the world believe she is your patient.'

## 14

Whenever he felt frustrated and out-of-sorts, as he did that day when forced to return home from Mossterton so early, Adam's first response was to shut himself away in his study and try to make sense of whatever it was that was bothering him. Sometimes it worked; often it did not. Lady Alice's swift grasp of the essentials and series of useful suggestions had made him feel more than usually discouraged by his own slowness and lack of determination in tackling the puzzle of the surgeon's death. She was correct, he decided. His impatience was getting in his way. He was rushing to deal with problems like finding a new home when there was still plenty of time before it would become a real priority. What mattered at the moment was to find the murderer in their midst.

Since sitting alone in his study, brooding on his sense of frustration, was certainly not going to help, he decided to take the short walk along the street to Peter Lassimer's apothecary shop. If his old friend was free and had the time, he was the ideal person with whom to talk through his problems. Luck was with him and he was soon seated in the apothecary's parlour, drinking punch and pouring out his troubles.

'I feel I'm no further forward than I was days ago,' Adam said.

'Something has to be behind this killing, but I'm damned if I know what it may be.'

'It's not nearly as bad as you're making out,' Peter said. 'What you need is patience. You say that the surgeon's former housekeeper is coming to see you tomorrow. She's also told you that she's been collecting information from some of the people in Millgate that you were intending to talk with anyway. Talking to people who won't talk openly to you, I think you said. Captain Mimms is seeing what he can discover about Mr Hawley's time in the navy. Meanwhile, you already have a good deal of general knowledge about the surgeon's relationships in the area; more than enough to make clear that it's most unlikely anyone there harboured some grudge against him. Finally, thanks to Dr Henshaw, you can rule out angry husbands and brothers. I know much of these items are negative, but they narrow the field of possibilities. Wicken has provided a definite indication that there could be more than simple, run-of-the-mill smuggling linked to the Navigation. I would say you've advanced a good way.'

'It doesn't feel like that,' Adam complained.

'Stop being so impatient! There's much still to do before you decide you've reached a dead end. For example, you have no idea what Miss Thoday might have discovered until you speak with her.'

'I suppose so, but what if she has found out nothing?'

'What a pessimist you have become! Why assume the worst? She may have discovered the key to the whole problem for all you know. Now, just in case she hasn't, why don't you and I apply our formidable brains to extracting something useful from what you've found out already.'

Adam could find no fault with this suggestion, so he waited quietly while Peter stepped into his shop and told his apprentice to call him only on matters of the highest urgency. When Peter returned, however, Adam felt curiously unwilling to apply himself to analysing what he knew already, as Peter had suggested. It was true he felt frustrated with his slow progress towards a solution to Hawley's murder, but that was not the main source of his dullness and lack of energy. It was time he admitted to himself that what he wanted most was to be able to tell the world the tremendous news about himself and Lady Alice. So long as he was blocked from doing so, he constantly fretted and worried his time away.

Peter, knowing nothing of Adam's true source of unease, put his friend's lethargy down to simple ill-temper. That could be cured, and the cure he had in mind was to refuse to allow Adam to leave without them taking some sensible steps towards solving the question of who had killed the surgeon.

'Very well,' Peter said, exuding energy and purpose. 'Let us start with the most promising reason for Hawley's death: that he stumbled on something going on in Millgate that was supposed to be secret. Let's leave it open for the moment whether this was to do with smuggling or some other activity. What would Mr Hawley do with that knowledge and how would those who wished it to stay secret find out?'

'Report what he had found to someone in authority, I suppose,' Adam said, his voice making clear his reluctance to join in this game. 'A magistrate, perhaps?'

'Exactly! So, let's think who the magistrate for that area might be. Not the same one as has responsibility in the town, I would imagine. Jackson? No, he lives over towards Reepham. Got it! Mr Thomas Mountneigh. Now there's a fine fellow for you — at least in his own eyes.'

'Mountneigh? I must have met him, but I cannot recall doing so.'

'He probably wouldn't have taken any notice of a lowly fellow like you or I, Bascom. Mere tradesmen in his eyes. Thomas Mountneigh thinks of himself as proper gentry: descended from a long line of eldest sons of eldest sons, all cherishing the lands which represent their claim to superiority over those who must earn their living by working.'

'Is he so very rich? Does he have a grand estate? If he does, how is it that his name means so little to me?'

'Right to the point, as usual. No, he is not especially rich. Indeed, his father is well known to have gambled and whored to such purpose that what estate his son inherited is weighed down with mortgages. It was never more than a modest holding anyway. I would imagine it may include seven or ten tenancies, no more. The rest is made up of the land surrounding Mountneigh's mansion and the home farm. The mansion I have not seen, but the word is that it was built maybe one hundred and fifty years ago and has been little improved since.'

'Yet its owner thinks himself above the rest of us?'

'Knows himself to be! He is a Mountneigh. According to him, the Mountneighs were — and still should be — amongst the premier families in this kingdom; if not for wealth and lands, then for purity of blood. His claim is that the original Mountneigh came with the Conqueror in 1066, fought alongside him when King Harold was slain, and should, by all rights, have been awarded at least an earldom for his pains. He wasn't, so the story goes, due to the jealousy of the De Lacy family, who poisoned the new king's mind against him. Since then, other families have risen and fallen, while the Mountneigh's have nursed their ancient grudge on their estate in Norfolk, waiting for the time when another king will recognise their legitimate claims.'

'Is all this correct?'

'Of course not. From all I hear, his direct line consists of merchants and farmers.'

'His pedigree is invented?'

'Entirely, so people say. I suspect that may be too harsh a judgement. To my mind, many people can claim some link to at least part of a family which was once from the gentry. Since younger sons do not inherit the lands, they must make their own way in the world, generally by becoming tenant farmers or through trade. The man is not such a fool as to claim his immediate forbears were gentry. According to his version, his great-great-grandfather was driven from his lands through his support for the royal cause during the Civil War. It is Oliver Cromwell's fault his part of the family had to turn to trade.'

'And the present Mountneigh believes this version of events?'

'Apparently. He's obsessed with restoring his family to what he claims is its proper status. As you might guess, I cannot stand the man.'

That was the trouble with Lassimer. His likes and dislikes were always extreme. He saw no good in anyone whom he found uncongenial, and little wrong with any of his friends. He was also prone to exaggerate for the sake of telling a good tale. Adam decided to take all that his friend said with a copious pinch of salt.

'I wonder if there's any way of finding out if Hawley did go to see Mountneigh; and what they talked about if he did?'

'I very much doubt Mountneigh will tell you. You could try asking Miss Thoday. She might at least know whether such a meeting ever took place.'

'Indeed. Let us hope she can tell me tomorrow.'

'What else should we consider? The smugglers, perhaps? I can't imagine the surgeon was about to hand them over to the authorities; not if he wanted to continue to live in Millgate and retain his patients. But what if they're smuggling something other than contraband?'

'Wicken thinks some may be involved in espionage,' Adam said. 'Carrying messages to and from the spymasters in France. Smuggling new spies into the country and helping those who have been discovered to escape.'

'There you are then! If the surgeon knew something that could get you arrested and convicted of treason, and you didn't trust him to keep his mouth shut, wouldn't you be tempted to kill him?'

'I suppose I would,' Adam admitted. 'It's just that I think the kind of people amongst whom the surgeon moved, and from whom he drew the majority of his patients, would be small-fry in the smuggling business. Wicken is not very interested in them. He wants to sniff out those who organise this kind of activity. They are hardly likely to be living in Millgate, don't you think?'

'Maybe, maybe not. I don't think it's sensible to assume you know the answer either way. There! We've been talking for barely ten minutes and I've already given you two extremely promising areas for further investigation. You could easily have worked both them out for yourself, if you'd tried. What on earth is the matter with you these days? If I didn't know you better, I'd say that you'd fallen in love.'

'How do you make that out?' Adam said, now feeling alarmed that Peter would work out more and then spread the word. If he did, could Lady Alice ever be convinced Adam had not let slip some incautious remark and set him on the right path?

'Your mind seems always elsewhere. You moon about, staring into the distance. You've lost interest in matters that were once of the greatest importance to you. All classic signs, believe me. As a result, you're well on the way to becoming useless to anyone. That's the trouble with love. It addles the brain, saps the energy and destroys the will.'

'How come you're so cheerful and busy then? Given the number of women with whom you've had love affairs, you should be in a coma by now.'

'But I don't have love affairs,' Peter said. 'I avoid love like the plague it is. To be in love is miserable and debilitating. To be in lust is far preferable. Love makes you moon over the very thought of your beloved. Lust encourages you to slip into bed with her at every possible opportunity. In my experience, women say they want to be loved, but what they really mean is they want you to lust after them so much that you shower them with presents and attention, then devote yourself wholly to giving them pleasure in every possible way.'

Adam could not stop himself from laughing, try as he might. 'You're incorrigible!' he gasped when he was finally able to speak. 'I swear you combine the glibness of a lawyer with the morals of a tom cat. I'm going home now, before you can say anything else calculated to corrupt me.'

'You won't argue, because you know I'm right,' Peter called after him. 'Lust is a wonderful state of mind. You should try it sometime.'

❦

MRS BRIGSTONE SERVED ADAM HIS DINNER THAT EVENING. Hannah, she told him, had developed a nasty cold in the head and was not fit to be near any gentleman's food. She had been given two bowls of strong beef tea, told to put on two nightdresses, one on top of the other, and sent to bed to sweat it out of her system. Mrs Brigstone had been looking for an opportunity to speak to the doctor in private, so this was an ideal chance.

Adam was intrigued. He was always very open with the servants and encouraged them to speak to him on any matter of concern, large or small. Why Mrs Brigstone should need a special opportunity to talk with him was therefore unclear. Still, she waited until he had finished his meal and she was clearing away the final dishes, so the least he could do was sit back in his chair and indicate that she had his full attention.

'It's about this business in Millgate,' she began. 'We all know you're off on another one of your hunts after a murderer. Hannah says we are wrong, and you're plotting how best to ask Lady Alice to marry you. Of course, she fills her head with silly romantic nonsense from those novels she and her friends pass around between them. The rest of us take no notice of her wild ideas.'

'You're right that I'm investigating the murder of Surgeon Hawley,' Adam said, carefully omitting to make any comment on Hannah's interpretation of his recent behaviour. 'Do you or any of the other servants know anything that would be helpful in this respect?'

'Not directly, as you might say,' Mrs Brigstone replied, 'but I do know that there's been odd things going on in Millgate for quite a few weeks now. My sister lives there, you see. She is married to a man who works for Mr Bale at the brewery.'

'And what has she told you?' Adam said. This was beginning to sound interesting.

'I suppose you already know that all the people in Millgate knew that the surgeon had been murdered, whatever that fool of a coroner tried to force his jury into recording. They also know there's been another murder, but this time the coroner got his way and it went down in the legal record as a suicide.'

'Someone else mentioned a suicide,' Adam replied. 'I believe it was a person called Laven.'

'That's right, sir, Mr Robert Laven, the elder of two brothers. Between them, the Laven brothers own the largest fleet of boats on the Navigation, as well as I don't know what else. Mr Robert was supposed to have shot himself with his own pistol, due to getting into debt through gambling.'

'And your sister thinks that wasn't correct,' Adam said.

'Not just my sister, sir, but just about everybody else whoever came into contact with those brothers. It's true Mr Robert was wild. He was a gambler, and a drinker, and never could keep his hands to himself either. They had terrible trouble keeping maidservants. But as for killing himself, that he would never do. He was far too arrogant.

Besides, he'd been in serious trouble many times before and always found a way out. Usually his brother provided the money to set him on his feet again. At other times, he either charmed his way past his difficulties, or lied and cheated his way out of them. He may have been wicked and a lecher, but he was never a coward. My sister reckons he'd have killed twenty other people before he would have killed himself.'

'But the inquest recorded a verdict of suicide you said.'

'That was all down to Mr Sleeth. He bullied all the witnesses and browbeat the jury to bring the verdict he'd decided on beforehand.'

'I wonder why he did that?' Adam said. 'Surely that would have upset the other brother and the rest of his family? Most families will go to great lengths to try to avoid even the suggestion that any family member would kill himself.'

'Nobody knows why he did it, sir. The family didn't make a fuss either. Not that there are many of them left nowadays. For the last few generations, according to those who know, the male members of that family have either never married, or lost most of their children in infancy. Mr Robert wasn't married either, sir, and nor is his brother, Mr Richard. So far as I know, they're the last of the line.'

'Thank you, Mrs Brigstone. That may prove very helpful. You may bring me the brandy now and then return to your duties.'

Another mystery, Adam thought, and Sleeth in the middle of it once again! It was obvious something strange was happening in Millgate. Could it be that the smugglers were forcing Sleeth to do their bidding? To imagine the reverse strained credulity too far, surely? What if he were being blackmailed? Adam could imagine the attorney tampering with his clients' funds or diverting them to his own use. Theft would be an ever-present temptation to someone charged with acting as executor of Wills or the trustee for an underage child. Aside from any question of illegality such actions would prompt, someone known to have succumbed to the urge to profit in that way would find it impossible to obtain new clients. It would only take a disgruntled clerk to see the chance of taking revenge for enough evidence to come into the hands of the smugglers to make Sleeth into their slave for ever afterwards.

Whatever the truth of these suppositions, it was plain something needed to be done urgently to remove Mr Sleeth from his post as coroner. Adam determined to write to Wicken that very evening, laying out the facts and asking for his help in bringing Sleeth's incompetence — or worse — to the notice of the relevant persons. With luck, he could then leave the matter in Wicken's hands and get on with finding Mr Hawley's killer.

## ❦ 15 ❦

The young woman whom Mrs Brigstone ushered into Adam's study the next morning bore little or no resemblance to the way Peter had described her. It was true Rose Thoday was somewhat unremarkable in appearance, being neither short nor tall and well-dressed without appearing fashionable. To Adam's eyes, she looked what he knew she had been: an upper servant in the household of a professional man of adequate means. She was neat, modest in her bearing and confident enough to wait patiently until he should address her.

Adam was intrigued by Miss Thoday's visit. It was true that he had wanted to speak with her, but he had never imagined she would come to him. Early on, his mind had been running on ways of calling at the surgeon's house without appearing impolite or overly curious. Lately, however, so many other things had demanded his attention that he had almost forgotten about her. None of the people from whom he had so far gained useful information had so much as mentioned her being involved in any way in the events surrounding the surgeon's death.

'Miss Thoday,' he said. 'I am delighted to make your acquaintance. Will it suit you for us to speak in this room, which I use as study and consulting room? If you would prefer it, we can go into the parlour instead.'

'This room is more than adequate, doctor. It has the advantage of windows which face somewhat towards the east, so we will be warmed by the morning sun. Spring has come late this year and it is well to take advantage of the warmer days. You house is a fine dwelling, sir. I have passed it many times, yet did not know until a few days ago who lived within.'

'May I offer you some refreshment, madam, before we begin?'

'Thank you, doctor, but I need none. I imagine you will be some-what surprised that I have sought you out in this way. As my note should have made plain, I do not come seeking your assistance as a physician. It is another of your skills of which I wish to take advantage. Everyone in Aylsham knows that you have been able to solve a number of taxing mysteries and bring more than one criminal to justice. I am determined to discover who killed my benefactor, sir, and come seeking your aid in the matter.'

She goes directly to the heart of the matter, Adam thought, without more than a minimum of the usual polite preliminaries. Fair enough. I will do the same.

'You were housekeeper to Surgeon Hawley, I believe,' he said. 'His death must have occasioned you considerable loss in many ways. From all that I have heard, he was a good man, so I expect he made a good master. Now that he is dead, you would, under normal circumstances, have lost your position. However, in your case I understand matters have turned out very differently.'

'Indeed, doctor. My late master, bless his soul, left me everything in his Will: his house and garden, his various assets and his medical equip-ment. I am my own woman, doctor, thanks to him, dependent on no man for my future.'

Yes, Adam told himself, there is another hint of the strength of character which had frightened Peter. I must tread warily.

'That is indeed fortunate, madam. What do you intend to do for the future, if I may ask?'

'Continue Mr Hawley's work as best I can, sir. I know I can never become a surgeon. Such work is restricted to men, though I have little doubt a woman, properly trained, could prove as able. Since I will not be allowed to do as I might, I will do what I can. I owe it to my master in return for all he has done for me.'

Adam was taken aback and showed it. 'But, madam—' he began.

'There are no "buts", doctor. Mr Hawley taught me all he knew of medical herbs, and I have increased my knowledge and skill beyond that point by diligent application to reading and practical experiment. I am not afraid to say that I am probably the most skilled herbalist for miles around, for I grow much of what I use — aye, and dry and prepare it too. Even Mr Lassimer, the apothecary, buys many of the herbs he uses from me. Mr Hawley also taught me much about the setting of bones and dislocations. I may not be able to claim to succeed him, but I can make myself useful to the same people he did.'

Adam did not know what to say. He could see now why Peter thought this woman extraordinary. Behind the polite words lay a rich vein of confidence, even assertiveness. He never doubted for a moment that what she was telling him was true.

'My apologies, madam. I did not mean to suggest doubt in your abilities or your determination. But it can be difficult for a young woman like yourself to make her way in the world without some male support. What you suggest — to continue your work as a herbalist — is entirely laudable, but I have my own practice to consider and have little time to spare to act as your guide.'

'Dr Bascom. If we continue simply following the dictates of polite conversation, I fear we will never understand one another. May I have your permission to speak plainly, sir? I assure you that I mean no disrespect.'

'Please do,' Adam said, 'for I confess I am a little bewildered about what you seek from me.'

'It is simple. I wish you to help me discover the identity of the man who killed my former master. You know how to go about this and I do not. You are a man and can go where you wish. As a woman, there are places I dare not venture and people to whom I cannot speak. I am not an especially wealthy woman, sir, even with the legacy from Mr Hawley, but I will willingly pay any reasonable fees for your time—'

Adam cut her off. 'When I act in my professional capacity as a physician, Miss Thoday, I charge as other physicians do. It is my occupation. I have never asked anyone for money to investigate a case of wrongdoing. In that area, I am merely a curious amateur, who has had some success, as much through good fortune as skill. There can be no question of taking your money.'

'I have offended you.'

'By no means. You asked that we speak plainly to one another, so that is what I have done. If I have expressed myself too harshly, I apologise. You have presented me with a series of surprises, Miss Thoday, and you must grant me the time to adjust myself to them. I may ask other things of you ...'

Rose narrowed her eyes, fearing what those might be.

'... but I will not ask for monetary payment. Let me consider what you ask and give you an answer tomorrow. If I judge your meaning correctly, you would wish to be an active participant in your quest to find this murderer. That puts me in a dilemma. Many people have assisted me during previous investigations, but always at my direction. To speak plainly again, what little I have been told about you before today, Miss Thoday, suggests that you would not take kindly to instructions. You wish to be a partner, not a mere assistant. I have never found myself in such a situation before, let alone when that partner is a woman. There are proprieties to consider. Even if I decide to set out along such a path, I cannot devote myself to it wholeheartedly without the agreement of the others concerned.'

It was Rose's turn to be taken aback. She had prepared herself for outright refusal. She had prepared herself, so far as she could, for agreement on terms she might find it hard to meet. What she had not expected was to be asked to wait while the doctor thought things over and consulted others. Her shoulders slumped and she could not hide her sense of dejection.

Adam smiled at her. 'I can see you are downcast, Miss Thoday. If it cheers you, let me confess I had already decided to look into the death of Surgeon Hawley before you came to my house. My assistant, Dr Henshaw, was involved in the inquest ...' He decided to spare her the mention of an autopsy. '... and he has shared with me the concerns which led him to argue with the coroner over the possibility that Mr

Hawley's death was accidental. I agree with him fully. Your former master was murdered, of that there can be no doubt. Yet, so far, the magistrate has done little beyond place the usual advertisements in local newspapers, appealing for information. I have no standing from which to launch an investigation, other than my inveterate curiosity. You, as Mr Hawley's heir, have every right to seek to bring the killer to justice. Have you been in contact with other members of his family? I believe they reside in Great Yarmouth.'

'I have not, doctor. The surgeon had not had dealings with them for many years. I imagine there must be a reason, but I do not know what it was. Since none were mentioned in his Will, I must assume the reason still stood.'

'Very well, let us forget about them. I have already said I mean to investigate. What I am unsure about is what part you can play in this investigation, other than providing useful information from your knowledge of the man. Being a woman—'

'You mean to confine me to the woman's place!' Rose said, her voice gaining an edge of irritation. 'Tell you what I know and let you and the other menfolk get on with everything else, while I sit at home and wait for such crumbs of news as you see fit to send me.'

'You see?' Adam said. 'Already you are taking issue with me; interpreting my words to fuel your anger at the world as it is. If I am concerned by your wish to become an active partner in seeking out the murderer, madam, it is mostly because I cannot yet see how such an arrangement would work. You said yourself there are places you cannot go and things you cannot do—'

'But does not the same apply to you, doctor?' Rose said. 'Come down to Millgate asking questions and no one is likely to give you an honest answer — if they give you an answer at all. You are an outsider, a wealthy man, the kind of person they have learned to fear. Will they assist you? I can assure you they will not. I live amongst them. They know me. They call me a Wise or a Cunning Woman — mere superstition in my opinion. Even so, the title has its uses. Many fear to lie to me in case I lay a curse upon them. That I cannot do — nor would I, even if I knew how — yet it clearly makes a difference to their feelings towards me. My great aunt, Goody Otley, was both respected and feared for her supposed powers. People say I look like her when she was young, and they know she taught me many things. They're certain I will assume her mantle as a Cunning Woman. She did teach me a great deal, doctor, but it was all about herbs and the various ways of bringing healing and comfort to others she had learned in a long life. Not witchcraft.'

She was right, of course. Hadn't he been wondering how he could set about persuading ordinary people to tell him what they knew? Here was the answer — if he dared to take it. What bothered him, of course, was how others would react. Miss Thoday was young, female and at least personable. To spend time with her on a regular basis, especially alone, would occasion gossip — even condemnation from the more puritanical. His practice might suffer as a result, to say nothing of his wider reputation. Then there was Lady Alice. She had urged him on, of course, but she might still feel uneasy at such a close working relationship coming on the heels of accepting his proposal of marriage. Adam was, in social matters, a conventional person. He suddenly thought of what his mother might say, if she found out, and experienced an icy feeling in the pit of his stomach. As for his brother, Giles . . .

'I will indeed help you, Miss Thoday,' Adam said, plucking up his courage, 'but only subject to putting certain practical arrangements in place. For a start, to avoid malicious gossip our meetings need to take place in the presence of a suitable chaperone.' He held up his hand to prevent her interrupting. 'Do you know of such a person? If you do not, the best we can do is communicate by letter. I can pass off your visit today as being of a medical nature. No one outside this room knows otherwise. However, I cannot expect you to feign some serious illness to provide an excuse for any future meetings. That would indeed render you helpless to do more than sit at home and wait for me to call.'

'I can set your mind at rest immediately on the subject of a chaperone, doctor. My Aunt Matilda has come to live with me. She was not happy with her previous accommodation and was delighted to take advantage of my changed circumstances. She is a most respectable lady of mature years, my late father's only sister. She is also a person noted for her discretion. I have acquainted her with what I know of the circumstances of Mr Hawley's death. Indeed, she has made a number of observations which I found most helpful. I have also engaged a kitchen maid and a housemaid, both of whom may be supervised by my aunt. You see, I am setting up my household in the appropriate manner. The lad to whom I entrusted the message asking for this appointment is also now in my employment. He will help me in the garden, as well as run errands. I think you will agree that there is nothing to stop us proceeding with my suggestion of full cooperation.'

'Indeed not, Miss Thoday. You seem to have anticipated me in every respect. I'm sure you think I am a fuss-pot, too concerned with what others may think. However, the plain truth is that, should the world take a wrong view of the way we proceed, I have much more to lose than you do.'

'Mr Hawley never worried about gossip, though we lived in the same house, with no one else present for much of the time.'

'Then you were a servant, Miss Thoday. If all the men who took advantage of their servants were laid in a row, it might stretch to the moon. Now you are an independent lady of means. It makes a difference.'

Rose considered this. It was only what most people would say after all. Strange how the happy accident of inheriting money could so rapidly change the way the world would interpret your circumstances. In her mind, taking advantage of the subordinate status of a female servant ought to be viewed more sternly than it was. Two adults, both unmarried, deciding to engage in intercourse was surely harmless enough.

'When can we meet next, doctor? I have told you almost all I know, but you have yet to reciprocate.'

'My time is already taken up fully for the next two or three days,' Adam said. I have already set certain things in motion which will not produce results for a few more days. There is also a person I am most eager to consult. He is elderly, so I need to go to him where he lives, some seven miles distant. However, that does not mean you need be idle.'

'What am I to do?' Rose could not be quieted for long. 'It is there that I most need your help. You need not doubt my determination or my enthusiasm. What I lack is a clear sense of where my time and energy might best be directed.'

'My suggestion is that you continue to find out all you can. Concentrate on what took place in the days immediately before the murder and on the night itself. Do not assume you already know all there is to know. In my experience, there is almost always something more to be discovered; something which may later prove crucial. All I can do is ask that you will share any extra knowledge with me.'

'Very well, doctor. Let us proceed on the basis we have agreed. However, I can do more than wander about asking folk if they know anything useful. If you will come to my house, I can show you something that must provide information you will get from nowhere else. I considered bringing some of it today, but being documentary, it is heavy and bulky. You can also meet my Aunt Matilda and satisfy yourself of her suitability as a chaperone.'

'Documentary evidence?' Adam was startled yet again. There seemed no end to the surprises this young woman had at her disposal.

'Yes, doctor. I have what I believe are Mr Hawley's medical notes and jottings going back many years. It will require both of us to make sense of them though. His handwriting could be nearly illegible at times and it will save much time if I am on hand to decipher it. He also used medical Latin freely. My late father taught me to understand some Latin, but only enough to read some of the works of the most famous classical authors. Medical Latin is beyond my comprehension.'

Another surprise. Most well-born ladies were entirely ignorant of Latin, yet this former servant claimed to know enough of the language to read the works of certain classical authors. Curiosity was never far below the surface of Adam's mind. Sometime soon, he told himself, he must find an opportunity to learn a great deal more about the enigma that was Miss Rose Thoday. Meanwhile, there were more pressing matters to be settled.

'Alas, as I told you, my time is fully occupied for the next two days at least — perhaps three. Then it will be Sunday. Let us agree to meet next Monday and I will come to your house. Will my coachman find it easily?'

'Ask anyone you see in Millgate and they will direct you. Very well, next Monday it is, since it can be no sooner.' Rose half rose to leave, then settled back in her chair. 'You have not yet shared much of the evidence you hold, doctor. I cannot take my leave until I am satisfied that you mean to keep your word about sharing information fully between us.'

'I beg of you, Miss Thoday. Bear with me until next Monday. By then, I should have heard from most of those who are currently seeking out fresh facts on my behalf. You have my most solemn promise to stick by all I have agreed. I have already written to a man I know, who is a former navy post-captain, now retired. If we are lucky, he may prove to have encountered your Mr Hawley during his naval service. That period of the surgeon's life may seem remote from his time in Aylsham, but we cannot exclude the possibility that what happened to him here had its origin in past events. I have also sent an urgent message to an important man in London who can look into Mr Sleeth's history for me and discover how he came to be appointed coroner, when he is so clearly unsuited to that role. If we are lucky, I may also have heard back from him by the time we meet next.'

'Let us act in complementary ways. You will attend to affairs and events beyond the narrow confines of Millgate. I will focus on local ones. It puzzles me why Mr Hawley went out when he did; even more why he was by the canal basin and staithe at the time he was attacked. I will look in detail at the last few entries in his medical records and hope to come upon an explanation there.'

'Very good, Miss Thoday. We will leave things there and each go about our investigations separately. Next Monday, we will share what we have found.'

By the time Miss Thoday left, all Adam wanted was to sit quietly in his study and think over what she had told him. His mind was still a jumble of seemingly unrelated facts and ideas. Left alone, he told himself, he might well be able to perceive some pattern forming that would make sense from the muddle. That wish was dashed the moment his maid, Hannah, came into the room. One glance at her face told him she had important news, for she was no more able to conceal her feelings on any matter than fly through the air.

'You are recovered already?' Adam said. 'No, I can see you are not. Your eyes are heavy and you keep sniffing. Are you sure you are fit enough to resume your duties?'

'Fit enough,' Hannah replied. If the truth were told, what had persuaded her to leave her room was the determination to see what impression that young hussy had made on her master. To her mind, it was obvious what had brought her to the house. The doctor was a most eligible bachelor.

'A man has just brought you a message from Captain Mimms, master,' she continued. 'An urgent one. Not a man I'd ever seen before either. A well set-up fellow, though. Strong-looking. Had that look about him that suggested he might have been a sailor. Handsome too.'

'Never mind the messenger, girl,' Adam said. Hannah was extremely susceptible to a handsome face and a winning manner. Adam thought it had something to do with all the cheap novels she borrowed from the circulating library. 'Why did he give the message to you? Why not speak to me himself?'

'Perhaps he felt uneasy about stepping inside a gentleman's house. He came to the kitchen door like a tradesman or a servant. My guess is he was hoping to leave his message with someone like me; someone he was more comfortable in dealing with. Anyhow, before I could do more than ask him his business, he blurted out what he had been told to say and was off down the street again.'

Adam sighed. 'Very well, Hannah. What did he say?'

'The captain says he has important news for you. Well, not him personally, that is. He's heard from a friend of his who lives somewhere over towards a place called Burnham Staithe. It's the friend who has the news. He wrote to the captain, and now the captain wants him to come to Holt to meet you and tell you what he knows. Can you visit the captain tomorrow or Thursday? In Holt. That's the message.'

If this information was as important as it sounded, hearing it must take precedence over everything else. Captain Mimms was not a man to exaggerate; nor would this friend of his travel to Holt from the Burnhams on a whim. The roads along the coast were not especially good and to get to Holt would require riding or driving more than twenty miles each way. Say at least four hours on the road in all. It would take Adam less than an hour to reach Holt from Aylsham in his carriage.

He told Hannah to send William to him, then told the groom he should go to Captain Mimms' home in Holt and confirm Adam would be with him soon after ten o'clock on Thursday. He had patients to visit tomorrow.

'It's too late to go now,' Adam said. 'It'll be dark before long and the road across the great heathlands between Edgefield and Holt is notorious for footpads and highwaymen after dark. Leave as soon as it is light in the morning. Give my message to the captain personally, if you can — and bring back any reply.'

Perhaps there would at last be something substantial on which to base his investigation. So far, Adam felt as if he was occupied in chasing phantoms and fragments of the truth. It was time his efforts produced some stronger indication of what lay behind the surgeon's death.

## ❧ 16 ❧

Adam always found the journey between Aylsham and Holt, though scarcely more than eight miles, somewhat trying. The most direct road wound its way along past the great mansion of Blickling Hall, backlit by the morning sun; past Corpusty Church, high on its hill and now entirely deserted by the village it served; past Saxthorpe and Edgefield, where began the great heathlands that stretched past Holt and up to the coast beyond. It was an excellent route for a man on horseback, but almost impossible for most carriages. About a mile outside Holt, the road plunged down a steep hill to cross the little River Glaven. Coaches — even chaises and light carriages — were too heavy for the horses to draw up this final obstacle.

They therefore took the more level route and entered the little market town via the road from Hempsted. Their route then took them past the grammar school founded by Sir Thomas Gresham, through the market place and along by the manor house. The town was now fully restored after the terrible fire of almost ninety years before and presented quite a modern appearance. Good brick houses for the most part, not the timber-framing and thatch which had sufficed before. Eventually, almost on the edge of the town on the other side, they came to Captain Mimms' home. A fine house too, with a commanding view from the top of a steep hill. Once past his house, the road took you steeply down to cross the Glaven a second time at Letheringsett, before wending its way onwards towards Fakenham. It was probably as close as the old seafarer could get, three miles inland, to standing on the quarter-deck and looking out across the ocean.

Captain Mimms and the friend he had asked to talk with Adam looked almost like brothers. Both were much of the same age, Adam judged, their hair and beards now white and their movements slowed by growing infirmity. They also shared that direct, clear-eyed look that comes from spending hours staring towards the horizon over strange seas and by distant shores. No one could ever take Captain Mimms for anything but a sailor. If anything, his friend looked even more the part of a retired naval man.

'Allow me to introduce Commodore Bartlett, doctor, once the terror of the French—'

'And would be again, Mimms, if I were allowed the chance. Give me a good frigate and a fair breeze and I'd send those damned Frenchies flying for harbour and safety, old as I am.'

'As you'll gather, my dear doctor, the commodore and I were both captains of frigates in His Majesty's navy. After I retired, Bartlett here went on to command a squadron in the Mediterranean for a time. Hence the rank of commodore. Your man Hawley served on Bartlett's last two ships, he tells me. I wrote to him on the off-chance he knew the man and struck gold. He can tell you a good deal about the fellow's time in the navy, but he has something else to relate which may well be of still greater interest.'

The commodore was obviously eager to tell his story. All Adam had to do, once the pleasantries were over, was sit back and listen, refreshing himself from time to time from the glass of fine Hereford-shire cider the captain had set before him.

'Hawley served as ship's surgeon on my last two ships, doctor. HMS Firedrake and HMS Brazen, they were. Both fine, 32-gun frigates, fast sailors and with sufficient armament to tackle even a ship of the line, if the need arose. We feared no Frenchie or Spaniard, but, by God, they feared us. The cowards fled at the mere sight of our topsails. We'd taken too many of their ships, you see, and sent the others home as shattered hulks, with blood running out of the gun-ports to show the state of them inside. My crews were the best trained in the fleet, able to fire three or four cannon shots in the time it took the Froggies to fire two. We had better guns, too. Heavy carronades. "Ship smashers" they call 'em. Fire a full broadside of those beauties into an enemy ship and you won't have to do it twice. It's the splinters, see? Fly everywhere inside and do more damage than fifty muskets or more.

'Surgeon Hawley was a fine man, doctor. Brave, hard-working and quicker at whipping off a leg or an arm than any surgeon I ever knew. Our ships didn't escape casualties in these fights, believe me. Many a good sailor went home lacking an eye or a hand or walking on a wooden leg. Many — too many — had to be sewn up in their hammocks and sent overboard to the fishes as well. But Hawley saved more than most and did so patiently and cheerfully. It's a brutal trade being a surgeon on a fighting ship, doctor. Takes its toll on a man. A good many surgeons end up bad-tempered, coarse fellows, or take to the drink and hasten their own ends in that way. Not Hawley though.

'What ended his naval career was a scrap we had with those damned Barbary pirates off the coast of Africa near Algiers. They loved nothing better than capturing a European ship and selling the crew into slavery. Couldn't have that, could we? My squadron was told to cruise off-shore and teach 'em a lesson. Send 'em back to port to lick their wounds and find some safer way to make money. We damn well did it, too. Came on a whole mass of them and smashed full half of them into matchwood. The rest fled. Your Barbary pirate is full of himself when things go well, but a miserable wretch if you stand up to him.

'They came off with severe casualties, I'd guess, while we lost scarcely a dozen men, and about twice as many as that wounded. Sadly, one of these was the surgeon. A cannonball smashed through the window of the room where he was operating. He took much of the flying glass and splinters of wood in his stomach and thighs. It's a miracle he didn't die there and then. A surgeon from one of the other ships patched him up as best he could, and we sailed for Gibraltar and the hospital there. I gather he was under their care for several months before he was shipped back to the naval hospital at Portsmouth, when he was fit enough to travel so far.

'Surgeons are treated as officers on board ship, doctor, so I got to know him during the time he served under me. You can't afford to make friends with your subordinate officers, doctor. Bad for discipline. Being a ship's captain is a damned lonely job at times. A surgeon is not quite in the same position. He's under your command, of course, like everyone else aboard, but he's not a junior you have to order about and sometimes discipline. It's far from unknown for captains and surgeons to become friends. That's what happened between me and Hawley. We liked one another. Even after we both retired, we kept in touch through occasional letters. He knew I'd retired to my family home in Burnham Overy Staithe. His family came from the borders of Norfolk and Suffolk, I believe. Fish merchants mostly, except him. I gathered he didn't get on too well with his only brother, so he decided to set up as a surgeon in Norfolk. I think he needed to be by boats and sailors, so he settled down in your town, close to where the trading wherries come up from the coast.

'When Mimms' letter came, telling me the poor fellow had been murdered, I was angrier than I'd been in many, many years, I can tell you. If you can help to see that foul murderer ends his days hanging on the gallows, I'll assist you by any means I can. Killing a man like Surgeon Hawley is a bloody disgrace! If it was up to me, I'd have the killer flogged raw, then hung up to choke out his miserable life as slowly as possible. No quick, merciful breaking of his neck.'

Commodore Bartlett's face had grown almost purple with rage by this time, so Adam thought he should intervene and try to find a way to calm him down. For all his fighting spirit, he was an old man. If he worked himself up still more, he might have an apoplexy or burst a blood vessel.

'Captain Mimms said you had something special to tell me, commodore,' he prompted. 'What was that?'

'What? Yes, of course. Hawley's last letter to me. Came about a month or three weeks ago. I replied within a day, as I recall. Didn't keep his letter after that, I'm afraid, but I can remember what it said in some detail. Damned odd, you see.'

'What was odd about it?' Adam asked.

'Wanted my advice. He'd never done that before. Neither of us were regular in our correspondence, nor very skilled in composition. When we wrote, we covered simple, daily matters: our health, anything interesting or amusing which had happened where each of us lived. That sort of thing. Sometimes we'd pass on a bit of news about a mutual acquaintance. This letter was different. Hawley wrote that he was greatly troubled in his conscience and wanted to know what I would suggest.'

'Troubled in his conscience?' Adam said, trying to keep the excitement out of his voice.

'That's right. He'd been involved in some medical case of sudden death. First time he'd been asked to take on such a thing. Had to examine a corpse and give evidence to the coroner on the cause of death. You'll know what I mean, I'm sure.'

'Conduct an autopsy,' Adam said. 'It's part of the process when someone is found dead in unusual circumstances. The coroner has to investigate and declare the cause of death, be it a crime, an accident or from some other reason. Usually, he assembles a jury to hear the evidence and reach a verdict. There's always an examination of the body by a medical man — assuming the body is available — who gives his evidence at the inquest.'

'Aye, you have it pat! This, Hawley wrote, was a case of suicide. A man was found dead, apparently after shooting himself in the head. No doubt about the cause of death. Bullet to the brain. That wasn't the problem.'

'What was?'

'Hawley was uneasy about the circumstances of the death. He happened to be visiting the house when they heard the shot, so he naturally rushed to where the sound had come from to see if he could do anything. There was something about what he saw that preyed on his mind. Something that he went over again and again, trying to explain away and could not.'

'Did he mention this in his evidence?'

'That was what troubled him most, it seems. He gave the cause of death — a gunshot to the head — then began to raise his other concerns. The coroner fellow would have none of it. Told him his job was to explain the cause of death, not engage in fruitless speculation on other matters. Hawley had never given evidence at one of these affairs before, you see, so he didn't go any further. Accepted the rebuke and stood down.'

'The court heard only his evidence pointing to suicide?'

'That's more or less what Hawley wrote. The verdict was suicide and that was an end of the matter, at least according to what most people thought. Trouble was, Hawley kept going over and over what he'd seen. He was convinced suicide was not what happened. The man had been murdered, doctor, then everything arranged to point to suicide.'

'Did he tell you in his letter what it was that he had seen, commodore?'

'He did not. All he said was that he believed suicide was not the correct verdict; and that his full evidence should have been heard. He didn't even tell me anything about the victim.'

'He said nothing at all to indicate why he thought it was murder?'

'Not really. He did say he couldn't see how it could have been accomplished. Something about the only door to the room being locked on the inside when he and the others got there, and the dead man being alone. I think if he could have explained how the man had been killed, if it were not suicide, he would have been more courageous in making his voice heard. But everyone else said suicide. He could only offer concerns and theories on the other side.'

'Did you give him any advice, sir?'

'Only the obvious. That, in his place, I would go to the relevant magistrate and tell him everything. It's the magistrate's job to look into possible crimes, isn't it? If I'd known then that you were nearby and had uncovered several criminals yourself, I would have told him to speak to you as well.'

'One last thing, if I may. Mr Hawley wrote to you some three or four weeks ago and you replied almost at once. Is that correct?'

'Certainly.'

'I imagine he would have received your reply within two or three days therefore?'

'I think so. I told my man to take it to the carrier in Burnham Market. He would have delivered it to the post office in either Fakenham or King's Lynn, and so on. Three days at the most, I would estimate. What do you think, Mimms?'

'My guess would be the morning of the third day, no later.'

'In that case, Surgeon Hawley would have received your letter well before the date of his death,' Adam said. 'I wonder if he acted as you suggested? Still, that is for me to find out. I am most grateful for all you have told me, commodore, and for you taking the time to make a special journey to Holt for the purpose.'

'No trouble, my good sir. No trouble at all. I'm always glad to see Mimms here and talk over old times, as you can imagine.'

'I've invited Bartlett to stay with me for a day or so,' Captain Mimms explained. 'It's not good for old men like us to be on the road for too long at any one time. Shakes up the liver. Now, another glass of cider before you leave, doctor?'

❧

DURING HIS JOURNEY BACK TO AYLSHAM, ADAM'S MIND WAS FULLY occupied with what Commodore Bartlett had told him as he worked out how he could discover what action Hawley had taken, if any, on receiving a reply. Who was the man who had supposedly committed suicide? What exactly had Hawley seen to make him doubt that verdict? Which magistrate had he spoken too — if he had spoken to any — and what had that man done in response?

The answer to the first of these questions he could surely discover from Miss Rose. According to Commodore Bartlett, Hawley said it was the first time he had conducted an autopsy and suicides were uncommon events. Rose Thoday would be bound to be able to recall when all this took place and who the dead man was. There were also Hawley's medical notes to consult. The refusal of the coroner to listen to anything that might upset his own views on the correct verdict sounded all too familiar. Adam would have taken a large bet that Mr Sleeth had been in charge of that inquest too. The fellow was a liability!

The other two questions would be harder to answer. Peter had already told him which magistrate Hawley would have approached, but it would be up to Adam to find out if Mr Mountneigh had undertaken any investigation. Adam could ask him, of course, but he was reluctant to do so. Something was telling him he would do well to keep his suspicions and actions secret. If Mr Hawley had let it be known that he was in a position to raise serious doubts about the verdict of suicide, that might well be the reason that someone had done away with him. It would be best to keep any potential conspirators in ignorance for as long as possible, at least until he had heard back from Sir Percival Wicken.

Once back in Aylsham, Adam wasted no time in seeking out Peter Lassimer yet again.

'Mr Mountneigh? Yes, I'm sure he would be the man. What can I tell you about him beyond what I mentioned the last time you asked? Probably not very much,' the apothecary said, in answer to Adam's questions. 'Not an easy man to deal with on any matter, as I think I told you already. Would he have taken action on the surgeon's suspicions? Maybe. However, if the suicide was someone Mountneigh reckoned to be amongst the lower classes, I doubt if the fellow bothered to make any further enquiries. It's ironic that the magistrate who claims responsibility for that area of this town most populated by working people has so little regard for anyone save the gentry. If it was someone of importance ... do you know who the suicide was?'

'All I know is that it was recent. Within the last three or four weeks.'

'If that's so, I would have expected even our Mr Mountneigh to be deeply concerned at any mention of fresh evidence. The only person I know of who killed himself that recently was Mr Robert Laven: not a member of the landed gentry, but a successful and wealthy merchant.'

'Aren't the Lavens that Catholic family that got caught up in the '45? Bonnie Prince Charlie's futile invasion I mean.'

'That's the family. The grandfather of the present Lavens was a Jacobite, through and through, and suffered as a result. His son was a womaniser and a most unpleasant character but still managed to do rather well in business. He established the family's present fortune.'

'Which is?'

'Five or six wherries on the Navigation and some sort of grain merchant business here in Aylsham. Any empty spaces in their own wherries are used to transport goods and passengers for other people. The younger brother, Richard, is the real businessman. Robert, when he was alive, was something of a liability. Drank heavily and gambled with a group who went in for high stakes. The tale at the time of his death was that he was caught cheating at cards to make up his losses. Shot himself rather than face the disgrace. Where were you that this passed you by? Mossterton Hall, I imagine.'

'I had gone to London as part of my royal duties and to meet with the president of the Royal College of Physicians.'

'Moving in high society in either case. You'll soon be too grand to bother with any local patients. Young Henshaw handles most of your practice already.'

Peter's remark caught Adam on the raw. He knew he was neglecting his practice in Norfolk; neglecting his role as a practicing physician even. All the honours heaped upon him at Wicken's instigation were gratifying, but he had not entered the medical profession to be a doctor in name only. From time to time, he was sorely tempted to resign all such positions and return purely to being a local physician. Only his desire to marry Lady Alice had stayed his hand. She was of noble blood and the widow of a rich baronet. She was used to moving in the highest circles and living in grand mansions with large numbers of servants. How could she ever be tempted to ally herself to someone who was no more than the younger son of an unimportant local squire? Especially if all he could offer her was the paltry income of a country doctor?

'Dr Henshaw is a most capable physician,' Adam said stiffly. 'He needs to strengthen his experience and I do not. Thank you for answering my questions, Lassimer. I will not trouble you further.'

'Bascom! Bascom! Don't take offence! I was only jesting—'

But Adam was already outside, making his way home while indulging in a bout of thoroughly bad temper.

It was fortunate for Adam's servants that there was a loving letter from Lady Alice awaiting their master on his return. He had mentioned the house and estate belonging to Mr Grandford Sawton in his last letter to her, stressing its fine position and probable suitability for enhancement and extension. To his delight, Lady Alice expressed an immediate interest in the property. She even suggested she should speak with her land agent to see whether it was indeed for sale. On their marriage, her wealth would be added to Adam's. The purchase of such a property as that owned by the late Mr Sawton would then be well within their grasp, even if Irmingland Abbey and its farms were retained as an investment.

His mind buzzing with images of Lady Alice presiding over Mr Sawton's former property as his wife, Adam at once collected pen and paper and replied in the affirmative. He had no qualms about her taking the initiative in this way. It was better coming from her. If he showed a sudden interest in a new house, especially one so much larger and grander than his current dwelling, his friends would soon put two and two together. Then the secret of his impending marriage to Lady Alice would be out. His friends? His mother he really meant. With Miss Sophia shortly to be joined in wedlock to Lady Alice's nephew, Mrs Bascom's urge to see her younger son married had now reached fever pitch. It would not do to give her the slightest hint of a change in his circumstances. If he did, she would pester him even more than she had been doing of late. Only the previous week, she had written to extol the virtue, wealth and beauty of one of her rich friends' eighteen-year-old granddaughters. Before then, her eye had fallen on two other young women, both seemingly amazingly handsome as well as heiresses. She had even tried, on one occasion, to match him up with a widow more than five years his senior.

## ❧ 17 ❧

The first substantial hole in the blank wall Adam felt was blocking further progress in his investigation appeared the next morning, though he did not notice it at the time. It was now more than three weeks since the surgeon's death. Indeed, they were almost into May, though the weather remained unseasonable enough.

He had asked Lady Alice when they met last if she was aware of anyone who might have known the people of Aylsham well over many years. In his experience, present actions usually had their roots somewhere in the past of those involved. The only people Miss Thoday had questioned in Millgate were either those directly involved in the events surrounding the surgeon's death or people who were nearby at the time. He had spread his net somewhat wider. His hunch that Captain Mimms might produce additional evidence had paid off handsomely. Now he proposed to follow the same approach regarding those people involved who were, so far as he knew, Aylsham born and bred. He needed someone old enough to be able to answer his questions about events up to fifty years ago. He also needed that person to be discreet enough to stay silent about what he asked.

There was, Lady Alice had told him, a very old lady who lived in a small cottage on the edge of the town. Her name was Miss Emily Mash and for most of her life she had operated a Dame school in the town. The time when that became too much for her coincided with Sir Daniel Fouchard's purchase of Mossterton Hall and estate.

'My late husband had strong ideas on the value of education,' Lady Alice had said. 'He was a man of great principle, not in religious but in social terms. He saw education as the best and most reliable source of the ethical outlook we all need to live a good life. That was why he engaged a person to teach the younger servants their letters and imbue them with a proper sense of reason and judgement. Miss Emily Mash had given up her school by then, but she was still eager to keep some links to her former occupation. She was very happy to accept his offer. The duties were light and she could find companionship amongst the upper servants.

'She was here when I came and I saw no reason to object to the arrangement. Indeed, I greatly enjoyed her company and valued her wisdom. Being so much younger than my husband, I felt somewhat at a loss in dealing with such a grand house, filled with servants of all kinds. Miss Mash became my helping hand. Only her increasing infirmity made it essential for her to leave me. Mossterton grew too large and chilly for her to cope, so Sir Daniel established her in a small cottage he owned and paid for a nurse to attend her. You will find her at Gable Cottage, Town Lane. She is rarely able to go out, I believe, so she is almost bound to be at home if you choose a respectable time to call. I will send a servant with a note right away, asking her to receive you and tell you all she can.'

When Adam called that afternoon, Miss Mash was indeed at home and very willing to receive him, according to the sturdy and capable woman who met him at the door.

'Miss Mash doesn't get many visitors, doctor,' she said, 'so this will be a treat for her. She has asked me to have tea available, if you would enjoy a dish or two. She's also partial to my small cakes. She'd eat them every day, if I allowed it, and end up too fat to breathe. However, since this is a special occasion, I have set a plate ready. Mind that you have your share! If you don't, you know what will happen to them.'

Adam happily accepted both tea and cakes, then followed the

woman into what must have been the best parlour. There he found Miss Mash, seated waiting for him. He was not sure what he had expected of a long-retired schoolteacher, but it certainly wasn't this: a tiny, almost bird-like figure, with white hair under her mob-cap, hands like tiny claws, skin stretched tight over her bones and the brightest eyes Adam had seen in many a year. Frail Miss Mash might be. Tiny she most certainly was. But there was nothing about her indicating any confusion, such as some old people suffer. Miss Mash's mind was as sharp as it had ever been, and her memory undimmed by the many years she had spent on this earth.

When she greeted him, Adam received another shock. The voice which issued from that diminutive frame was as rich and strong as that of a woman of twenty.

'So, doctor,' Miss Mash said, after the usual polite preliminaries. 'Lady Alice has sent you. Indeed, she recommends you with unusual warmth as a person of acute perception. Are you married, sir?'

Adam, bewildered by such a question, admitted he was not.

'Good. When you do marry, see you choose well. You seem to me to be a well set-up young fellow, so you should have a wide choice. Neatly dressed. Polite. I've seen too many fine young men ruined by making a disastrous marriage, typically for the chance of laying their hands on a substantial dowry. Are you a good doctor?'

'That is for others to say, madam,' Adam replied. 'So far, my patients seem content with what I can do for them.'

'Which won't be much, if you're typical of most physicians. However, that is hardly your fault. The business of medicine has advanced little since the time of Julius Caesar. There are encouraging signs of progress, but too much lethargy for my liking. Do you like Lady Alice?'

'Lady Alice is a fine person, Miss Mash. It would surely be impossible for anyone not to be aware of her many good points.'

'Very smoothly said, sir. Now tell me the truth. Have you a strong affection for the girl?'

Adam found himself lost for words. Lady Alice was hardly a girl — unless, of course, you looked at her from the perspective of such extreme old age. He wasn't used to being questioned so bluntly on what was surely a most personal matter. He could feel himself blushing.

'Cat got your tongue, has it? Never mind, I can see the answer in your face. Hurry up and ask her to marry you. That would be my advice. I've known young Alice ever since she first came to Norfolk, bound in matrimony to a man old enough to be her father. Fortunately, Sir Daniel was the best of men and she made him the best of wives. We used to talk together a great deal, you know. It was hard for such a young woman to be thrust into running that huge place they called home. Still, she coped, and I did my best to help her. I could always tell what she was thinking. Plain enough in her letter to me too. Take my advice and seal the bargain right away. Wives like that are few and far between, believe me.'

'Um ... I'll bear it in mind,' was all Adam was able to say.

'Now I've embarrassed you, haven't I? Privilege of old age. Very well, we'll move on. You wanted to know about some long-term residents of Aylsham, I believe.'

'I did.' Adam was back on firm ground. 'Four people in particular. Robert and Richard Laven—'

'Robert's dead, so I hear. D'you know who killed him?'

'I do not. But why do you ask who killed him? The verdict of the inquest was suicide.'

'I wouldn't trust any statement associated with Jacob Sleeth; not if he told me my own name. He never said anything without there being some profit in it. Of course, it wasn't suicide! Robert Laven kill himself? He'd sooner have cut off his privates and worn them on his head.'

This startling suggestion left Adam groping for what to say next.

'Stop staring at me like a fish on a slab, sir! At my age, you don't have time to waste on niceties. When I was younger, I practised all the social graces and minded my tongue. Now I'm done with all that and say what comes into my head. Robert Laven was far too fond of himself to spoil his looks by blowing out his brains, as they said he did. Besides, since the man believed the world would never be able to manage without him, I can't see him leaving unless Old Nick in person got him by the feet and dragged him off to hell.'

'What of his brother?'

'Richard? Slippery Dick? I don't think I've ever seen brothers so different in character. You know their fool of a great-grandfather managed to lose the family lands and fortune by dabbling in treason? Jacobites? Pah! Their grandfather was arrogant and pompous, but you have to give him his due; he worked himself into an early grave making a start on rebuilding the family fortunes. The land had gone by then, so he turned to trade. Even though it wasn't what he'd been brought up to do, he still managed to prosper. Their father took up where he left off, then left his business jointly to his two sons. Worst thing he could have done.'

'Why was that?' Adam asked.

'Neither of them could accept what had come upon the family. Robert dabbled in the business but hadn't the brains or the application to do any good. A typical spoiled elder brother, to my mind. Richard is totally different. He's the clever one. He's also been obsessed since his childhood with the aim of restoring the family to where he thinks it belongs: amongst the ranks of the landed gentry. For that you need money, so he set out to make and keep every penny he could muster. The trouble was his elder brother. As fast as Richard made it, Robert believed it was his God-given right to spend it. Fine clothes, loose women, gambling, drink. They've spent years wrangling with one another. Richard found ever more secure places to hide what he'd made, while Robert sought out ever more wild and foolish ways to get into debt. Since the business was jointly owned, Robert worked out his brother could never allow him to be sent to a debtor's prison; not unless he was prepared to ruin the reputation of their business.'

'That sounds as if it was a recipe for trouble between them.'

'Of course, it was.' Miss Mash pulled her shawl more tightly around her. Adam noticed it was of the finest Norwich cloth, probably a gift from Sir Daniel or Lady Alice. 'Recently, I believe, things had become even worse. The word is that Richard, desperate to stop his brother bringing them both to ruin, finally refused to meet his brother's debts. Told him to find the money himself. Maybe that brought Robert down to earth at last. He didn't change his ways though. He somehow must have found another source of cash — a rich one too. First, he paid off his debts, then he started to live more flamboyantly than before. Even his younger brother suddenly became less of a critic.'

'Their relations improved?'

'I doubt it was all sweetness and light, but they had at least stopped arguing in public. Of course, with his brother now dead, Richard can run things as he wishes.'

'You already mentioned Mr Sleeth—'

'That vile toad! He'd sell his grandmother for sixpence and his soul for the chance to be treated as a gentleman. I remember Master Sleeth creeping about in the mud of the street, trying to find lost hap'penies. He grovelled then and he grovels now. An attorney? Rubbish! He finds wealthy men, insinuates himself into their good graces by any means he can, demonstrates his willingness to do anything for money, then acts as their agent to do their dirty work.'

'Did he work for anyone in particular?'

'He used to spend most of his time crawling to Robert Laven and his brother. Mr Robert wanted someone to be the butt of his jokes and Sleeth would accept any indignity, so long as he could see how to turn it to his profit. Robert Laven was a fool. It never occurred to him that Sleeth was becoming privy to a great many things his "friends" didn't want to become generally known. Not just Robert's gambling and womanising — everyone knew about those — but their business dealings as well. He may even have discovered Richard's taste for corrupting young boys.'

'Richard Laven is a sodomite?'

'Always has been. When he was fourteen or fifteen, I caught him myself with a boy of maybe eight. His father promised to give him a good beating, but I doubt it would have done any good. Simply made him more careful the next time. But we weren't talking about Richard Laven's sins. I was telling you about Sleeth.'

'You said he was spying out anything detrimental to Robert and Richard Laven.'

'Worse than that, he was well on his way to turning the tables on them. The Laven brothers somehow discovered what he was doing and didn't like it. There was a time, not so long ago, when Mr Sleeth could be seen walking with a stick and with his face all black and blue. He said he'd been in an accident in a friend's carriage, if you'd believe such rubbish. After that there was a cooling off in his relationship with the Lavens. They began to use another attorney some of the time, and he kept himself away from Millgate Manor.'

'What can you tell me about Mr Thomas Mountneigh?'

'I hope you don't move in such circles, doctor. Lady Alice will never marry you if you do. Thomas Mountneigh. There's another fine fellow, I declare! Gentleman, magistrate and thoroughgoing knave. The Mountneighs of former years had mostly been tenant farmers and local tradesmen. It was the great-grandfather of the current Mountneigh, the first Thomas, who set up in business and prospered. His son, Thomas's grandfather, Edward, inherited. He was a charming person and always kindly, so not equipped to prosper in trade. Under him, the business was never capable of producing more than a modest income. After him came Everard, his son, who was a mediocre businessman at best. Everard tried to better himself, but he lacked both brains and common sense. He believed every hard-luck story which those who owed him money offered him. Kept giving them more time to pay. Filled his account books with lists of unpaid bills. Finally, with bankruptcy staring him in the face, the wretched fellow hanged himself.'

'His son began with nothing, then?'

'Almost. Today's Thomas took over a business with few assets and a mountain of debts. However, he had a very different cast of mind to his father. No more indulging people with unpaid accounts. Within a few weeks, he had armies of bailiffs seizing goods and the worst offenders thrown into the debtor's prison. He made the business into a thriving concern — but with a reputation for ruthlessness and sharp practice.'

'Someone told me he owns an estate outside the town. Is that not so?'

'It is. Once his family business was making money, he sold it, right down to the smallest item, together with the house his great-grandfather had bought in the town. With the proceeds, he bought an estate of some three thousand acres in Burgh and the substantial mansion which was part of it.'

'Was that where all the money came from? Surely he couldn't have sold the business for that much?'

'No one knows for sure. He certainly borrowed heavily, even though, at about the same time, he married and got his hands on his new wife's wealth. He'd never shown much interest in marrying until then. It was only after he began claiming a fancy pedigree that he looked for a wife. It was the talk of the town.'

'Did the lady — and her father — believe his claims to gentility?'

'Who knows? Mountneigh married the woman for her money and probably had no other use for her. Either way, she soon embarked on a lengthy affair with Robert Laven. I imagine she was glad to experience something of the pleasure a wife expects from her husband, even though it came via another man. Mr Robert had plenty of practice in the art of pleasuring women.'

'Didn't her husband take exception to their behaviour?'

'If he did, he had an odd way of showing it. He was quite thick with Robert Laven at one time.'

'So Mountneigh and at least one of the Laven brothers were close friends?'

'Close? No. Never that. The Lavens had been gentry and lost their lands. Mountneigh had bought his lands and his status and wanted to be accepted for the gentleman he makes himself out to be. The Lavens were useful to him in that regard, but no more than that. When Robert got into serious financial problems about six months ago, Mountneigh was said to have cut him dead in the street. Turned his face away and pretended not to know him. So far as I know, the only recent dealings between Mountneigh and the Lavens were business ones. Mountneigh instructed his agent not to sell his grain to the miller in Aylsham, claiming his prices were too low. He then had it shipped down the Navigation and sold in London. Since the Lavens own the most wherries on this upper part of the Bure, he must be one of their more important customers. He can't do without their wherries and they can't do without the trade he brings them. Liking doesn't come into it.'

'Do you know if Mountneigh has paid off any debts he inherited to buy his estate?'

'I don't, but I doubt it very much. I imagine a good many of his creditors have held off, seeing the ruthless way he has begun to make those estates yield better profits. If they pressed him hard now, they'd be lucky to get perhaps half their money. How long they'll stay patient is anyone's guess. He likes to live the high life does Mr Mountneigh. I can't see that estate supporting him in such an extravagant way.'

At this point, the nurse came back into the room and took Adam by the arm.

'You must stop now, doctor, I beg of you. See how flushed Miss Mash is. I warrant she'll pay for all this excitement after you've gone.'

'No! No!' the old lady said. 'Leave him alone! We haven't finished yet. I am perfectly well and not at all tired.'

Such had been her agility of mind and forcefulness of speech, Adam had forgotten he was dealing with a lady of such advanced age. Now he felt thoroughly ashamed of himself. He was supposed to be a doctor! Before she could move her hand out of the way he took her wrist and felt for the pulse. For a moment, he couldn't feel it at all. Then he found it: weak, fluttery and irregular.

'You're tired, Miss Mash. Your nurse is correct,' he said, trying to sound as calm and reassuring as he could, while inwardly raining down curses on his thoughtlessness. 'It's time for me to go. I am most grateful for you telling me all you have. Indeed, you have told me so much I need to go away and give myself time to digest it properly.'

One glance showed him Miss Mash had already admitted defeat. She was slumped back into her chair and her breathing had become shallow and fitful.

'Will you come and see me again?' she asked. 'So few people do nowadays. Lady Alice, sometimes, when she can manage it, but no one else. I am lonely for fresh company.'

'When the mystery of the surgeon's death is solved — if it ever is — I promise to come and tell you all about it,' Adam said, meaning it. 'Now rest. Your nurse will bring you something to help you put some strength back into you. Good day to you, Miss Mash, and thank you again.'

'Beef tea,' Adam said to the nurse as they walked back to the front door. He felt in the bag he almost always carried and took out a small bottle. 'Three drops of this — no more — in a small glass of wine will help her sleep. I could curse myself for not noticing how tired she had become. I'd even forgot her age. That voice!'

'It happens to us all, doctor. When she's talking, you forget she's almost ninety years of age. That's why I took the liberty of peeping in from time to time. To ask you to stop before any real harm was done.'

'I'm relieved you did,' Adam said. 'Now, hurry back to her and see she does as you tell her. Sleep and nourishment are what she needs. I won't forget my promise to return to tell her what I discover, though that will not be soon, I imagine. Ask her to be patient, please. I have many demands on my time over the next few months, but I will come again, whatever the outcome. It's the least I can do.'

## ❧ 18 ❧

A letter from Sir Percival Wicken, Under-Secretary at the Home Department, arrived next day and Adam settled himself in his study to read what the great man said. Wicken was not just a powerful civil servant, with the ear of the prime minister and even the king himself, but was also responsible for most espionage and counter-espionage activities other than those run by his opposite number at the Admiralty. The government of Mr William Pitt operated an extensive system of agents, informers and correspondents, and collected regular reports from local postmasters, magistrates and officials of all kinds. Sifted and collated, the most important elements of all this intelligence found their way to Sir Percival. He chose what to pass on to ministers and the king. People might dub the king "Farmer George", but that did him a disservice. He had a keen eye for anything which might threaten the monarchy and showed a close interest in secret intelligence. It was even said he expected daily reports on such matters.

After the usual opening pleasantries, Wicken's letter swiftly turned to business.

· · ·

*MY DEAR DOCTOR,*

*I have sometimes thought that you possess powers of divination denied to lesser men. Your last letter reached me when I was on the point of communicating with you on a somewhat similar topic. As you must guess, the possibility of those engaged in smuggling using such a useful way inland as the Bure Navigation had not escaped us. The matter was discussed several times with the Commissioners of the Revenue. They, however, were of the opinion that its usefulness to the free-traders was somewhat limited. Contraband would hardly be landed at a major port like Great Yarmouth. Even if it were landed somewhere along that wild, desolate coast to the north and transported to the nearest village staithe on the Navigation, it would be impossible to unload it openly for onward travel. The wherries on the Navigation are far smaller than regular ones. Bulky goods like barrels of brandy or tobacco take up a good deal of space. You might hide a few amongst the legitimate cargo, but it would take far too long to move a significant amount to Aylsham, to say nothing of the problems of distributing it from there.*

*If there is significant smuggling via that route — and there must be; the people who live along the northern and eastern coasts of Norfolk are inveterate smugglers — it will be of small-sized luxury goods, such as lace or silk. The Revenue and Preventive Service would be delighted to stop such trade and catch those involved, but that is their problem, not mine.*

*What concerns me is the virtual certainty that documents and messages from the spies those damned French revolutionaries have planted in our country are still travelling through Norfolk with comparative ease. The same goes for representatives of seditious groups from Ireland, eager to break away from this united nation and looking to French support to stage a rebellion. The ports and coves of the south coast are tightly watched. What were once the most favoured routes have become far more difficult and risky for the men I wish to catch. I do not say nothing passes that way, but our enemies are too cunning to risk all on well-known and traditional routes like those.*

*You have helped us before to stop up new routes via the Norfolk coast. However, we are yet more convinced nowadays that our enemies' eyes are once again fixed on that part of the realm. They are hopeful of making an armed descent upon our land, and their need to spy out our defences and preparations has therefore increased. The sea journey from Norfolk to the Low Countries or*

*northern France is relatively short. The German Ocean is also infested with*
*smugglers and privateers, all eager to earn extra money by conveying messages or*
*people in secret. Packets of papers are easily hidden, and an extra " sailor"*
*amongst a crew might easily pass unnoticed.*

*I have already spoken with a colleague about your man, Sleeth. Be assured*
*he will not remain coroner for much longer, once I give the word. However,*
*what you have told me of him is most intriguing and I need more time to*
*discover all I wish on that matter. I pray you, do nothing to alarm the man until*
*you hear from me again. If he is, as you suggest, acting on behalf of the smuggling*
*gangs, they will help him escape our grasp the moment they sense suspicion.*

*Expect to hear from me again very soon.*

*I am, doctor, your most appreciative and humble servant,*
*Percival Wicken.*

AFTER HER MUCH DELAYED MEETING WITH ADAM, ROSE WAS
greatly disheartened. Nevertheless, she did not mean to sit idle while
she waited to meet with the doctor again to hear what he had discovered. To do that would undermine her status in this investigation. By
claiming to be an equal, she had assumed an obligation to uncover the
same amount of useful evidence as the doctor.

What was puzzling her most at this stage was why the surgeon had
gone out so late at night and why he had been at the staithe when he
was attacked. Had he been called out on an urgent medical matter, he
would surely have turned in the opposite direction, towards the road.
He would only have gone to the staithe at the canal basin if that had
been where he would find his patient. But no one would be working
there so late at night, and there were no boats tied up there either. His
movements were a mystery, but one that she was determined to
unravel if she could.

Her first action was to read through his medical notes for the two
weeks before his death. She might not be able to understand all the
terms, nor make sense of the medical Latin words, but she would be
able to read enough to discover which patients he had seen and when.

At first, the results seemed disappointing. She found only one case that involved an amputation, two people who had suffered broken bones, and one man who, if she read the surgeon's writing correctly, claimed to have inadvertently swallowed a wasp. He firmly believed the wasp was alive inside him and its stings were the cause of the pains in his stomach. At the end of the note, the surgeon had written, 'Severe indigestion, probably caused by overeating.'

Finally, when her eyes were watering from the strain of trying to decipher the surgeon's tiny, cramped handwriting, she found what she was looking for. There was mention of the case of someone noted as being near to death and in great pain. She could make no sense of the details about the treatment and the cause of this person's suffering, since most of it was written in Latin. However, it was clear that, for a time, the surgeon had been visiting almost every other day.

The last entry mentioned this patient was last seen four days before the surgeon's death and Mr Hawley did not expect to need to go again, since death was imminent. He had also made a note that this would be a patient treated pro bono. That Latin tag she did understand. The surgeon had determined not to charge for his services, probably because the household was too poor to be able to pay him his normal fees.

Since she could find no other patient who was at all likely to need an urgent visit, she decided to go and discover whether the man's family had called for the surgeon on the night in question. It was, of course, possible that he'd been called out to a completely new case. If that were so, his death would have prevented him from making any notes about it afterwards. It would then be impossible to discover any more. Rose, determined not to be defeatist, set that possibility aside, took her cloak and a small basket of vegetables and made her way to where she believed the patient had lived.

She had to ask two people before she found exactly the right place. As she had expected, it proved to be a wretched, tumbledown hovel badly in need of fresh thatch on the roof. Two children, dressed in rags, were playing in the dirt outside the door, watched by a child of perhaps two years, whose meagre clothing revealed skin covered in dirt and sores. While she was glad she had brought the vegetables, Rose at once determined to send Jack down later with a large jar of a salve she had found useful in treating many skin complaints.

Rose found a woman, who she thought must be the mother of these children, sitting in what passed for a kitchen and stirring what looked like a thin gruel of oats. Rose handed over the vegetables, dismissed the thanks with a wave of the hand, and sat on the only other chair in the room that looked capable of bearing an adult's weight.

The woman readily agreed that there had indeed been a death in the family recently. Her husband's father had been taken by a disease of the lungs, even though he had scarcely reached his fiftieth year. Yes, Surgeon Hawley had tried to treat the man, but the disease was too far advanced. By the end, all he had been able to do was give them a small bottle of medicine to ease the man's pain. He had told them to put about fifteen drops into a small glass of brandy and give it to the patient to drink.

Rose winced inwardly at the size of the dose, for it was surely laudanum. Such a large dose would certainly take away the man's pain. It would be equally certain to hasten his end, though that too was probably a blessing.

Returning her attention to what the woman was telling her, Rose was able to confirm that the surgeon had made no charge for attending on the dying man. While deeply grateful for his kindness and concern, the family had felt badly about accepting his charity. They had therefore given him a brace of hares, which her husband had caught for him specially. Rose remembered those hares. She had hung them in the larder and cooked them the day before the surgeon's death. The poorer people often paid the surgeon with such gifts in lieu of money. He knew they were poached but accepted them all the same. The owners of the grand estates round about the area could easily stand the loss.

No, the woman said, they had not called the surgeon out on the night that he was killed. There had been no purpose in doing so. He had already done all he could. Her father-in-law had died late the following day. That had not been the only misfortune they had suffered either. Her eldest son, a lad of fourteen, had managed to obtain work only two months previously. It wasn't much, under-groom at Millgate Manor, but it had meant he could contribute a few shillings from time to time to bolster her husband's income.

Had he been hurt in some way? Rose asked. Perhaps this was the reason why the surgeon had gone out that night.

No, the woman told her, he was well enough. What had happened was that he had lost his job. Dismissed without a character, which was bound to make it impossible to get a similar job anywhere else. His crime had been to steal a small amount of brandy, so they could give the surgeon's medicine to his grandfather. There was no way they could afford to buy brandy, even from the smugglers. The boy had begged for mercy and tried to explain exactly why he'd taken the brandy, but it made no difference. Mr Richard had even held back the payments still owing on his wages, saying he was treating it as recompense for what had been stolen.

Rose asked what he was doing now and was told that he was trying to obtain a casual labouring job at the yard where they repaired the wherries. The Lavens were bad people to work for anyway, which was why they had so much difficulty getting servants to stay. While he was alive, Mr Robert had tried to force his attentions on just about every woman in the household under the age of fifty. Mr Richard, who paid the wages, was mean and shifty. He was always finding reasons to hold back some of the money due on account of some minor fault in work or behaviour. Her son had also told her — but only after he'd been dismissed — that Mr Richard had managed to catch him on his own on two occasions and tried to kiss him. As far as the family were concerned, while they missed the money, they were glad he wasn't working there anymore.

Thinking about it all that evening, Rose wasn't exactly certain what she had learned. She hadn't discovered why the surgeon had been called out, unless someone else had known about the man who was dying and sent a message purporting to come from his family. The surgeon had known he could do no more, so he would hardly have rushed out in the middle of the night if that had been the case. Yet her intuition told her that she had learned something of considerable importance, if she could only see where it fitted into the picture. It was all most perplexing. She wondered if all Dr Bascom's investigations were like this; full of gaps which could not be filled and information which could not be fitted into any of the gaps. She rather suspected they were.

## ❧ 19 ❧

**M**onday came and Adam made good on his promise to attend on Miss Thoday at what was now her home in Millgate. William found where it stood easily enough. They had begun by going down from the Market Place and White Hart Street, across the bridge over the river, then turning right into Mill Row; then on past the great mill itself to the right, with the miller's house nearly opposite it. Finally, they drew up by the canal basin and staithes, from where the canal followed the River Bure until they joined a little way downstream. Rose's house was on their left, close to the basin, yet set enough apart in its surrounding gardens to present more of a rural image than one associated with commerce. Like those about it, it was built of good red brick, with a roof of pantiles: two windows on either side of the main door, both edged with dressed stone from Northamptonshire, and five above them. That it was the house of a prosperous personage of the middling sort was attested by the plasterwork about the door, consisting of fluted columns supporting a triangular pediment — all in the best classical style.

Rose herself must have been looking out for the chaise's arrival, for she was waiting for Adam at her front door as he made his way up the path from the road. He bowed, she curtseyed and stood aside for him to enter, but his attention had been caught by the abundance of blossoms in her garden and he was in no hurry to go inside.

'Some of these flowers I know,' he said, 'yet many are new to me. Do you grow them as herbs or simply to brighten and adorn this pathway? If the latter is true, they indeed make a brave show. Have they any medicinal uses?'

'Some do,' Rose said, surprised at her visitor's degree of interest. 'These daffodils, for example. If you dig up the bulbs and crush them, then apply them to wounds or bruises, they lessen any inflammation and hasten the natural process of curing. However, doing that destroys the flowers for next year. I must admit I generally prefer to see them as ornamental rather than useful. At the end of winter, such spring blooms lift the spirits, do they not?'

'And these? I am sure I have seen them before but cannot recall the name.'

'It is called Alexanders, doctor, and grows abundantly in these parts, though always nearer to the sea than here. I planted them in my garden because the seeds are useful to comfort the stomach, disperse windiness and promote urination.'

'Sometime, you must instruct me further in such matters, Miss Thoday. I can see my understanding of the powers of herbal treatment is greatly defective. However, let me not delay you here any longer, for the wind is still chilly and you are not dressed for walking out of doors as I am.'

Adam followed his hostess inside, where a young maidservant took his hat and coat. William would see all was well with the horse and carriage, then doubtless make his way around to the kitchen door, hoping to find a welcome — and something to eat and drink — from the cook.

'May I introduce my aunt, Miss Matilda Thoday, doctor?' Rose said, after showing Adam into a small, neat parlour. 'I have asked her to join us, so that you may meet her and assure yourself that your reputation will remain unsullied as a result of this visit.'

'I am delighted to make your acquaintance, Dr Bascom,' the lady said. 'Please forgive my niece for her strange sense of humour. It is entirely proper that she should be chaperoned, as I believe you have already told her. She has conveyed to me the subject of your discussions, at least in general terms, so you may speak freely. I will sit here and try not to interfere.'

Matilda Thoday turned out to be a well-built, neatly-dressed woman of middle age, eminently respectable in her appearance and polished in her manner. The physical resemblance to her niece was obvious enough on first meeting. Only when Adam came to know both of them better did he discover that the two women shared the same determination and an equally lively intelligence. Now, he thought Aunt Matilda looked somewhat severe, but this may have been a manner assumed during her lengthy stay with her cousin. Rose had described that household as consisting of a dull and puritanical husband and a constantly critical wife.

'Aunt Matilda somewhat disapproves of my intention to seek out the murderer, doctor,' Rose said. 'She believes it is not a proper occupation for a young woman. Nevertheless, she has agreed to play a part in our endeavours. As she says, you may speak openly. I can assure you she will not betray any confidences between us.'

'How kind of you to say so,' the elder Miss Thoday said, her voice heavy with sarcasm. 'What my niece says is only true in part, doctor. I think she is taking on something best left to others with greater knowledge and experience in such matters. I also fully understand her reasons for doing so. Mr Hawley showed her great kindness during his life and has now provided for her most handsomely in his Will — neither of which he needed to do, for he was no relation to the Thodays. Whoever ended his life committed an act of blatant wickedness and should be brought to justice.'

'I am delighted to make your acquaintance, Miss Thoday,' Adam said. 'I also tried to persuade your niece to step aside from the course she has set for herself. My presence here today proves I failed.'

'I am all too well aware of the futility of trying to dissuade Rose from anything upon which she has set her mind,' Aunt Matilda replied, smiling for the first time. That smile quite transformed her face, revealing something of her natural kindness. 'She is too like her father in that respect. To attempt to sway my late brother from the path he had chosen had as great a chance of success as standing in front of a coach going at full gallop and commanding it to stop. In either case, you risked some hurt while achieving nothing.'

It was becoming obvious to Adam that he stood little chance of remaining in control of any conversation with these two ladies unless he asserted himself.

'I can only thank you for agreeing to help us in this way,' he said, returning the smile. 'Attempts to dissuade your niece from becoming involved are clearly a waste of breath. That said, I must add that I am sure I shall find her assistance invaluable. She can speak with those who will not speak with me—'

'Which is what I have been doing to some purpose, doctor.' Rose was bursting with eagerness to explain all she had discovered. All these more or less polite preliminaries were beginning to cause her intolerable frustration. It was time to get down to some serious talk, even at the risk of interrupting in a most unladylike manner. Ignoring her aunt's raised eyebrows and the doctor's surprise at her intervention, she plunged at once into all she had learned from Samuel Nugent, the man who worked at the wherry yard. Then she explained how she had tracked down the poor woman whose father-in-law the surgeon had been treating and heard of the unpleasant nature of the Laven brothers.

As she set out her story, Rose could see that Dr Bascom was becoming more and more interested in what she had discovered. At the end, she sat back on her chair, waiting for the applause. Instead, she faced a barrage of questions.

'Do you think this Samuel Nugent is a reliable witness?' Adam asked her. 'By his own admission, he was asleep immediately before the surgeon's murder. Might not his tale of an intruder at the yard and the first splash he heard be an invention to conceal his poor performance as a watchman? Maybe even a dream he later decided would make him sound important? If he was a witness to all that happened — not an eye-witness, of course, since it was dark, but still someone present close by — why did he not come forward at the inquest? Why wait until you came to speak with him?'

Rose's mouth fell open. She had not expected such scepticism; nor to have to justify the conclusions she had drawn from all she had been told. And Adam did not stop there.

'This woman whose father-in-law was dying. Did you sense that she might have been telling you what she thought you wished to hear? All you learned for certain was that neither she nor anyone else in her household had summoned the surgeon on the night he was killed. Almost everyone in Millgate could assert as much. Has the fact that her son was dismissed from his position coloured her view of the Lavens?'

This was too much for Rose. 'Just because I found this out and you did not; and because I am a mere woman and not a learned physician with a reputation as a solver of—' she began.

'Rose!' Aunt Matilda said, as much shocked as angry. 'Behave yourself! That is no way to speak to our guest. Dr Bascom will have every justification in leaving this house right away and refusing to deal with you at all in the future if you continue in such a vein. I can see you expected him to lavish praise on you at once for what you have done. He has great experience in matters such as these, and his questions are entirely reasonable to my mind.'

It was time for Adam to intervene, before matters got out of hand.

'Please,' he said. 'Miss Thoday and ... err ... Miss Thoday—'

'For heaven's sake!' That was Rose.

Her aunt joined in. 'Hush, child! Let the poor man speak. Dr Bascom. Despite the conventions of politeness, I really do think it will save us from a great deal of confusion if, in these exceptional circumstances, we dispense with excessive formality — at least in private. Our names are Rose and Matilda and I suggest you use them. We, naturally, will continue to address you as doctor, since that will cause no confusion.'

'Why not Dr Adam, since you would have him use our Christian names, aunt?'

'Because the doctor is a gentleman and a learned physician, Rose, and you and I are mere nobodies.'

'Ladies!' Adam said, more sharply than he intended, so that there was a sudden silence, and both looked at him in surprise. 'You may address me however you wish. I do not care. I, however, will gladly accept Miss Matilda's suggestion, purely for the purpose of avoiding confusion. Now, Miss Rose. I most humbly apologise for responding to your narrative as I did. You have done extremely well in finding out so much in such a short space of time. You also showed considerable initiative both in realising your garden boy's uncle might be in possession of useful information and in using the surgeon's notes as you did. You deserve praise, and I am happy to give it. My only excuse is that I have never before been in the situation of co-operating with another in investigating a mystery. The questions I asked were those I would put to myself in my own head. It was unfortunate that, spoken aloud without any preliminaries, they must have sounded far too critical of your efforts.'

Rose blushed and avoided Adam's eyes. 'I too apologise,' she said. 'My rudeness was unpardonable. Indeed, I behaved like a spoiled brat who expects a treat and receives a slap instead. Let me answer your questions, if I may. I observed Mr Nugent closely while he was speaking with me, and I detected nothing to suggest he was telling a tale prepared in advance. Nor, to be frank, do I think he would have the imagination to think up such a story. If he did not come forward at the inquest, I suspect it was simply that he was not asked to do so. To the best of my knowledge, no one sought out witnesses in the way your words implied. Save for the wherryman who found the body, I think you will find the only other witnesses called were those necessary to identify the body and reveal the cause of his death. As for the woman—'

Adam stiffened. 'Miss Thoday ... Miss Rose, I mean. You have just made a most important point. Why were no other potential witnesses sought out? No coroner worth his salt would assume anyone with relevant information who had not been called by him would stand up at the inquest and demand to be heard. My assistant, Dr Henshaw, has already told me that much of his own evidence would have been excluded, had he not persisted in a way that the coroner could not ignore. Now, it appears, the possibility of there being further information on what took place was ignored also. The question we need to consider is whether or not this was incompetence or a deliberate action. Is someone — someone powerful probably — intent on consigning the murder of Mr Matthew Hawley to oblivion? Did that someone collude with the coroner for this purpose — or even issue an instruction the coroner felt he had to obey? These are deep waters indeed.'

'Yet even with the evidence from Mr Nugent we are no further forward,' Rose said. 'We already knew when and how Mr Hawley met his death. Nothing Mr Nugent could tell me helps us identify who killed him. It was dark and he could not see what was going on. All he could tell me was what he heard.'

'That is true,' Adam said, 'but his story tells us a great deal about how the killing must have been done. Let us try to reconstruct events in our minds. Please join in, Miss Matilda. The more minds brought to bear on a matter such as this, the better.'

'And the woman's story?' Rose asked. 'Is that of use to us?'

'Indeed, it is. I had been wondering whether Mr Hawley was summoned to visit anyone that evening, probably as a matter of urgency. If he was, however, it was not to the dying man. However, if someone else knew of his concern for that family, might they not have pretended to bring him a message from them, asking him to come at once?'

'You said this woman had several children, Rose,' her aunt added. 'What about a message to say that one of them was stricken down with some serious illness?'

'Both suggestions seem good ones,' Rose replied, 'yet can there be any way to know for sure? I was tired, having spent that evening in the kitchen preparing food for the next day. I therefore retired to bed somewhat earlier than usual and must have fallen at once into a deep sleep. So far as I knew, Mr Hawley was either here, in the parlour, or in the room he called his study, on the other side of the front door. He seemed to need little sleep. It was his custom to retire late and rise early, often before I was awake myself.'

'You did not hear him go out that evening?'

'I did not. My bedroom is upstairs at the back of the house. Anyone coming at night and wishing to speak to the surgeon might easily tap on the window where he was, having seen the light within.

People knew we kept no maid who lived in, so the only ones they might speak to would be the surgeon or myself.'

'Was it not his practice to tell you that he was going out and where he was going?'

'No. I helped him where I could in his work, and he taught me much. However, all was at his behest. Mr Hawley was a private man, doctor, who had spent years as his own master. I doubt it would have occurred to him to account to me for his actions in such a way.'

'Pity. Still, we know he did go out, and I suspect he was summoned by someone. Who that was, and what the nature of the summons might have been, we cannot yet tell. I assume, since it was dark, he would have taken a lantern?'

'Certainly. One was always set ready by the door.'

'Was it found by his body?'

'If it was, no one has returned it.'

'Then I imagine it now lies at the bottom of the canal basin.'

'Why is the lantern of importance, doctor?' Matilda asked. She had been following the conversation closely, but could not see the relevance of such a mundane object as a lantern.

'A man with a lantern illuminates himself, as well as his path,' Adam replied. 'As I see it, Mr Hawley left this house, carrying a lit lantern and intending to go wherever he had been summoned. That summons was almost certainly false; a ruse designed to bring him out of the house at a specific time. His killer was waiting, hidden in the shadows. His next task was to make sure Mr Hawley turned away from the road and walked down towards the canal basin.'

'The odd sound!' Matilda said in triumph. 'The noise like a child or a cat.'

'A child, I would guess,' Adam said. 'No one would turn aside on hearing a cat in the night. But a child, and one down by the water ... would you not go at once to investigate? Especially if that childish cry was followed by a splash.'

'The first splash,' Rose said. 'Of course!'

'That was the first piece of wood going into the water. Not thrown, since the noise would be too great to mimic a small child falling in. I imagine our killer stood the piece of wood on end and let it topple over.'

'Are you saying Mr Hawley went down to the water expecting to rescue a child from drowning?'

'Exactly. He was carrying a lantern, which meant he could be seen as well as see. He would almost certainly have stopped right to the edge of the staithe, holding the lantern up and moving it about, trying to catch sight of where the child might be. The murderer could come up behind him swiftly, strike him on the head with the second piece of timber and watch him fall head first into the water. That was the second, much louder splash.'

'And the third?' Matilda asked.

'You will recall all that I am telling you is no more than guesswork,' Adam said. 'Albeit guesswork based on what someone nearby told you they heard. It is not fact. I could easily be wrong.'

'We know,' Rose said, 'but go on, please.'

'Very well. What might explain the third splash is this. The killer did not expect there to be anyone nearby. Having toppled the surgeon into the water, he may well have intended to use the second piece of timber to first hold the body under to make sure the surgeon downed, then to push the corpse as far away from the bank as possible. That way, it might not be found for hours, even days. A corpse sinks at first, then rises again only when the gasses of decomposition lift it to the surface.'

Both women shuddered at Adam's words and he cursed himself for being so explicit. He might be used to death and corpses, but they were not. He hurried on, hoping to distract them again.

'As it was, I expect the killer heard the wherryman approaching. The fellow might even have called out as well. Either way, safety and concealment would now be paramount. The third splash, on this basis, was the murderer disposing of the second piece of wood; the one with which he had committed the crime. All he had to do then was slip aside into the darkness and wait in some place of concealment. We know a small crowd soon assembled. It's certain everyone's attention would have been on the water, the recovery of the body and the reali-sation of who it was. The murderer only had to choose a suitable time to join the edge of the crowd as if he had just arrived. Either that or walk away openly, his job done.'

'If it wasn't like that, it should have been,' Rose said. 'You have accounted for all the evidence I have been able to gather and woven it into a totally convincing narrative. I am amazed. What do you think, aunt?'

'I think as you do,' Matilda said. 'I also wonder how, even in the absence of important evidence, the events of that night could have been interpreted as proving the death was accidental.'

Adam looked grim. 'Because that was how someone wished it to be seen,' he said, 'and the simplest way to understand such a wish must be to assume that person was closely connected to the killer; or be the killer himself, of course.'

'Occam's Razor!' Rose said. 'The simplest way of answering a problem is usually the correct one.'

'Your father has much to answer for in giving you a sound education,' her aunt said sadly.

'If what I imagine happened on that night is at all close to the truth,' Adam continued, 'it also tells us something of considerable importance. The events I have described point to the two likely facts about the murderer. Firstly, that he is a man of intelligence and cunning. A mere hired ruffian would have hidden in wait for Mr Hawley, then struck him down and simply walked away. He would not have cared what verdict the inquest reached on the death. He would have felt quite secure in the knowledge that the crime would never be traced back to him. This killing seems to have been planned with some care, and that indicates the murderer feared he might be traced. Only that would account for wanting to have the death recorded as an accident so no further action would be taken.'

'Yet how could he be traced?' Rose asked. 'Isn't that what we have been attempting to do, so far with little success?'

'Do not dismiss our efforts — your efforts — so lightly,' Adam replied. 'We have come a long way since the inquest was held. No, if the murderer feared discovery, he must have assumed there was a way — maybe even a simple way — to track him down. My guess is that he is someone known to have had some contact with the surgeon. Either that or he lives locally and has been involved in events he wishes to remain secret, but fears the surgeon both knew about and threatened to make it public.'

'Mr Hawley would never have resorted to blackmail!' Rose said angrily.

'That was not what I meant, Miss Rose. I fear I expressed myself somewhat clumsily. What was going through my mind is that Mr Hawley, knowing of some illegal or disreputable activity on the murderer's part, might have felt duty bound to put a stop to it — even bring it to the attention of the authorities.'

'Do you have something in mind, doctor?' Miss Matilda asked.

'Let us leave that for the moment and take things in their proper order,' Adam replied. 'Miss Rose's discoveries point the way to understanding what took place that night—'

'Now you must tell us what you have found,' Rose interrupted, eager as always to move on and ignoring her aunt's warning frown yet again.

'Before I tell you what little I have discovered,' Adam said, 'I'd like to ask one or two questions. Do either of you know anything about Mr Sleeth, the coroner?'

'Personally, no,' Rose said. 'I know of him, of course. Nor, from what I have heard, would I wish to make his acquaintance. Do you know him, aunt?'

'No,' Matilda replied, 'I do not, I'm glad to say.'

'May I ask each of you why you have responded to my question as you have? Miss Rose?'

'Because what I have heard of him suggests he is rude, pompous and overbearing. Mr Hawley disliked him intensely, that I know.'

'Miss Matilda?'

'I agree with my niece. My brother encountered him once or twice and told me Mr Sleeth was the kind of man who seeks to lord it over anyone he feels to be his inferior, while acting as the most odious toady towards his superiors. What is he, after all? An attorney, they say. Insofar as that means anyone who acts on behalf of others, the description is fair. If you take it to mean a person with sound legal training and knowledge, my brother said Mr Sleeth was no attorney at all.'

'Do you know how he came to be appointed coroner?'

'Almost certainly through patronage, doctor,' Rose said. 'Mr Hawley said the man revelled in the position, since it allowed him a suitable platform from which to proclaim his importance.'

'I thank you both,' Adam told them. 'While I have no proof that Mr Sleeth has abused his position as coroner to try to ensure the surgeon's death was treated as an accident, I have heard nothing to indicate such a suggestion would be false.'

'He would need someone to urge him into such a course, doctor,' Rose said. 'According to Mr Hawley, the man was a typical bully; autocratic to a fault when he felt secure, but the most arrant coward in the face of anyone with more power than he could muster.'

'You're almost certainly right, Miss Rose,' Adam said. 'What I cannot see at present is who that person might be.'

'My brother said Mr Robert Laven always ordered Sleeth about, when he was alive,' Matilda added. 'Both were bullies, but Mr Laven was considerably more powerful and well-connected than the wretched Sleeth.'

'Until he committed suicide.'

'That's right. Only about a month or six weeks ago. The gossip is that he was in far too deeply with a group of serious gamblers, could not meet his losses, and was caught cheating to try to make up the difference. Rather than face up to his inevitable disgrace, he shot himself.'

'I suppose there's no doubt of what happened?'

'He was found alone in his room, with a discharged pistol fallen from his hand and a hole in his temple. He entered the room — several people confirmed that — bang! — a servant rushes in and there's Laven dead on the floor.'

'Another blind alley, I fear. I seem to be fated to find them. There are still one or two people who have yet to reply to my enquiries, and others who came up blank, but are now seeking answers by other paths. The only potentially useful information is that there is a suspicion the Bure Navigation is being used for smuggling.'

'Suspicion? Absolute certainty would be better.' Rose was contemptuous of Adam's cautious words. 'Of course, there is smuggling using the Navigation. There's smuggling everywhere along the coasts near here. Nearly everyone is involved in the free trade in some way. The poor give assistance to landings and are paid more for one night than they can earn in a week of legitimate work. The rich rely on the smugglers to keep their cellars full, their tobacco pipes lit, and their ladies dressed in rich lace and silk.'

'The doctor is speaking only of the Navigation, my dear,' her aunt said. 'I think you will find that nearly all the contraband is landed on the coast, especially heavy items like kegs of spirits and tobacco. There might be one or two items like that brought up the Navigation to be delivered to someone. I dare say that happens quite regularly. But no one is going to use the Navigation as the means of getting a substantial amount of contraband away from the coast.'

'Why not?' Adam asked.

'The wherries that sail along it are too small. You'd need a whole fleet to transport a large amount of illicit goods, especially if you had to hide the contraband amongst a legitimate cargo. The wherries also sail only by day. It's too dangerous by night and you couldn't negotiate the locks. That means there are many people about during loading and unloading, any one of whom could be an informer for the Revenue. Finally, as a means of transportation it's too slow. Contraband brought from the coast would have to be unloaded and reloaded at Coltishall, which is where the Navigation begins. Normal wherries are too large to go any further. In addition, the boats on the Navigation stop to load and unload at six or so villages before they get here. All must present opportunities for unwanted observation by the Revenue or the Preventive Service.'

'To be plain with you both,' Adam said slowly, 'I wasn't thinking of normal contraband. Please keep this entirely confidential, but the word is going about that things like packages of letters and certain people are being smuggled into and out of this country by this route.'

'Spying? Is that what you mean? Helping the French?'

'Perhaps. Perhaps seditious material like pamphlets or books. Maybe troublemakers keen to stir up rebellion.'

'The Irish? They're always making trouble.'

'Maybe. Is it possible that Mr Hawley came upon some smuggling of that kind and was about to report it to the authorities? Might that be why he was killed?'

The two ladies looked at each other for a long moment, clearly startled by this unexpected turn in the conversation. It was Rose who first broke the silence.

'It's impossible that Mr Hawley should not have seen evidence of normal smuggling. He must have done so many times. Would he report it? By no means. For a start, in these parts free trading is seen as legitimate business. People don't consider it a crime. Most of them see the element of concealment as something of a game; a chance to outwit the government agents and make fools of them. For the rest, the authorities are always forcing various indignities on ordinary folk. This is their chance to take revenge. Besides, the smuggling gangs are ruthless with anyone even suspected of being an informer.'

'The people behind the transporting of espionage and fomenters of rebellion are ten times more ruthless than those, Miss Rose. They are also outsiders. I imagine most of the people involved with normal contraband are local people.'

'That might well make a difference,' Miss Matilda said. She had been silent for a few moments, allowing her niece to speak for them both. 'Those who are native to these parts hold all outsiders in deep suspicion. They are also loyal Englishmen, save in minor matters like cheating the Revenue and assaulting its servants. Stubborn, argumentative, fiercely independent and disrespectful of authority are all terms that could be applied to them with little fear of contradiction. But if they felt one of their own — or a man like Mr Hawley, whom they regarded as a valued friend — had been killed by some outsiders, especially French outsiders, they would close ranks to bring justice down on their heads.'

'No one will talk to you — or even to me — about smuggling, doctor,' Rose added. 'It's never a topic of open conversation, beyond an occasional celebration of some especially daring exploit by the smugglers. Our only hope is to make people believe we are genuine in caring only about espionage and the like. Then they might talk, if they are not too frightened.'

'Do not consider putting yourself into danger, Miss Rose, I beg you. I meant it when I said those behind espionage and other forms of treachery are pitiless in protecting themselves. Besides, there is no need. I know people who are used to dealing with such matters and paid well to face the risks involved. If this type of activity does lie behind the surgeon's murder, I can call upon them.'

Rose stared at him, her eyes wide open with shock and surprise. This was not something she had expected to encounter when she set out to persuade a local physician to help her solve the mystery of who had killed her benefactor and mentor.

'I do not know what to make of you, doctor,' she said after a long pause. 'How many medical men know people like that, I wonder? Even more strange, how many speak with such confidence of having the ability to call upon them when needed?'

'That I cannot say,' Adam replied, his voice as calm as it might have been when telling a patient to stay in bed and build up his strength with beef tea. 'That I know of such people is mostly chance. However, let us not dwell on what or who I know. What we need now is information on where such people's attention should be directed. Maybe someone has seen some odd activity taking place along the Navigation. Perhaps one or two strangers have been seen to visit a boat before it departs or are noted while waiting for one to arrive. Eyes and ears are what we need, not tongues to ask dangerous questions.'

Rose, still uncertain from shock, said she would see what she could do, though she sounded far from confident.

'How many men crew each small wherry, do you know?' Adam asked her.

'Only one, I think. Occasionally two, if there are many stops to be made along the way, with loading and unloading at each stop, an extra person is taken to assist.'

'Are passengers carried?'

'Oh yes. If you wish to go to Great Yarmouth, gliding along on a wherry is much to be preferred to bouncing up and down in a stage-coach and facing the dangers of the road. It might take a little longer, but it's a pleasant way to travel, especially in fine weather.'

'How many passengers can be taken at one time?'

'Only a few on a single wherry — unless it had almost no cargo. Say three or four at the very most. They're small boats.'

'So, no one would remark on seeing a wherry with passengers?'

'No one at all.'

'Short of stopping and searching every wherry then, I can see no way of focussing attention on boats which may be carrying French spies or Irish rebels, let alone packets of papers destined for transmission to Paris.'

'I can,' Matilda said. 'You need someone amongst the crew to let you know of anything suspicious taking place. Perhaps odd packets quickly tucked away in whatever the principal member of the crew sees as his own private place. Passengers with foreign accents or those who try to keep out of sight of anyone on land or in other boats. If it's handled carefully, that kind of warning would never be noticed. You might have a code to signal which wherry should be stopped and searched.'

'I was apprehensive about sharing this task with Miss Rose. More concerned when it was clear you, Miss Matilda, had been enlisted by her as well. Now I am very glad you are both here. But do you think we can find a crew member — better still, several — who will play the role you've outlined?'

'We can try, doctor,' Rose said. 'We can try.'

As it turned out, their efforts were not needed. The very next morning, Adam received an urgent letter from Sir Percival Wicken in London.

## ❧ 20 ❧

This time, Wicken's letter was delivered with all the speed and security offered by his use of a King's Messenger. That he had written in great haste was also apparent from the poorly formed letters in various places and the occasional ink smudge where his hand had rested before the ink was fully dry. Adam's previous letter had clearly started a chain of actions which now claimed the great man's undivided attention. The contents of his letter made this plain.

UNTIL NOW, WE HAVE FOUND OURSELVES POWERLESS TO TAKE THE ACTION *needed to put a stop to whatever is going on between Great Yarmouth and Happisburgh to the north. Stopping and inspecting every ship would occupy half of the navy — and they are already stretched too thinly about the globe for comfort — while patrolling sufficiently to block up every channel for espionage would require more men than the Revenue and Preventive Services possess in the country as a whole. At least half of the men in the militia or other local units are either in league with the smugglers or fear for their families, should they be identified as government agents.*

*We can only act on clear, direct evidence which points to a specific person or group. We had learned already from other sources that the beaches to the north of Great Yarmouth are a favoured place for privateers to land agents and collect reports to take back to France. We have mounted extra patrols and done our best to intercept those engaged in this treachery with negligible results. If anything is being landed, or lifted off, from that part of Norfolk, it is not to be found on the coast. It is whisked inland before we can intercept it, or, on the outward journey, moved to the coast only at the last minute.*

*To be honest, until I set certain investigations in process after your last letter, I had not thought of the Bure Navigation. I can see that was a mistake. You may indeed have discovered the very centre of activities; maybe even one or more of those who are closest to the heart of an organisation seeking to under-mine the government and people of this realm.*

*I am therefore sending you some assistance, which should be with you within a week at the most — I hope it will be less. Once again, you have managed to penetrate to the heart of a situation which I suspected but could not fully make out. Once before, I gave you a free hand to take what action you deemed necessary. I did not regret it then, and I am sure I will not regret it this time either. Use the resources I am sending you entirely as you wish. If you need more, ask and they will be provided.*

*A word of warning. You will find yourself dealing with dangerous and desperate men, more than ready to kill to protect themselves and their activities. At the slightest sign of a personal threat, doctor, stay clear and send me a message. The men I am sending are paid to risk their lives. Your life is one I will never willingly put at risk.*

SO, ADAM THOUGHT, WICKEN HAD ALREADY PICKED UP HINTS OF the Bure Navigation being used in the service of espionage, not just to carry ordinary contraband. Might the surgeon also have learned of such activity, or even stumbled upon it? Was he killed to make sure what he knew was not passed on to the authorities? It was far from unlikely. Unfortunately, if that was the reason for his murder, it left Adam as much in the dark as before. Unless he knew the identity of those involved in such secret activities, he could not even begin to work out who might have been the killer. To assume Mr Hawley had been assassinated by some agent of the French government to stop him telling what he knew was as bad as assuming he was killed by a passing vagrant. In either case, the identity of the murderer would never be known.

Adam had placed considerable hopes on Wicken telling him something to get the investigation moving in the right direction. Now they were dashed. All he had left was a vague notion that the Navigation might be employed to convey reports from spies down to the coast for onward transmission to some privateer or smugglers' vessel. It was enough to plunge Adam into a mood of near despair. Weeks had passed since Surgeon Hawley's murder and Adam knew little more now than he had then.

For a while, Adam's enthusiasm for the whole investigation wavered. It was all very well Wicken giving him a free hand to proceed, and whatever resources he needed to do so. His problem was not knowing the correct direction his investigation should now take, let alone how the men referred to in Wicken's letter might be used to greatest effect. When he had returned from Millgate the day before, there had been a number of pressing matters awaiting him connected with his medical practice; matters which demanded his personal attention. As a result, he had not even had the opportunity to examine Surgeon Hawley's medical notes. Miss Rose had agreed to let him take them away, rather than expecting him to go through them immediately. He had little doubt, however, that she would be expecting his verdict on their usefulness at the earliest possible opportunity.

He put Wicken's letter down and began pacing up and down his study. It was the usual problem: too much to do and too little time in which to do it. What was most important? The medical notes, he imagined. There was a patient in Aylsham he must visit that morning. Once that was done, he would shut himself away and give his whole attention to deciphering anything in Hawley's writings which might be of use. After that was done, if he could stay awake for long enough, he would write Lady Alice a letter to bring her up-to-date on his progress. He had found that reducing his thoughts to a coherent narrative, short enough to fit onto a sheet of paper, was a sound practice for sorting what was useful from what was not. Besides, when he did not do so, the shifting mass of impressions, facts, conjectures and theories in his head always kept him from sleeping.

No sooner had Adam left his house on the way to visit his patient, when his plans were thrown into complete disorder. Almost the first person he encountered, coming across the Market Place from Red Lion Street, was Miss Matilda Thoday.

'A fortunate encounter, doctor,' the lady said, after the usual polite greetings had been exchanged. 'Rose and I have ventured into the town on a number of errands, one of which was to call at your house and see whether you might be able to receive us. We have been thinking about the task you left with us. There is someone Rose would like you to meet; someone who is in an excellent position to notice anything unusual about traffic on the Navigation. I do not know the man well, but Rose seems certain that he can be trusted with a confidential assignment like this. He is, she tells me, an ardent patriot and supporter of king and parliament.'

'Unfortunately, I am on my way to visit a patient and have little time to discuss what you propose,' Adam said. 'Please convey my regrets and apologies to Miss Rose and say I will perhaps be able to call on you both tomorrow.' Adam was certainly not going to admit he hadn't looked at Mr Hawley's notes and was setting aside the rest of the day to do so. 'Where is she, by the way?'

'While I was attending to other matters, she went to Mr Lassimer's shop. He sent a note asking for fresh supplies of various dried herbs and plants. He likes to buy from my niece. He says she has the best quality of herbs and takes the most care in seeing they retain their full potency when they are dried. I had expected to find her outside your house waiting for me to join her. Ah, here she comes now.'

Rose had already seen Adam and her aunt, for she began to hurry, quickening her pace as much as the pattens she was wearing would allow. She had an empty basket on her arm, doubtless the one used to hold the bunches and packets of herbs she had delivered to the apothecary.

'The doctor is on his way to see a patient,' her aunt said, as soon as Rose came up to them, 'and is unable to spare us any of his time today.'

'A very good day to you, Dr Bascom,' Rose said. 'I hope you are able to listen for a short while at least, before going to torment your patient in one of the many ways beloved by physicians.'

'Rose!' her aunt said in horror. 'Must you shame me so by your rudeness? What possessed you to make such a remark?'

'Mr Lassimer, aunt. I mentioned that I was hoping to meet with Dr Bascom this morning, and Mr Lassimer said he had found him extremely touchy and bad tempered of late. He warned me to take care, lest I too should provoke the doctor to take offence at some innocent remark.'

'Our good apothecary is using you to take his revenge on me,' Adam said. 'He made a most wounding remark to me recently, as a result of which I discontinued our conversation and went home. There was nothing innocent about what he said, I assure you. However, he knows very well that I cannot remain angry with him for long. He therefore seeks to prime you to twit me in this way. I cannot imagine why he has done so, since he claims that you frighten him.'

'Frighten him! How do I do that? I have always dealt with him in a most polite and business-like manner.'

'That, I imagine is how,' Adam said. It was his turn to tease now. 'Friend Lassimer is happiest dealing with young ladies of a much more flirtatious nature.'

'Older ladies of that kind too, so I hear,' Aunt Matilda added. 'His reputation for amorous dalliance had reached even to the small village where I lived until recently.'

Rose looked disappointed. 'He has never tried to flirt with me,' she said. 'Indeed, he treats me with great respect. Am I so unattractive, doctor?'

Adam decided teasing Miss Rose Thoday was an activity fraught with danger, best left for another day when his mind was less preoccupied with serious matters.

'Rose,' her aunt said, her tone again one of warning. 'One day you will go too far.'

'To tease is to risk being teased in return, Aunt. I'm sure the doctor understands that. I am just better at doing it than he is.'

'You are, indeed, greatly my superior in such matters, Miss Rose,' Adam said. 'I never had a sister. My only brother is something of a dry stick and my mother, whom I love dearly, is a most formidable lady. Few would dare to trifle with her in any manner. My experience of flirtatious ladies is therefore sadly limited. I am far more at ease on the safe ground of science and facts.'

'Then let us turn to facts, sir. My aunt may have told you that I think I have found a way to accomplish what you asked of me yesterday.'

'She did, Miss Rose. But let us not stand on the street to converse. Please be so good as to step inside my house for a moment, where we can carry on our conversation seated in warmth and comfort. It must not be for long though. I have a practice to run and my patients expect me to visit when I have arranged to do so. Fifteen minutes and no more!'

When they were all seated, with Rose presenting a picture of demure respectability, Adam invited her to begin.

'I gather you wish me to meet someone, Miss Rose,' he said. 'Someone who is well-placed to observe what is going on at the staithes and on the Navigation itself, without attracting notice by doing so.'

'That is correct, doctor. My aunt has stolen my thunder, I fear. After you left, I realised the miller has constant contact with most of those who sail the wherries. His mill also stands part-way across the river, very near to the canal basin itself. Aside from his own servants going to and fro with sacks of flour to be transported to his customers, many of the local people visit the mill to buy supplies of flour. He is not a gossip, but there can be no doubt he must hear about everything that takes place in Millgate and its surroundings.'

'Can he be trusted?'

'He's the greatest patriot I know, doctor. Tell him you want him to help you track down an escape route for French spies and he'll bless you for the chance to serve his king and country.'

'Very well. Let me know when it will be convenient to meet with him. I don't promise I'll tell him anything. This matter is too important for me to trust anyone until I am completely satisfied that I am right to do so.'

'You trusted me.'

'So I did.'

The two stared at each other for several moments. She's infuriating and awkward and far too full of herself, Adam thought, yet I trusted her without even thinking it through. He's awfully pompous at times and hopeless with women, Rose told herself. Clever though. No doubt about that. I hope one day some woman takes him in hand and helps him become what he has it in him to be. Not me though, even if I was in his class. I'd probably throttle him first. Still, you can't help feeling fond of him, can you?

'Let's get back to the murder of Surgeon Hawley,' Adam said. 'I haven't had time to read the surgeon's notes fully, but I did notice a lengthy entry about an autopsy. Do you know if this was on the body of Mr Robert Laven? He had been found dead and was suspected of killing himself, I believe.'

'Yes, it was. Mr Hawley had never done an autopsy before, so it worried him that his first was to be in connection with the death of such a prominent person.'

'Do you know why he was asked to do it?'

'All he told me was that whoever usually carried out such examinations was not available for some reason, and he was approached instead.'

'Who approached him? Do you know that?'

'It was Mr Sleeth, the coroner.'

'Now, please think carefully. Did Mr Hawley mention anything to you at the time about his concerns with what he found?'

'No. I knew he was anxious before the inquest, but he'd explained why that was.'

'And afterwards?'

'You have to understand that Mr Hawley was a very private person. I doubt if he would have thought it appropriate to confide in me. After all, despite his willingness to teach and encourage me, I was still only his housekeeper. I know most people assumed we shared a bed, but I assure you that wasn't the case. If it was your assistant who examined his body after he was killed, I expect you know why.'

'You knew?'

'Of course. He told me himself. I don't imagine he thought I had what people call "designs" on him, but he told me anyway. He claimed it was to set my mind at rest when he suggested I moved in, but that was just him being polite. I never told anyone else, of course. Not until I told my aunt here, just before you came the first time. Mr Hawley would have been terribly embarrassed if his secret had got out. Now he's beyond all that though, isn't he?'

'Commodore Bartlett considered him a brave man and the best surgeon he had ever had under his command. What happened was unfortunate, to say the least, but he received all his wounds in the service of his country, that one included. You can feel proud when you remember him.'

'Thank you, doctor.' Rose's eyes were betraying her. She bent her head and fumbled with a handkerchief to cover her confusion. If Dr Bascom went on showing so much compassion, she was going to break down completely and howl her eyes out. She felt her aunt touch her on the arm and managed a watery smile.

It was time to hurry on. 'Do you know whether Mr Hawley took his concerns to the authorities, Miss Rose? The commodore had suggested he should talk to the appropriate magistrate.'

'If he did talk to Mr Mountneigh, doctor, I very much doubt he would have done much good by doing so. However, the truth is that I have no idea what Mr Hawley did or didn't do.'

'That is a great pity, Miss Rose. We have advanced so far, yet once again come upon a wall I can see no way over.'

'Would finishing Mr Hawley's medical notebooks help, doctor? He was a careful and organised man. Almost every day, he would sit at his desk and write down the symptoms of each case, what he had diagnosed, and the treatment he had recommended or the action he had taken. I believe he used a fresh page for each case, so there would be space to add comments about the patient's progress. That must be why there are so many books.'

'Indeed, it would help, Miss Rose. You may be assured I will undertake the task just as soon as I have the time. Now, if there is nothing else, I really must go to my patient. I am grateful to you for thinking about the miller. It may well be worth speaking with him, as you suggest. However, let us leave that as merely an idea for the moment. I have received news only this morning that may change all our plans. Please forgive me if I do not share it immediately. Would it be convenient for me to visit you tomorrow afternoon, perhaps? If it is, I will share everything with you then, including what I may have found in Mr Hawley's notes.'

## 21

That evening, Adam sat with the pile of notebooks at his side and began with the most recent of the surgeon's medical notes, reasoning that the most pressing matter was to understand precisely what had bothered him so much about the death of Mr Robert Laven. It proved a wise decision, for he struck gold right away. So much so, indeed, that he left off reading any further back than that and devoted his time instead to trying to work out what his new discoveries might mean.

He had for some time been convinced in his own mind that the reason for Mr Hawley's murder would be found to be tied up with Mr Robert Laven's death and the subsequent inquest. Now he was certain. Sleeth had done his best to conceal the truth. When news had reached him that Mr Hawley, pricked by his conscience, was setting himself to get the verdict of the inquest jury overturned, he would have realised Hawley had to be silenced permanently.

At that point, Adam paused. Damn it! Every answer in this most frustrating business served merely to provoke further questions. What was it that Sleeth feared? The surgeon's notes showing Robert Laven had been murdered. But why? Had Robert also been involved in some way with espionage? He and his brother owned a good many of the boats on the Navigation, which suggested his involvement would be of great benefit. Yet if he were involved, why had he been killed? What could he have done to merit such a response? Had he been about to betray the operation in some way?

Another question. Was Sleeth the mastermind behind the use of the Navigation or merely another useful pawn to be moved about by superior minds? The man's determination to see a verdict of suicide brought in was odd in the extreme. Suicides were always more likely to be concealed than proclaimed to the world. Popular thought still saw killing oneself as committing a mortal sin. Although the legal wording of "suicide while the balance of the mind was disturbed" proclaimed self-murderers insane to entitle them to be buried in consecrated land, killing oneself was still thought to bring shame on your family. If the Laven family were as obsessed with restoring their position amongst the gentry as he had been told, it seemed incredible that they had not brought pressure to bear on the coroner to bring in another verdict.

Well, he would sleep on it. Perhaps turning to it with a fresh eye next morning would produce some useful ideas before he needed to face Rose and her aunt later in the day.

⁂

'HAVE YOU READ HAWLEY'S NOTEBOOKS?' PETER ASKED, WHEN Adam sat with him next morning in his compounding room. 'Did you find them of any use?'

'I sat up from late evening far into the night going through the most recent ones,' Adam said. 'By God, Lassimer, that fellow's handwriting was hard to read! Not only was it small and cramped, but he saved space by using abbreviations of his own, as well as the Latin ones we all know about. Still, there's no doubt he had a methodical approach to his work. His notes were a good deal fuller, and better, than the ones I keep. At times, he also added comments — rather like parts of a diary.'

'And the autopsy on Robert Laven?'

'Written up in excellent detail. What was even better is that he added extra comments afterwards as they came to his mind. Many cases occupied only one page. In the case of Robert Laven, he began with one page, then changed his mind, setting aside a whole book for writing up what he found. He copied his original note into the new book and went on from there. Wasteful, but extremely useful to me.'

'What did it say?'

'I'll start with his description of the scene—'

'He viewed the body in situ?'

'Yes, but completely by chance. According to his notes, he was visiting Laven's house to treat one of the servants who had fallen down the stairs and badly sprained her foot. Hearing the shot — he'd been in the navy remember, so knew what that sound must be — he rushed upstairs to see if anyone needed medical help. By the time he arrived, others had broken down the door. There was Robert Laven, stretched out on the floor of his dressing room, facing away from the door. According to Hawley's notes, he lay on his face, with his right arm folded underneath him. The left arm was stretched out fully and the pistol was lying just by that hand.'

'He was dead?'

'Clearly so. The room smelled of the powder and there was a trickle of blood from the wound. As was said at the inquest, the cause of death was straightforward. Laven was killed by a single shot through the left temple. The ball was presumed to have come from the pistol that was found on the floor by his body. It entered his skull, ricocheted off the inside and doubtless did a great deal of damage to his brain. He must have died in an instant.'

'Simple enough,' Peter said. 'Suicide.'

'Maybe. There were one or two oddities however. Hawley had noted them down carefully, obviously expecting to have to explain them to the coroner and his lay jury.'

'Which Sleeth gave him no chance to do?'

'If our information is correct, he did not. Probably because they must have undermined his case for suicide. For a start, there was no sign of any powder-burns or discolouration to the area around the wound. A pistol spits out a good deal of smoke, mixed with unburnt powder and ashes. Fired at close range, these strike the place around the point where the ball enters, leaving characteristic marks. There were none.'

'That must mean the shot came from further away. How far?'

'We don't know any more than Hawley did. However, the next piece of evidence seemed to confirm the idea that it was further than the length of a man's arm. The pistol ball was still inside the skull. As I said, it had probably bounced around in there, before coming to rest. Unless Laven deliberately charged the pistol with far less than the usual amount of powder, that should not have happened. In the case of a pistol fired close to the head, the ball would smash its way straight through and make its exit on the other side of the skull, leaving a large hole as it did so.'

'Was it an unusually small pistol?'

'It seems not. It appears to have been one of a pair of what are usually known as duelling pistols.'

'It looks as if the man was shot from further back and the pistol laid down to make it look like suicide. Is that right?'

'That would have been my conclusion. There's a third point as well. The entry-wound was in the left temple, remember? If you were going to shoot yourself in the head, how would you do it?'

'I would take the pistol, charge and cock it and hold it up against the side of my head. Then fire.'

'In which hand would you hold it?'

'My right hand, of course — Ah! Laven shot himself, if he did, using his left hand. Was he left-handed, do you know?'

'I do not, and neither did Mr Hawley. I expect he thought the coroner, having taken his evidence, would raise the point at the inquest. Robert Hawley's brother would be bound to be present. He would know.'

'But this evidence was never given, so no such question was asked.'

'Precisely. Our good surgeon did not leave it there, however. He must have asked people who knew Robert Laven, for later he added a note stating that all he had spoken with said Robert Laven used his right hand — as most of the rest of us do.'

'Could he have been ambidextrous?'

'Possibly. To my mind, none of these oddities are conclusive on their own. Remember, the surgeon happened to see the body before anyone had a chance to correct any problems which might have the image of suicide. At the time, Sleeth didn't know that, nor did he expect to have to ask Mr Hawley to make the autopsy. Had it been otherwise, someone could have said they cleaned the dead man's head before the autopsy took place. People have done stranger things. Maybe Laven did skimp on the charge of powder, knowing the shot would be from close range. Perhaps he feared a bullet which travelled straight though the head might still not kill him, so he set out to ensure it did as much damage as possible. Perhaps he was ambidextrous or was using his right hand to steady himself. It's when you take them all together that the explanations start to sound false.'

'You think Robert Laven was murdered?'

'I do. So did Matthew Hawley, and his conviction grew stronger as time passed. That must have been what bothered him so much. A man had been publicly branded a suicide, when all along he had been murdered. Thanks to Mr Sleeth's determination to be right in every particular, the verdict of the jury had been reached without all the facts being presented.'

'But if someone else fired the shot, how did he escape without being seen or heard by anyone?'

'An excellent question. Nothing in Hawley's notes gave a direct answer until almost the final entry. The problem must have bothered him a good deal. The trouble was that, during the short time he was in the room itself—'

'Just a moment,' Peter interrupted. 'I don't think you ever said where it was the body was found.'

'Didn't I? I'm sure I did. It was in the man's dressing room, next to his bedroom.'

'Fine. Go on.'

'As I was explaining, by the time Hawley reached that room, there were several other people present, all attracted by the sound of the shot. So far as he could recall, all were servants.'

'Not the man's brother?'

'No. He wasn't in the house, it seems. Anyhow, there was so much confusion, Hawley didn't get a good look at the room. All he could recall was that the window was shut and the door onto the passageway outside had been locked on the inside. Otherwise, it was just a dressing room, with the usual chairs, a small table, a mirror — which had been knocked over — and two chests with drawers, probably for clothes.'

'Was there a door into the bedroom?'

'There was. The butler tried it and said it too was locked. Since there was no key visible, it must have been locked from the other side.'

'Wouldn't it be odd to lock the door between your bedroom and your dressing room?' Peter said.

'This didn't occur to the surgeon until later. When it did, he guessed the killer might have slipped through that door, locked it behind him and made his escape that way.'

'Risky enough though, wasn't it? If he left the bedroom to go down the stairs, he might well have met someone running to see what was going on. People might even have entered the bedroom first, unsure of where the sound of the shot had come from.'

'All very true. From his notes, Mr Hawley was grappling with just such problems as those when he was killed himself,' Adam said. 'However, all this is moot. Mr Sleeth ensured a verdict of suicide was reached, so none of what we have been discussing was ever mentioned at the inquest. As far as the law was concerned, that was that.'

'Not for Mr Hawley though.'

'As you say. He wrote that his conscience was increasingly troubled as he thought over all he had seen, together with what he found at the autopsy. It was all in his original written report, of course, but nowhere else. Sleeth even made him rewrite his report, on the grounds that it had to go into the official record and must not include anything ruled irrelevant by the court.'

'So, the murderer would have thought he'd got away with his crime, only to find afterwards that the surgeon was determined to get the matter re-examined ...'

'Precisely. The surgeon wouldn't let the matter drop. So long as Matthew Hawley was alive and well, the murderer was in terrible danger. Killing him became a necessity; a desperate act of self-preservation.'

'Do you know if Hawley took any action before his death to bring all this out into the open?' Peter asked.

'We know already that he wrote to Commodore Bartlett. That's mentioned in his notes as well: "Wrote to B— to ask for advice." We also know what Bartlett told him to do: go to the magistrate.'

'Do you know if he did?'

'Not clearly. The only clue is in the very last entry, which reads: "M — today". Could be Mr Mountneigh, but could easily be someone else. If the surgeon did talk to Mountneigh, he left no record of it. The murderer of Robert Laven got to him first.'

'By all that's holy, I think you have the answer! That was why Hawley was killed—. Just a moment. Why did our murderer not do anything to destroy the records Hawley had left? He had only to set fire to his house or break his way in and steal them.'

'I imagine because he didn't know they existed. Would you have expected a humble local surgeon to keep records with such care? Most probably don't keep any records at all. They know all their patients too well to need written reminders of past illnesses and treatments.'

'You're right. Most of us deal with the same patients over and over again. Writing everything down doesn't seem necessary. You know what treatment you gave, so it's easy enough to follow it up. Once the patient recovers—'

'Or dies,' Adam added quietly.

'—there's no further need to think about that particular illness at all. With the chronic cases, you see the person often enough to have everything at the front of your mind anyway. Mr Hawley's records leave me amazed. Do you know why he kept them in that way?'

'I asked Miss Thoday, but she had no idea. He was doing it before she came to look after him, and she accepted it as normal, not having any experience of other medical practitioners. Indeed, it appeared so normal that she copied it for herself. I gather she already has at least a dozen notebooks filled with information on the herbs she has grown and how she has used them to provide medicines. She tells me she also notes down details of the cases where she has prescribed them and the effect they had. Not in proper medical terminology, of course, for she knows little or none of that. In plain, common sense terms. She says reviewing past cases often helps her add to her knowledge.'

'I am beginning to feel inadequate, Bascom. You said you also write case notes?'

'I do, but not with such detail or care as Hawley did. I'll also admit there are times when I'm too tired, too pressed for time, or simply too lazy to do it at all. This has been a useful jolt to be more disciplined in the future.'

'I admired Matthew Hawley before. Now my admiration has doubled.'

'Of course,' Adam said wickedly, 'he did not face the same demands on his time as you do. He could devote himself to writing as much as was needed. Why, he might even have been as conscientious in that pursuit as you are in satisfying the needs of the lonely widows of this town.'

'Never!' Peter said. 'That, as you know, is my mission in life, not some mere fad of clerking and record-keeping. And before you ask, I do not keep notes on my experiences with them either. Now go away and leave me in peace! Just remember to tell me what else you find out about Hawley. I presume you're not going to drop the matter, are you?'

'Definitely not!'

⚜

HIS MOST URGENT PROBLEM, ADAM DECIDED LATER, WAS JUST AS before: knowing what to do next. There was also the complication caused by his concern not to let the community which lived and worked on the Navigation become aware of his interest in the surgeon's death. From what he knew now, it seemed unlikely that the killing had anything to do with the commonplace smuggling of contraband goods. Of course, he could not rule it out, but Wicken's last letter had made it clear that, since espionage was most probably involved, he must take the greatest care not to alert those involved — or their masters — that their activities were being watched. If he did, they would simply shut down and all hope of apprehending them would be lost. Miss Rose could ask questions of the local people freely, because she had been Mr Hawley's housekeeper and was now his heiress. He could not.

What was she doing? The question stopped him in his tracks. Did she realise the true danger she might be placing herself in, if she managed — even by accident — to come close to the truth? It was possible that the people involved would simply dismiss her as a nosey woman. Even if she went to the authorities, he could imagine Sleeth, for example, dismissing everything she said as evidence of hysteria, brought on by the loss of a man she loved. If he and any others thought otherwise, she would definitely bring danger on herself. He needed to warn her to lie low as he was doing. Most of all, it was imperative he tell her not to speak with the patriotic miller at this stage or give him the slightest hint of what might be taking place. The fewer people who knew of their suspicions, the better.

In the end, Adam decided he must meet with the two Thoday ladies again in person. Then he could tell them what he had discovered from the surgeon's notebooks and warn them in the plainest terms of the twin dangers of causing the local people involved to take flight, and making whoever had murdered twice already decide a few more deaths would be of little consequence compared with facing the gallows themselves. He therefore sent William — on foot this time — to ask the ladies to meet him in his house next morning. It might even be best if William indicated they must come up into the main part of the town on their own. Adam wished to avoid appearing in Millgate at all at this stage, if he could possibly avoid it. Even seeing his carriage there might be sufficient to tip off those they wished to apprehend. He was sure he was extremely close to discovering all he needed to know. No sense in spoiling it by impatience now.

Once he had sent William on his way, Adam sat down to compose a lengthy letter to Wicken. He would first bring him up-to-date on what else had been discovered so far, then seek the great man's views on the most appropriate course of action. He was certain Wicken must have access to excellent sources of information on anyone of interest to him. Four local men had featured in various ways in the matter of the surgeon's death so far: the coroner, Mr

Sleeth, the magistrate, Mr Mountneigh, and the two Laven brothers. Whatever Wicken could discover about these four might prove invaluable.

Meanwhile, it was back to waiting. His letter to Wicken would take several days to arrive. Then there would have to be time for Wicken to assemble all the information his people could find and write a reply. A week seemed the shortest possible time for all this to take place. Would Wicken's 'reinforcements' arrive before then? There was no sign of them so far. He only hoped they would not announce their presence in Aylsham too openly, nor their links with him. Local physicians did not usually have a need to assemble a body of rugged supporters around them.

Feeling depressed and frustrated, Adam took up his pen yet again and set his mind to writing a loving and cheerful letter to Lady Alice.

❧

ADAM'S MEETING THE NEXT DAY WITH MISS ROSE AND MISS Matilda produced just one item which carried the investigation forward — and that only by a small step. The two ladies were alternately fascinated and horrified by the account of Robert Laven's death which Adam had managed to extract from the surgeon's medical notebooks. Rose had known Mr Hawley was troubled by the autopsy, but she had never understood why. Now, hearing what her former master had discovered, she professed herself convinced that it was no suicide, but another murder of an especially devious type. Her aunt readily agreed, but, as Peter had done before, at once put her finger on the problem of how the killer had managed to escape without being seen or heard. To this she added another question. Assuming the killer had made his way into the house, how had he known where to find Robert Laven alone and vulnerable?

Next it was Rose's turn to insert a complication. She pointed out that the surgeon had thought the pistol used was one of a pair of duelling weapons. How had he worked this out? Was there anything special about such pistols to make the identification obvious? If it was one of a pair, where was the other one? You would have expected the killer to bring his weapon with him, not rely on finding something suitable once he had arrived.

Adam could supply answers to none of these questions. So far as he knew, a pistol was judged to be a duelling pistol only if it was one of a matched pair. Even then, such a pair had to be of fine manufacture and probably heavily decorated. There was nothing different about the mechanism or design. Plain, workaday pistols were often called horse pistols, simply because they were the kind of weapon you might carry when you went out riding or driving your carriage. Many roads were well known to be frequented by footpads or highwaymen. In this case, no one had mentioned seeing or knowing of another pistol matching the one which lay by Robert Laven's hand.

Another thought. Wouldn't it have been seen as odd if the man had killed himself with a weapon no one in the house recognised? If you shoot yourself in your own home, surely you would use one of your own pistols?

All the three of them could agree on was that the verdict of suicide became less believable the more you looked into it.

'Three people seem to me to be associated with Robert Laven's death, besides the man himself.' Adam said, changing the subject in his frustration. 'Mr Sleeth, of course. The other Laven brother, the younger one, Richard. Yet he wasn't even in the house at the time. Finally, Mr Mountneigh — but only if he's the M— mentioned in the surgeon's notes. Of these three, only Sleeth is also associated with the murder of Mr Hawley. I have a question for you; for Miss Rose, in particular. If Mr Hawley had taken his concerns to the magistrate, Mr Mountneigh just before his death, it would be reasonable to assume he would have carried out some sort of enquiry. Did this happen? For example, before I arrived, had anyone questioned you about the surgeon and what you knew of his movements on that evening?'

'No one,' Rose said. 'Nor have I heard of anyone else in this area being questioned. Now that you mention it, even the constable did not return. All treated the matter as an accident.'

'Not even after the inquest? Thanks to my young colleague Dr Henshaw, the verdict was murder. Did no one seek new information as a result of that finding?'

'No one.'

'I smell a rat!' Miss Matilda said firmly. 'We know the inquest on Robert Laven was manipulated to produce what someone wanted the verdict to be. The same trick failed in the case of Surgeon Henshaw. Yet even then, no one came to investigate further.'

'I believe the magistrate did insert the usual advertisement into the newspaper offering rewards for information, aunt.'

'Much good that would that do, child! Especially if those with information were the ones most concerned to make sure it was not discovered.'

'I agree,' Adam said. 'It looks as if the magistrate did as little as possible, mostly keeping quiet and hoping the matter would be forgotten. Who was it who had the advertisement put in the newspaper, Miss Rose? Can you recall? His name would usually be given as a guarantee of authenticity—'

'—and whoma to ask for payment,' Miss Matilda added.

'I'm certain it was Mr Mountneigh,' Rose said slowly.

All three looked at one another in silence. Then Adam said what everyone must be thinking.

'Unless anyone comes up with a good reason against, I am adding Mr Mountneigh's name to Sleeth's as someone involved in both the murder of Mr Hawley and that of Robert Laven.'

'What about Richard Laven, the brother?' Rose said. 'Robert clearly can't have anything to do with a murder after his own death.'

'I don't know,' Adam said. 'There is something which niggles at my mind about the Lavens. On the face of it, they cannot be suspected of anything. Richard Laven was out when his brother died — or rather was murdered, as we are now sure. I grant he might have ordered the killing, but he could not have carried it out. Now let's deal with the second killing. On the night when the surgeon was killed, Richard Laven says he was at home, heard the commotion and went out to see what it was about. He didn't therefore reach the staithe until well after the murder had taken place. If that's correct, he's not the murderer there either. There's a point too against assuming he was somehow involved. Why would he wish to prevent the surgeon giving evidence that would prove his brother's death was not suicide?'

'So, you're convinced he's not our man in either case?'

'Everything points to the man's innocence, yet I'm still worried that I've missed something. If I have, I have no notion what it may be.'

'Have you given up the notion that Mr Hawley's death was caused by the smugglers, doctor?' Rose asked.

'Not altogether, Miss Rose. Once again, I'm in two minds. It's a tempting solution, although a link with the murder of Robert Laven provides a much more satisfying reason for the surgeon's death. If we assume the smugglers were his killers, the business of Laven simply hangs in the air.'

'Maybe they really aren't connected. Perhaps Mr Hawley was killed for some reason unconnected with Robert Laven's death.'

'That's the trouble. There's nothing to indicate it was either way. A smuggler would certainly know his way around the staithes and canal basin here. But would such a man be able to enter a gentleman's house, unseen; find his way unerringly to a suitable place for the murder; carry it out exactly enough to simulate suicide; then escape again, for all the world as if he had never been there? Your average smuggler is a rough-and-ready person who can rarely be accused of subtlety. A member of a smuggling gang might have killed Mr Hawley. That was much more of a rough-and-ready affair. On the other hand, neither of us has come up with any reason for the smugglers to want the surgeon dead.'

'What about the people who carry out spying?'

'They certainly seem more likely killers. The persons who plan and organise smuggling people and papers into and out of the country mostly rely on local ne'er-do-wells and seamen for ordinary tasks. They themselves are far more cunning, ruthless and ready to risk all to avoid being detected. But which of the two men had provoked them enough to want him dead? Again, we have nothing to suggest an answer.'

'Perhaps one killing or the other was about smuggling and the other was not?'

'No, no, Miss Rose. Please don't dream up still more explanations. I suggest we stick to investigating the plain facts surrounding the surgeon's murder. We have no proof his death had anything to do with Robert Laven's. If it were not for Mr Hawley's doubts regarding the verdict of suicide in that case, we should not be considering it at all.

Why don't we leave Robert Laven aside for the moment? We don't need more mare's nests.'

'But we can't!' Rose exclaimed. 'You said yourself you can't see why the smugglers would have wished Mr Hawley dead. If we leave Robert Laven aside, what do we have as a basis for our investigation? Nothing!'

'I have to agree,' Matilda said. 'Some link to the earlier death is the only viable way to proceed at present. That being so, I have another question. One murderer or two?'

Adam sighed and shook his head. These two ladies were not about to let him take any easy way out of his dilemma. The mare's nest would have to be disentangled.

'My guess would be two,' he said. 'The first killing was cleverly done, albeit with several mistakes. The second seems to have been simpler and more brutal.'

'A gang?'

'Perhaps.'

And so it went on, with no firm conclusions possible without gaining more facts. As Adam pointed out, he had only just been able to ask truly specific questions of "his friend in London". If he was able to provide the answers, that might yet bring the breakthrough they needed. Without that, it appeared they had reached another dead end. Two killings. Two attempts to hide the truth. As to why this had been done and who lay behind it, they were little further forward. Though it was never discussed or formally agreed, none of them saw Mr Sleeth as the mastermind behind it all. At most, he might have been a useful tool in someone else's hands. Nothing more.

After the ladies went home, Adam sat in his study and tried to busy himself with medical matters, but his mind kept returning to the deaths in Millgate. The whole matter now seemed insoluble, mostly because they lacked sufficient evidence to rule any solution either in or out. For the moment, all they could do was wait and hope for some additional evidence to turn up and help them move forward.

## ❧ 2 2 ☙

'There's a gentleman to see you,' Hannah told her master, soon after noon the next day. 'Come from London urgent, he says.'

'Show him in,' Adam said, putting down the pen he had been using and standing up. If he'd come from London, it was certain to be the man Wicken had sent.

The day had not begun in an auspicious way. Despite it being almost the end of May, dense fog had rolled in from the sea and was proving slow to clear. Above the fog, the clouds were thick enough to make a man think it was the depth of winter, not a day in early spring. It was cold, the air felt dank, and those people who were about wrapped themselves in their thickest clothes and hunched themselves against the chill. It was so dark inside the house that Adam had even contemplated telling Hannah to light the candles. He did have one lit on his desk — he could not have read or written anything without it — but the rest of the room was filled with shadows. The best thing he could do was greet his guest where he was, then suggest they moved to the parlour, where the walls were painted in a pale blue and large mirrors reflected whatever light came in through the windows back into the room.

The man who entered with Hannah was in his early middle age; a well set-up fellow, neatly but soberly dressed. He looked more like a prosperous yeoman than whatever he was.

'George Gwatkin at your service, Dr Bascom,' he said, stepping forward and shaking hands. His grip was firm, but not too tight. 'Principal Surveyor with the Post Office.'

All this was said in a voice loud enough to carry to any listening ears outside the room, should that be required. Once Hannah had gone and the door was shut, Mr Gwatkin lowered his voice a good deal and stepped closer.

'That was for public consumption, sir. Sir Percival Wicken has sent me, as you may have guessed. He asked me to give you this letter of introduction.'

'It is too dark in here today for comfort, Mr Gwatkin. We will move into the parlour and I shall tell my maid to light the candles. When that is done, she will bring us some refreshment and we can talk like gentlemen. I will also be able to make out what Sir Percival has written. I recognised his writing at once. Nowadays, he always seems to be in the greatest hurry when he writes. His words dash across the page. Some are smudged and others contain letters so badly formed they can only be guessed at. I will need light and time to read what you have brought me. Follow me, please? Would you like coffee or something stronger?"

Once they were seated, each with a dish of good coffee, Adam turned his attention back to Wicken's letter. Fortunately, it was brief and to the point. Mr George Gwatkin, it said, had been sent to provide additional support and could be trusted in all matters. Since it was better not to commit certain matters to paper, Mr Gwatkin had also been instructed to disclose his other instructions. It had already been arranged that he and those who accompanied him would be given accommodation in suitable quarters at Blicking Hall. They would be operating outwardly to satisfy the needs of the Post Office. In reality, they were to be entirely Adam's to command.

'Sir Percival writes that you will explain all to me, Mr Gwatkin.'

'Of course, doctor. Ostensibly, I am here to lead a small group of surveyors from the Post Office, despatched to find ways to improve the speed of messages sent from the Norfolk coastline to London, in case a French invasion takes place somewhere around Weybourne. At present, a man can cross by sea from Norfolk to the coast of the Low Countries in a day. To get to London, which is almost exactly the same distance, will take him at least three days. A French commander in Amsterdam would thus receive reports up to two days before the same information reached London. I assure you I can talk with great eloquence on the topic if necessary.'

'I thought there was to be a chain of beacons,' Adam said.

'Quite right, doctor. I am also supposed to be ensuring that chain follows the best route. All nonsense, but it gives me and my men a suitable excuse to roam around the countryside. To keep up the pretence, we'll pay special attention to any high ground — such as there is around here. While we're doing that, we'll keep eyes and ears open and make sure not to stray far from the Bure Navigation.'

'What have you been told about that?'

'Sir Percival had already become suspicious of certain people and activities in this general area, doctor. Our informants have reported an unusual number of dubious strangers passing to and fro along the Navigation. Some are likely messengers, bearing letters and other documents to be smuggled abroad. Others are persons of greater interest to us. This now appears also to be a well-established route for bringing contraband printed items from the continent. What this mostly means is seditious writings and pamphlets, such as the works of the traitor Thomas Paine. It is not the first time this coast has been used in this way. This time, Sir Percival means to close it off for good, if he can.'

'Easier said than done, I imagine,' Adam said. 'Smuggling is rife in these parts, while the whole coast between Great Yarmouth and King's Lynn is a mass of lonely marshes, remote beaches and low cliffs. However, let us return to the Bure Navigation. Is that of particular interest?'

'We believe so. Thanks to extra efforts by the Revenue and Preventive Service at the coast, the smugglers are finding their life harder. The fear of invasion also tells against them. Militia units from elsewhere in the country and dragoons patrol much of this coast, especially at night. Clandestine movements are now more likely to be noticed and investigated. In the past, the local men ignored them, since many were involved themselves in smuggling. When it comes to individuals, lonely coasts and remote villages are also poor places for strangers. Too many suspicious eyes. Anyone unusual stands out like a lit beacon.'

'But isn't the Navigation a rather public place?'

'Indeed so, doctor. Yet that can work to these men's advantage. Passengers travel along the Navigation all the time and many of them are strangers to these parts. What are one or two more? The best place to conceal a package or a person is amongst others which seem outwardly the same. As you may know, Sir Percival thinks the murderers you are investigating may be operating an established route for conveying more than contraband.'

'That may well be so,' Adam said. 'Yet from what I have been able to gather, whatever lies behind these grave events has a more local set of causes. Nor do all those I judge to be involved have any obvious interest, financial or personal, in the Navigation. It's true the business of the Laven brothers was — and still is — based on transporting goods and passengers between here and Coltishall. They own — or rather, the remaining brother now owns — at least five or six boats on the Navigation. But the other two I have my eye on are an attorney and a gentleman and justice of the peace.'

'I see, doctor. Nevertheless, I have my orders.'

'And I would not wish to obstruct you in carrying them out. There is something that links my suspects together — something more than childhood friendships — but I'm damned if I know what it may be. They don't even seem to like one another.'

Gwatkin was a bold, confident fellow and Adam feared he might prove to be the kind of man to seize on one way of interpreting events, then rush into action without considering other options and alternatives. There was no way he was going to be hurried into decisions that might have profited from greater reflection.

'If you'll be guided by me, Mr Gwatkin,' Adam said, 'you won't be in too much of a hurry. Both Richard Laven and Mr Mountneigh strike me as clever men; the kind who won't easily be caught out or give themselves away. I don't intend to approach either without having plenty of firm evidence on my side. At present, all we have is supposition and guesswork.'

'Then we'll have to get that evidence, won't we, sir. Is there some place from which we can keep a close eye on what — and who — passes along the Navigation?'

'There's the mill. I'm told the miller's a most patriotic fellow. It would certainly be an excellent place to see all that goes on at and around the canal basin. He might even be willing to keep an eye open and report any strangers he saw hanging around that area.'

Gwatkin shook his head. 'Best leave that to my men, doctor. Amateurs can be unreliable and cause more harm than good.'

'I'm an amateur,' Adam said drily.

'Oh ... I didn't mean ... I do apologise, sir.' Gwatkin's embarrassment amused Adam. The man was altogether too sure of himself for comfort. 'We'll get the evidence you need, you may be certain of that.'

'That's more easily said than done. My advice would be to spend a few days getting the lie of the land, before taking any action. Once I let you stop and search one of the boats, you'll no longer be able to pretend that you work for the Post Office. The longer you can move about unseen and unchallenged, the better your chances of springing your trap at the best possible moment.'

'So, what do we do?'

'Watch and wait. Send your men singly to the villages along the route of the Navigation, looking for the best route for this imaginary chain of beacons. Let them keep their eyes and ears open, but show no particular interest in the Navigation itself or the boats along it. Above all, make no move without speaking to me first. Sir Percival wrote that you are to operate under my direction. You can be certain he will not take kindly to any unwanted initiatives. You are concerned with espionage, while I am also seeking a murderer and need additional evidence, if I am to see justice done. Watch and wait, Mr Gwatkin. Watch and wait. Those are my orders.'

THAT EVENING, ADAM WAS TO ATTEND A DINNER PARTY HELD BY A

number of the more affluent townspeople, including several members of the legal and medical professions. It was a regular occasion, though Adam was not the most diligent of attendees. Today, however, he was glad of a chance to turn his mind away from his problems. Perhaps he could then return to his investigation refreshed and reinvigorated.

These dinners were mostly about good fellowship and good cheer, both seasoned with a liberal sprinkling of gossip. Those who attended met in a large, private room at the Black Boys Inn, where they ate a substantial meal and washed it down with copious amounts of wine and champagne. Afterwards, they drank port and brandy, smoked their cigars, and generally put the world to rights — at least until some of them became too drunk for rational conversation. At that point, the rest decided it was at last time to make their way home to bed. It was rare for anyone to leave before midnight or one o'clock in the morning.

When he had first come to Aylsham, the demands of building up a practice — and the cost of attending — had given Adam a plausible excuse to avoid evenings of this nature. He was not by nature especially sociable and found the raucous bonhomie hard to bear. Nowadays, his growing wealth had produced a more relaxed attitude to money. He had also realised, belatedly, that others expected him to attend — if only to show he was not the kind to turn up his nose at those who had been his friends in leaner times. Staying aloof did nothing for a man's reputation in a small town like Aylsham. The better class of people put great store by willingness to take a full part in what was known as 'polite society' — his mother especially. The fact that he found the evenings more enjoyable than he had expected had proved an unexpected bonus. Peter Lassimer was nearly always present and was universally judged to be excellent company, as well as a deep fund of salacious stories and anecdotes for later in the evening, when the alcohol was beginning to take its toll.

Somehow, that particular evening, the conversation turned to the subject of gambling and someone mentioned the name of Robert Laven. It seemed his gambling habit had been notorious, as had his liking for strong drink and weak-willed women. Various tales and jokes about him were passed around the table. Adam was immediately on the alert. Here was his chance to seek out any fresh information which might be of use to him. Amidst general surprise, he told the group that he had never encountered either of the Laven brothers until very recently.

'You're lucky!' one of the others said and all agreed. It was clear the Laven brothers had been generally disliked and distrusted. Frederick Andrews, who was Adam's own attorney, summed up the general feeling.

'There's no way they can live as they do on the profits from running a few wherries up and down the Navigation,' he said. 'They have to be involved in something else — something illegal. We all suspect they smuggle goods on those wherries. I've bought one or two things I believe came from them in the first place.'

'What kind of things do they smuggle?' Adam asked.

'Silks, laces, fine china — things like that. Anything fairly small and highly valuable. Why? Are you looking to buy a present for Lady Alice?'

It took some time for the general mirth to subside at that remark. Adam might like to believe his personal life was his own, but that was far from the case. The growing frequency of his contacts with Lady Alice since her husband's death had been carefully noted and remarked upon. So much so that several large wagers had been placed on the exact time when their intention to marry would be made public.

When calm had been restored, Adam decided to continue his enquiries about the Lavens as far as he dared.

'I'm sure that you cannot just go to the captain of the wherry and ask to see what goods he has on board, can you?' he said. 'Do you have to place an order with someone in advance, or is there someone you can contact to discover what might be available?'

'He's definitely looking for a present for a lady!' Peter called out from further down the table. 'I wonder which one. Lady Alice or Miss Thoday?' There was more laughter.

'Just curious,' Adam protested.

'You really are an innocent, aren't you,' Andrews said. 'If you spent more of your time in and around Aylsham and less time roaming about the countryside finding excuses to call at Mossterton Hall, you would know these things. That fellow Sleeth is the one to speak to — if you can hold your nose long enough!'

'What has he got to do with the Laven brothers?' Adam said.

'He used to be their attorney until recently. Still has dealings with them, only now he tries to keep them secret. Nasty piece of work. That's why he's never been invited to these gatherings.'

'Secret dealings with the Lavens? Is everyone aware of that?'

'Everyone but you! Look, nobody likes the fellow and nobody trusts him, so he gets precious little work from anyone else in this town. The Laven brothers had been his most important clients for years. He'd hardly let them go entirely. I suppose it's just Richard Laven now, since his brother committed suicide.'

'I'm surprised he managed to do it before somebody else killed him,' said a voice from the other end of the table. 'I imagine he'd made plenty of enemies one way or another.'

'He certainly wasn't too scrupulous in his business dealings.' That was Mr Wickes, the tanner. 'If you didn't keep a close eye on the fellow, he'd cheat you in a host of clever ways.'

'I agree,' Mr Curties, the grocer, added. 'It's my guess Laven had his fingers in a good many pies; many of them not on the right side of the law either.'

'You're probably right,' Andrews said. 'Those two brothers and Sleeth had to be getting a good deal of money from somewhere else, not just from their smuggling. Heaven knows from where though.'

The drink had been flowing freely and most of those present were quite tipsy by this time. It wouldn't be long before they got bored with this topic, but Adam decided he could risk one last attempt to get some more useful information.

'I notice Mr Mountneigh never attends these dinners,' he said to the room in general. As he hoped, his remark produced a roar of laughter and derision.

'We'd rather invite the devil!' came one shout.

'I'd rather invite my wife's father, and he's a foul, whoreson old bastard!' came another.

'I wouldn't trust him to tell you his own name, even if he swore it on the Bible.' That was the voice from the far end of the table again.

Mr Andrews leant over and put his arm around Adam's shoulders. 'Poor old Bascom,' he said. 'Everyone knows the truth but you, it seems. Mountneigh's grandfather and father were both corn chandlers. The grandfather started the business and the son made a fortune from selling grain to the government, even if it meant the local people went without bread. That's our fellow's real pedigree, whatever he claims otherwise. Today's Mountneigh always fancied himself as a gentleman, so as soon as he inherited, he sold the business and bought a run-down house and estate just outside the town. With that, and his made-up family tree, he's been trying to transform himself into a gentleman — a man of leisure and property. He also married a plain but wealthy wife and, thanks to lobbying from her family, got himself appointed as a Justice of the Peace. Now he acts as if he was a peer of the realm.'

'From what I hear,' the rector said, 'his wife's money is already gone and he's finding it hard to sustain that grandiose lifestyle on the income from his estate and investments alone.' The rector had been quiet up till now, though he'd been keeping pace with everybody else in the matter of drinking. It had obviously brought him to the point where the wish to be part of the conversation overcame his natural, clerical reticence. 'There are rumours that he too has got involved with the Laven brothers and their shady dealings,' he continued. 'I pray it is not so.'

'That's a prayer that's likely to go unanswered,' Andrews said. 'You'll tell me it's never too late for repentance, but in this case I'm not at all sure that can be true. Mr Mountneigh's sin of pride is as great as Lucifer's, to my mind.'

There were nods and murmurs of agreement from all around the table. Then somebody else began to talk about a cricket match that was scheduled to take place on the following Saturday and the conversation moved on. Still, Adam was well pleased with what he had heard. There, at last, were the links he had sought between the three men he believed were involved in the death of the surgeon. What remained now was to decide how best to make use of this knowledge.

IT WAS SEVERAL DAYS LATER WHEN MR GWATKIN ONCE AGAIN CAME to Adam's house, this time in a state of extreme excitement. Hannah had barely showed him into her master's study before he had blurted out his news.

'We have them!' he cried. 'All we have to do now is put them under arrest.'

'What are you talking about?' Adam said. 'Who is it that you have?'

'Three men, doctor. Two of them are certainly French spies. We believe the third is an Irishman, sent to ask the French government to supply weapons and money to support yet another rebellion on that island. Our men have tracked them right across the country as they made their way here. When they arrived, they went at once to see an attorney in this town, a man called Sleeth. He took them down to the canal basin. They are now aboard one of the wherries there, waiting to be taken downstream. All I need is your agreement that I should arrest them.'

'You will do nothing of the kind, 'Adam said. 'If Sleeth has gone with them openly, it must be because he thinks he has nothing to fear. Tell me this. Did they themselves pay for their journey?'

'I think so,' Gwatkin said. 'But what has that to do with anything?'

'A great deal. If you arrest them now, and we confront the conspirators with what is going on, they will say that they have no knowledge of anything untoward. The three men, they will tell us, arrived and asked to book onward travel, probably to Great Yarmouth. As far as our suspects are concerned, they are just passengers. Those boats carry passengers almost every day of the week. How were they to know these three were traitors? You see? You have no evidence at all to link their passage to any prior arrangement or regular activity.'

Gwatkin's downcast look almost made Adam burst out laughing, but he managed to restrain himself in time.

'Here's what you must do,' he said. 'Let them proceed on their journey, with your men keeping track of them as before. You should only arrest them when they are at the coast and on the point of securing their passage out to a waiting ship. That way, you will prevent them from leaving the country, and at the same time be able to arrest whoever it is who is willing to take them to what I imagine will be a waiting privateer. Let there be no provable link in any of this to an organisation pledged to secure their safe passage down the Navigation. Please be patient, sir. We must not alert our conspirators before we are ready.'

'Very well, if those are your orders.' Gwatkin's voice was sulky. He did not like being held back from the course of action which he had decided upon. 'I'll send a messenger at once to our men at Great Yarmouth. Those who have followed these traitors across the country may continue to do so. What shall my other men do?'

'We need to find something being carried on those wherries which must have been put there with the agreement of the owner. I have been told from reliable sources that our conspirators are also engaged in regular smuggling; mostly small but valuable items, such as lace and silk from France and porcelain from the East. Finding that would be a start, but still less than we truly need. What we really want is evidence of treasonable activities. Packages of papers and letters destined for spies in England or their spymasters overseas for example.'

'Won't these conspirators take fright at the seizing of these latest "passengers", even if it is not done until they reach Great Yarmouth? It will be plain how they travelled there.'

'That's so, I admit,' Adam said. He was reluctant to risk all on what still seemed to him to be links to the men in Aylsham they would struggle to prove. 'Left to myself, I would still wait a little longer, but I sense that you and your master are eager to move more quickly.'

'We have experience of men such as these,' Gwatkin said. 'You will not take them unless you do it by surprise. It is a significant risk, but I don't believe there is any better option.'

Adam still hesitated. What Gwatkin wanted would certainly put an end to the Bure Navigation being seen as a safe route for espionage purposes. Whether it would provide the evidence needed to hang the surgeon's murderer, maybe Robert Laven's murderer as well, was much more uncertain. Then an idea came to him; still a considerable gamble but possessing a greater likelihood of success than focussing only on the traitors now sitting on a boat at the canal basin.

'Very well,' he said. 'I respect your greater experience on matters of espionage, so we will take a calculated risk. First, send someone as messenger to Great Yarmouth. Then despatch a single man to Coltishall to make sure these traitors do not leave the Navigation there and make their way to Great Yarmouth by some other route. I doubt they will, but we should be sure. After that, collect all the rest of your men together. How many will still be available to you?'

'Six, including myself.'

'That ought to be sufficient. I want you to detain and search every one of the wherries owned by Richard Laven. If they are tied up do it right away. If they are moving, do it the moment they tie up. I believe there are five of them, including the one carrying the Frenchmen, I imagine. Leave them until Coltishall. Arrest them while the passengers are transferring to the larger boat which will be waiting there.

'Fix all the other seizures for the same time and do them all together. As soon as the spies are taken and the first additional boat is searched, news will spread up and down the Navigation at breakneck speed. We must therefore prevent any of the captains from disposing of items before we can find them. Your search should be as thorough as possible. Some things may be found fairly easily — probably including the contraband — but the things we're more interested in are likely to be hidden with some care. Don't miss anything! When you have done all that, come and tell me what you have found. Then we will decide what to do next.'

Gwatkin hurried out, happier now that he had a specific course of action to follow. Adam still felt that this move was premature. He could only hope the outcome would be a positive one.

❧

THE NEXT MORNING, GWATKIN WAS BACK, LOOKING TRIUMPHANT and waving a handful of sheets of paper.

'We found a good deal of contraband on the boats heading for Aylsham, doctor, as you predicted,' he said. 'French silk, lace, some boxes of fine cigars, some porcelain. These papers are the prize, however. Some are in code or cipher. Others are in French but written to read like something friends might write to one another. Those may either conceal secret writings, or use some kind of code, based on words or letters.'

'Where did you find them?' Adam asked. 'Were they well hidden?'

'The contraband was not particularly well hidden. It was mostly just tucked amongst the rest of the cargo. The papers had been concealed with greater care. There were false bulkheads in the cargo areas and false sides or bottoms to certain crates. We even found one set of papers, wrapped in two layers of heavily oiled cloth, wedged into the bottom of a bucket that the crew had been using as a privy. I imagine they felt sure nobody would look there.'

'I congratulate you on doing an excellent job,' Adam said — and meant it.

'Do we go and see this Laven fellow right away?' Gwatkin asked. 'Surely we have all the evidence we need to put him and his fellow conspirators under arrest?'

'Perhaps. Even so it will be better if we can get a confession from one of them. Let's start with Mr Sleeth. I feel certain he is the weakest link. If we can frighten him sufficiently, he may denounce the others to save his own neck. What we need now is a constable or a magistrate, so that we can make a legal arrest.'

'I am a constable for the Bow Street Magistrates Court, doctor, as are several of my men. I also hold a special commission from the king to root out spies and saboteurs,' Gwatkin said. 'Any arrest I make will be entirely legal.'

'Excellent,' Adam replied. 'Let us go together. When we get there, I want you to stay silent and let me do all the talking.'

The two men hurried to Mr Sleeth's house and Adam knocked at the door. When a maid came to see who it was, he announced himself as Dr Bascom and asked to see the attorney on a matter of urgency.

'Stay here,' he said quietly to Gwatkin after the maid had departed to find her master. 'I want to give Sleeth as violent a shock as I can. If you come in with me, he'll be on his guard right away. Try to stay close to the door so you can hear what I'm saying. You'll know when it's time to come in.'

'Mr Sleeth will see you now, doctor,' the maid told him. 'Please follow me.'

'My friend will wait here,' Adam said to her. 'I will not keep Mr Sleeth long.' With that, he followed the maid into the room which the attorney obviously used to receive visitors.

Sleeth was seated behind a large desk but stood up when Adam entered. Adam thought he looked nervous. Whether that was because he suspected what was to come, or simply because Adam was an unusual visitor, he did not know. Sleeth tried to look relaxed, but his voice shook a little as he wished his visitor good day and enquired how he might be of service.

'You can start by telling me the truth,' Adam said. 'How long have you and the others been engaged in treason against this realm?'

The effect of Adam's question was as startling as he could have wished. All the colour drained from the attorney's face and he fell backwards into his chair. In doing so, he also dislodged his wig, which fell onto the floor beside him, revealing an almost perfectly bald head. From that ungainly position, Sleeth stared up into Adam's face, his eyes wide with shock and his breath coming in rapid, irregular gasps. Adam had never seen anyone reduced to so pitiable a state quite so quickly.

'Well?' he snapped. 'We know all about the three men you so recently put onto one of Mr Laven's wherries. Two of them are French spies and one is an Irish rebel. How much are you being paid for your part in this conspiracy?'

Since Sleeth appeared still to be incapable of speech, Adam pressed on. 'Was this your clever idea? Not content with smuggling, you have to turn to espionage? That makes it treason, doesn't it? You and your colleagues will all hang outside Norwich Castle, I expect, which is all you deserve. Mr Gwatkin! Come in now, please.'

At the sight of Adam's burly assistant, Mr Sleeth seemed to squirm back in his chair even further. He had still not managed to speak.

'This gentleman has come from London,' Adam continued. 'He is an official of the Bow Street Magistrate's Court with a special commission from the King to track down spies and traitors. He will now arrest you on charges of treason and assisting an enemy in time of war.'

Sleeth found his voice at last. 'It wasn't my idea,' he gasped. 'It was Robert Laven. He was always short of money. Gambling, you see. We were doing quite nicely from the profits from the smuggling, but he was spending his share faster than the money was coming in. He didn't tell us of this new source of income in advance, of course. The first the rest of us knew about it was when our monthly receipts doubled. By then, it was too late.'

'You mean your greed took over,' Adam said.

'Not that. We wanted him to refuse any further contact, but he said it had been going on for long enough that no one would believe the rest of us were not involved. Besides, the French would find another route, then hand us over to the authorities as revenge.'

'And you believed him?'

'If we had crossed him, he would have handed us over himself. He was that kind of person. He would have gone to the authorities and claimed to have discovered the rest of us had deceived him, by entering into illegal arrangements to transport documents and spies for the French.'

By this time, Mr Gwatkin had the good sense to step back a little and delay any formal arrest. Like Adam, he was intent on the story that was now unfolding and feared any interruption would deprive them of valuable information.

'How long ago did this arrangement start?' Adam asked.

'We first found out about it around six months ago, but Robert Laven must have been doing it in secret for months before then. He was right to say we'd all be implicated, whatever we did. Laughed at our confusion. We three got together and tried to work out what to do next. Mountneigh reckoned that if we were caught, we were doomed anyway, so we might as well continue and enjoy the extra profit.'

'What went wrong? Why was Robert Laven murdered?'

'Oh God! You know about that too?' Sleeth began to cry and looked more repugnant than ever. Adam could feel no pity for him. His downfall was of his own making.

'Which one of you shot him and faked the appearance of suicide?' he snapped. 'Was it you?'

'Not me! I swear it!'

'Who then?'

'It was his brother. Robert Laven had started drinking more than ever. His gambling became more reckless too, so that he lost even more than he had done before. He even tried cheating, but was soon caught. Richard thought it was only a matter of time before he was thrown into a debtor's prison. He had also started to refuse to give his brother any more money. Good money after bad, he said. Mountneigh and I met and talked the problem through. We agreed Robert had to be stopped before he gave the rest of us away. Then we spoke in private with Richard. He agreed with us and offered to do what was necessary.'

'His own brother killed him? You expect me to believe that?'

'He did! I swear it's true! Richard killed him and my job was to make sure that the verdict was suicide. Mountneigh was too much of a coward to get involved at all. It would all have worked well if that wretched surgeon hadn't decided to interfere. The man I usually used to carry out autopsies was sick, so I had to find someone else at short notice. Surgeons are supposed to be at the lowest level of the medical profession; just about good enough to hack off some limbs and nothing else. It was my bad luck to pick one with brains. I managed to shut his mouth at the inquest, but he wouldn't let matters lie there. Fortunately, he decided to take what he thought he knew to Mountneigh.'

'I think that's all we need to know,' Adam said. 'You can arrest him now, Gwatkin. Then get him out of my sight.'

'No! No! I want to turn King's evidence!' Sleeth leapt to his feet and began waving his arms around wildly, but Gwatkin seized him by the shoulder and pronounced the words of the arrest.

'You can't turn King's evidence until you've been arrested, my friend,' Gwatkin said. 'Then it will be up to the judge when you come forward for trial.' He turned to Adam. 'I left several of my men outside. They'll keep him close until we can pick up the other two.'

'I'll let you pick up Mountneigh on your own,' Adam replied. 'You don't need me for that. In fact, you could send two of your men to do it, while you come with me to seek out Richard Laven. Just make sure he doesn't try to browbeat them with the fact that he's a magistrate.'

They took Sleeth outside, dressed as he was and without his wig. Adam didn't know whether he had a wife, but if he did, he didn't ask to see or speak to her. Gwatkin called his men over and detailed two of them to take the wretched fellow to the local lock-up and keep him close.

'When we've got all three,' he said to Adam, 'we'll take them under armed guard to Norwich Castle. These prisoners are too important to trust to a local gaol. I wouldn't be surprised if they aren't sent down to London for trial.'

The arrest of Mr Mountneigh proved to be relatively straightforward, although, as Adam had predicted, he tried to bluster and claim some sort of immunity as magistrate. When that proved useless, he demanded to be given the evidence on which he was being arrested. That only caused the two London constables to laugh.

'Your fellow conspirator, the man Sleeth, has confessed and wants to turn King's evidence against you,' they told him. 'There's your evidence. You'll hang, sure enough.'

'At least let me say farewell to my wife,' Mountneigh protested. 'Surely you can't deny me that?'

Alerted by the noise, Mountneigh's wife had already entered the room, so she heard this final request.

'Maybe they can't,' she said, 'but I can. I've been listening outside the door. I've long regretted marrying you, Thomas Mountneigh, even when I only thought you were a cruel, selfish, pompous, arrogant fool. You only married me for my money. Now I know you're a traitor, I hope you rot in hell! Take him away, gentlemen. His presence causes a foul smell in the house.'

While this was going on, Adam and Gwatkin had made their way down towards Millgate and turned along the driveway to Millgate Manor. As before, Gwatkin left one of his men outside, while he strode up and banged on the door. This time, however, they were to be disappointed, for the maid servant told them her master had left the house a few minutes before they arrived. No, she didn't know where he was going, but he seemed in a great hurry. Had anyone been to the house within the past hour or so? Yes, a young man had come. He was dressed like a clerk, so she supposed he had come from Mr Sleeth's office. He didn't stay long, so his business could not have been complicated.

'It never occurred to me that Sleeth would have a clerk,' Adam said.

'He must have been listening to everything we said to his master. Once he realised what was happening, he thought he could earn a few shillings by carrying the word to Richard Laven before we could get here. Do you think our bird has flown?'

'I fear so,' Gwatkin replied. 'He can't have got far though. I'll have my men get horses and set out after him. Where do you think he will be heading?'

'He'll most likely try to escape overseas, which means he'll be heading for Great Yarmouth. Might it not be better to have your men go there at full speed and try to pick him up while he is looking for a captain to take him on board?'

'Maybe I'll do both those things,' Gwatkin said. 'Sir Percival will be furious if we let him escape. I'm no coward, but the idea of facing Sir Percival when he's in a temper is enough to make my knees shake.'

As Gwatkin turned away to talk to his men, a boy rushed up to Adam. 'Doctor! Doctor!' the boy cried out. 'You've got to come quick! A man 'as broke into the 'ouse and taken my mistress prisoner. He's got a pistol too! He says 'e'll kill 'er, if I don't bring you back right away.'

Adam recognised the boy as the one who worked in Miss Rose's garden and understood in an instant the terrible danger in which his mistress must now be.

'Gwatkin! Leave all that!' he shouted. 'It's Laven! He's gone to the house where the surgeon lived. He's taken the women there hostage! We've got to get there right away! He's killed twice, so I'm sure he won't hesitate to do it again. Hurry, man! Hurry! We're their only chance.'

'Why has he gone there?' Gwatkin asked, waving to his men to gather around him. 'If he lets us catch up with him, he has no chance of escape.'

'I can think of two reasons straightaway,' Adam said. 'If he thinks we only know about the smuggling, he may be trying to take hostages to bargain with. The alternative is that he believes the surgeon told his housekeeper enough about the death of Robert Laven to make her a possible witness against him. If that's the case, he's going to kill her.'

'But ...'

'Look, he won't be thinking clearly,' Adam said, silencing Gwatkin's protest. 'He's in a panic. The only chance Miss Rose has of surviving is if we can interfere with his plans. Here's what you must do. I'll go to the house as fast as I can; you collect as many of your men as you can find and follow after me with all speed. If you can, surround the house. Whether he kills again or not, that devil is not going to escape! As soon as I get there, I'm going inside. I want you to stay outside unless you hear shooting or sounds of a struggle. Then come in as fast as you can.'

He turned to the boy who brought the message. 'You come with me lad. When we get there, I want you to go around behind the house — wait! Do you know what room they're in?'

'When I came away, sir, they was in the kitchen.'

'Is that at the back or the front?'

'The back.'

'Right! You stay by the window and pick up ten pebbles or small sticks. Count up to ten, not too quickly, and put one pebble in your pocket. Do the same thing with the next pebble and so on. Will you do that?' The boy nodded his head. 'When you put the last pebble in your pocket, bend down, pick up a good-sized stone and throw it through the kitchen window. Now, let's run like the very wind.'

## ✿ 23 ✿

Adam and the boy rushed headlong towards what had once been the surgeon's house. The amazing sight of a gentleman and a scruffy boy running hell-for-leather caused those people who were about their business along the way to stop what they were doing and stare after them. A few of the loungers and idlers tried to join in the fun, shouting encouragement and looking back to see if the two runners were being pursued. Fortunately, there was no attempt to stop them.

Adam was not used to proceeding at a faster pace than a sedate walk. Before long, his breathing became laboured and he developed a painful stitch in his side. All that drove him on was his fear for Rose and her aunt. If he was right in his understanding of past events, Richard Laven had killed twice already and would not hesitate to kill again. If he had so far stayed his hand this time, it must be in the hope Adam would buy Miss Rose's safety at the price of helping him escape. Once it became clear his plan would not work, there would be nothing to stop him carrying out his threat.

By the time they reached where Rose lived, Adam was completely out of breath and felt nauseous from the unaccustomed effort. With a gargantuan effort of willpower, he therefore forced himself to stand still until his breathing calmed enough to allow him to speak. Then he signalled to the lad to wait behind and to start counting. Only then did he open the front door and go inside.

All was quiet. Was this a trick? An ambush by Richard Laven to destroy the man whom he knew had now succeeded in bringing his treachery to light? Were the two women already dead? Slowly, walking on tiptoe, he began making his way to the rear of the house where the boy had said the kitchen was to be found. He was still painfully short of breath from running and his heart was beating faster than he had ever known it beat before. If it came to a struggle, he wouldn't be of much use against a desperate man in full possession of his strength. All he could do was hope he was right and Laven had decided to take Miss Rose — and hopefully her aunt, Miss Matilda — as hostages. If he had gone to the house only to kill the former housekeeper, he would have done it by now and left to make good his escape.

Laven had not left. When Adam at last stepped into the kitchen, he found the man standing right behind Rose. He was holding her tightly by the arm and had a pistol, fully cocked, aimed at the side of her head. Miss Matilda was a few feet away, standing by the kitchen dresser and seemingly frozen in horror.

'Ah, Dr Bascom at last,' Laven said, his voice calm and steady. 'The boy found you then. Listen now and listen carefully. I'm not going to make the mistake of boasting or answering any foolish questions. That would give your bully-boys time to get here. Your choice is simple, and you must make it immediately. Either you call your men off and allow me to leave this place unmolested — taking Miss Thoday with me, of course, to guarantee my safety — or I shoot her right away. I know all about your reputation for catching criminals, and I'm determined not to add to your successes. I don't doubt that the other two will admit to our smuggling, even if they try to put all the blame for it on me. If that wretched surgeon hadn't worked out that I killed my brother, none of this would have happened. Everyone knew he was sweet on his housekeeper, so he almost certainly shared what he knew. That's why I'm going to keep her with me until I can leave this country. Just to make sure she can't give evidence against me.'

'If you kill her, you'll hang anyway,' Adam said. 'I'll have seen you do it.'

'Don't treat me as a fool, doctor. I see you are unarmed, while I have this pistol tucked in my belt and a knife in my pocket too. If I have to die, I'll make very sure that I take you and the other woman with me.'

At that moment, there came a loud crash and tinkling of glass as the boy, Jack, hurled a sizeable stone through the kitchen window. As Adam had hoped, it proved sufficient to distract Laven's attention for a split second. At once, he darted forward and grabbed hold of Laven's arm, trying to twist the gun away from where it was pointed at the side of Rose's head. Laven, realising the trick, fought back with all his might. In the ensuing struggle, he managed to twist the gun around towards Adam and pull the trigger. The gun went off and the ball — more by chance than by any effort at avoiding it — missed Adam's head by a tiny fraction of an inch, before burying itself in the wall and throwing out a large cloud of plaster.

By then, Adam was wrestling with Laven for possession of the knife the man had said he was carrying. His could feel his energy, much depleted by his headlong dash from Laven's house, steadily ebbing away. All the while, desperation and fear were adding to his adversary's strength. Things might have gone very badly for him indeed, if the two women had not taken a hand in the matter.

As the door flew open and Gwatkin and his men tumbled into the room, Miss Rose twisted out of Laven's grasp, snatched up a small dish that was standing on the table, and threw the contents into Laven's face. His head was at once enveloped in a cloud of the powder, so that he rubbed furiously at his eyes and began to cough and gasp for breath. That dish, Rose later explained, contained a substantial amount of finely ground pepper. Next, Miss Matilda stepped forward, snatched up a saucepan from the dresser, and brought it down firmly on the back of Laven's head. There was a sound like the distant striking of a church bell, Laven's eyes rolled back into his head, his knees buckled and he and Adam, still locked together, slumped to the floor.

It took longer to lift Adam to his feet and disentangle him from his adversary than it did to drag Laven upright. Despite what must have been a fearsome blow, he was still alive, though unconscious. Adam, ever the physician, made the foolish remark that he should be treated with great care, since he would certainly have suffered a severe concussion. Gwatkin simply ignored him, telling his men to drag the traitor outside, bind his arms and legs fast with rope and commandeer a cart in which he could be carried up the hill and over to the lock-up, where they should lodge him with the other two.

'We'll keep him there with the others,' Gwatkin told Adam, 'but only for tonight. At dawn, my men and I will set out for Norwich. Once we arrive, I'll see him and the others locked up in the castle and send post haste to Sir Percival for further instructions. He'll decide where best to hold all three securely and decide where their trial should take place. I'll therefore take my leave of you now, doctor. It has been a pleasure — and an education — to work with you, and you have my most sincere thanks for all you have done. I am quite certain I could not have done this without you. Doubtless Sir Percival will write to you to convey his own thanks and the gratitude of the government and the nation. Farewell, sir. Maybe we will meet again someday.'

It had all happened so quickly, Adam felt almost as stunned as Richard Laven. Was it truly over? Had they succeeded in capturing the remaining members of the group responsible for providing the French with a safe espionage route — and solved the mystery of Surgeon Hawley's murder at the same time?

He had no more time to ponder these questions, however, for Miss Rose had planted herself before him and was demanding to know if he was badly injured.

'There's blood on your face, doctor,' she said, 'and you look as white as a ghost. Here, sit in this chair and get your breath back. I'll just find something to bathe your face. That pistol ball must have come close enough to scrape your scalp. No? Let me look. No, there's no mark. aunt, boil water for some calming camomile tea. Now, doctor, are you quite sure you have no other hurts?'

'Leave the poor man alone, Rose,' her aunt told her. 'Fussing over him as if you were his mother isn't going to do anything except convince him you've lost your mind. He'll do best if you give him space and time to recover on his own. If you must do something, give him a sound kissing for saving our lives.'

'Aunt Matilda!' Rose squeaked. 'That is a most improper suggestion!'

'I'd do it myself, if I were thirty years younger,' her aunt replied. Relief was making her lightheaded. 'That's the trouble with you young people. You're so tied up in convention, and far too easily shocked. Thank you, doctor. Rose and I will never be able to repay you for what you have done for us today. Rose! Set to and make that camomile tea. An old lady like me needs to take life easy. Since coming to live with you, I swear I've aged ten years in as many days.'

IT WAS NOT QUITE THE END OF THE EVENTS OF THAT DAY AS FAR AS Gwatkin and his new prisoner were concerned. By the time he and his men went back up the hill into Aylsham itself, a sizeable crowd had assembled, attracted by all the noise and excitement. Moreover, as is the way with such crowds, the rumour swiftly spread that the man in the handcart was none other than Mr Richard Laven and that he was the one responsible for the death of the surgeon. As a result, such an ugly mood now spread through the crowd that Gwatkin and his men had to produce their guns and truncheons to prevent their uncon-scious prisoner from being dispatched to the next world there and then. All the crowd could do to vent their fury was scoop up handfuls of mud and filth from the roadway and throw it over the recumbent body in the handcart. By the time the procession left Millgate, Laven, at last struggling back to consciousness, found he possessed a thick coating of stinking muck from his head to the soles of his feet.

Nor did drinking the camomile tea end the day for Adam. He was covered in bruises from his struggle, while the emotions of what had taken place — fear, anger, hatred, excitement, and relief — now left him drained and exhausted. Not so Miss Rose. Being held hostage and threatened with imminent death seemed to have left her unaffected. While Adam remained slumped in his chair, his eyes smarting from the pepper which had missed Laven and fallen on him, the young woman looked around the room, smiled at her aunt, who occupied the only other chair, and said, 'We'll have to paper over that window until we can find someone to repair it for us. I wonder who threw the stone through it?'

'Is that all you have to say on the matter?' Adam gasped.

'What else is there to say? Richard Laven just told us he killed his brother, and we're all certain he killed the surgeon as well. Mercifully, we are still alive and can therefore give evidence against him. We also have the notes that Mr Hawley left. Unless our system of justice fails us, the wretched man will hang — as he so richly deserves. Oh, perhaps I should thank you as my aunt did.'

'He will certainly hang,' Adam said. 'What you do not know is that he has been found to have been engaged in espionage on behalf of the French. Since he's committed treason as well as two murders, his fate is assured, believe me. But forget Laven. You and your aunt could have been killed.'

'So could you, doctor, if we had not intervened. If we are grateful to you for saving our lives, the same applies to you. The man was desperate, and despair often gives people unnatural strength. He'd missed you with his pistol shot. If he'd managed to reach his knife, he would have used it and taken your life for certain. I was not prepared to let that happen without doing my best to stop him.'

'Nor was I,' Miss Matilda said. 'There was also something wonderfully satisfying about the noise that saucepan made when it struck him on the head. Just like a bell.'

'It will definitely have made his head ring too, I imagine,' her niece added. 'Cheer up, doctor. We've all survived. That has to be what matters most, don't you think?'

'You are quite correct, Miss Rose,' Adam said, 'and I am extremely grateful for all that you did. Both of you showed bravery and considerable presence of mind.'

'Does that mean you will ask us to help you in the future?' Rose asked, attempting to look as innocent as she could.

Adam decided that was a question best avoided. 'If we are fortunate,' he said, his own face as expressionless as hers, 'the requirement will not arise.' He was already wondering just how much of what had taken place could be reported to Lady Alice. She might very well take grave exception to her future husband risking his life in such a thoughtless manner. There would, in times to come, be more to consider than his own safety before he threw himself into dangerous situations.

As he lay in his bed that night, reeking of the embrocation he had applied to his many bruises, Adam reflected that there were times when some women's strength of character far exceeded his expectations. Whether he should be grateful he was not so sure. He had an uneasy feeling that Lady Alice, for all her diminutive size, would also prove a person to be reckoned with. Just like his mother. And probably Miss Ruth. And ...

But by then he had fallen asleep.

## 24

A week passed, then ten days, until June was upon them. No news came from London or Norwich. Life began to return to normal. Only Adam's fading bruises and lingering aches reminded him of all that had taken place. The story might have ended there, but Adam decided he must host a dinner to show his gratitude to those who had been most involved in unmasking the use of the Navigation for smuggling and espionage.

There were five of them around the table: Adam, Miss Rose and Miss Matilda, Peter Lassimer and Dr Harrison Henshaw, Adam's assistant. Only Mr Gwatkin was absent, since he had returned to his normal duties in London. Mrs Whitbread, the cook, had provided them with a magnificent meal. There had been white soup or pea soup to start. The fish course was a whole turbot, accompanied by a rich oyster sauce. Then came a choice of chicken, lamb cutlets, venison pie or roast beef, accompanied by a variety of vegetables. The meal had ended with syllabubs and jellies, two fruit tarts, cheese and walnuts. They had drunk champagne, hock and claret, and the gentleman were now passing the port between them. It had been decided to break with convention, and the ladies had not withdrawn, so that all might explain their part in the capture of the three men, who were now on their way towards London and a certain appointment with the hangman.

Adam began. 'Mr Gwatkin was quite right when he said that he thought the conspirators would be sent to London for trial,' he said. 'I had the briefest of notes from Sir Percival Wicken this morning. The Attorney General has asked that some of the evidence should be given behind closed doors. I expect they don't want the French to know Wicken's men tracked those spies across the country, or how they did it. Now, everyone here played an important part in achieving that success. I suggest we each relate the parts we know best, starting with Lassimer here and Dr Henshaw, without whose eagle eyes at an autopsy the murderers of Surgeon Hawley might have escaped.'

They all agreed to this, so Peter and Henshaw begun by explaining the roles they had played in determining the cause of Surgeon Hawley's death and forcing Mr Sleeth, as coroner, to allow the jury to return a true verdict. While Rose and her aunt knew the outline of those events, neither had been present at the inquest itself, so all the details were new to them. After that, the two ladies explained the parts that they had played in the unfolding drama, ending with the moment when Richard Laven burst into the house and took them hostage.

'He pushed us both into the kitchen,' Rose explained, 'waving that pistol around and demanding to know exactly what the surgeon had told me about the death of Robert Laven, his brother. Several times I explained that he had told me nothing, but either he was too distracted to understand what I was saying, or he was determined not to believe me.'

'He was like a madman,' Miss Matilda added. 'I believe he thought I was one of the servants, because he virtually ignored me and kept shouting at Rose. I was on the point of deciding to try to slip out and fetch help, when he seemed to notice me at last, for he pointed his pistol at me and told me to stand completely still.'

'Of course, he had only the one pistol and there were two of us,' Rose said. 'He hadn't known that Aunt Matilda had joined the household, I expect.'

'He also had a knife,' Adam said. 'He tried to get to it after his pistol had discharged into the wall.'

'That's true,' Rose replied. 'Yet I believe his intention in seeking me out had been mostly to discover what I knew about the death of his brother. He was certain Mr Hawley must have shared his discoveries with me.'

'An irrational belief surely,' Henshaw said. 'If you had known — and decided to share that knowledge — there had been abundant time since the surgeon's death for you to do so. The fact that you had not done so should have told him all he needed to know.'

'Perhaps so,' Peter added, 'but fears can easily overcome rational thought. There is also the point that Miss Rose was now known to be talking with Bascom here. She might have told him. He would have known very well what to do with that information. Unless Miss Rose convinced him that she genuinely knew nothing, I am sure he would have killed her. He was trying to eliminate anyone who could act as a witness in a trial.'

'Whatever was in his mind,' Rose said firmly, sweeping aside these interruptions and resuming her narrative, 'finding that there were two of us put him in a dilemma. He could have shot me and tried to make his escape before the hue and cry was raised. As it was, he either had to find another way of disposing of my aunt or accept that she would raise the alarm the minute he fired the pistol.'

'Not quite,' Matilda said. 'I would have done my best to kill him first.'

'How was it that your garden boy came to seek me out?' Adam asked.

'I saw him peeping in through the window,' Rose said, 'so I kept nodding and pulling faces at him, trying to make him understand what he should do. When he disappeared, I didn't know whether he'd understood or simply assumed I was playing some silly game and gone about his work.'

'It was fortunate he found us when he did,' Adam said. 'When we went to Laven's house and he wasn't there, we assumed he was trying to make his escape immediately. As the lad ran up, we were just about to scatter in all directions to try to pick up Laven's trail. I ran down first to give Mr Gwatkin time to assemble his men and give them instructions.'

'You've no need to tell us what happened after that,' Peter said, interrupting what he feared would be a lengthy narrative. 'Henshaw and I know all about the heroic actions of these two ladies and your own, much more meagre, part in those events. I don't know about the others, but I'm rather less interested in all this business about spying than I am in discovering how and why the two murders took place. Has Richard Laven confessed to both of them?'

'So far as I know,' Adam said, 'he has refused to say anything at all. That was certainly the case during his period in Norwich, and I doubt that going to London will change his mind.'

'Does that mean we'll never know exactly what happened?' Dr Henshaw said. 'How frustrating! I suppose, Dr Bascom, you've already worked it out for yourself.'

Adam smiled. 'I do have some ideas ...' he said, trying to sound modest. 'I cannot be sure, you understand. However, if you put all the information together, you can produce a story which makes good sense, and is at least as plausible as anything else.'

'Tell us then!' Peter said. 'I know you. I'm sure you're dying to tell us. Spare us the false modesty, Bascom, and get on with it.'

'Very well,' Adam said. 'If that's what you want. Just remember that this is a story and not necessarily the truth.'

'Please, doctor,' Rose said. 'Don't keep us in suspense.'

'Very well. All our conspirators,' Adam began, 'share one thing in common: they were desperate for money. Robert Laven was a gambler, a drinker and a womaniser. He was heavily in debt as a result and Richard, his brother, was refusing to assist him any further. What had caused this change? Richard was obsessed with the idea of restoring the family to the status of landed gentry. To do that he needed a great deal of money, yet his brother spent it almost as fast as he could make it. He must finally have realised Robert was the greatest barrier to his ambition. Mr Mountneigh was obsessed with status. He'd left commerce behind and bought himself an estate; he'd even married a moderately wealthy wife. Even so, his income was insufficient for the type of life he thought he deserved. Mr Sleeth was a poor attorney and a deeply unpleasant man. Few people in Aylsham were willing to entrust their business to him, so he found himself constantly short of money. It must have felt like a miracle when Robert Laven asked him to undertake some confidential business on his behalf.

'I say Robert because the two who are willing to speak assert the idea of the smuggling beginning with him. Richard, his brother, joined in, doubtless hoping that an increased income would allow him to set some of it aside for the future. The two of them owned a fleet of wherries on the Navigation. They were thus ideally placed to collect contraband from the coast and transport it back to Aylsham. Barrels of brandy and packets of tobacco would have been too conspicuous. They concentrated instead on small, highly-priced items, such as silks and laces. Unfortunately, Robert's gambling losses swiftly outpaced whatever his share of the profits on the contraband amounted to. He needed another source of income and preferably a much more substantial one.

'How and why he got the idea of getting involved in espionage, we will never know. The others are adamant he began by letting the boats carry packages of secret writings. At that stage, they claim, they knew nothing of what he was doing. Then he added the business of transporting individuals, who wanted to enter or leave the country unnoticed. The earnings were substantial, of course, and the others quickly spotted their share had suddenly increased. They say then, and only then, did Robert Laven confess what he had been doing to produce such profits. They claim they were horrified, though I noticed that none of them turned down the extra cash produced.'

'Why did the other three have a change of heart?' Peter asked. 'Unless they were detected, all of them stood to gain by Robert's stratagem. You said they wanted money. Here was a way to produce enough to make them rich.'

'According to Sleeth and Mountneigh, Robert's behaviour grew wilder and more unpredictable. With extra money in his purse, he drank more heavily and gambled more outrageously than ever. Soon he was back in debt more deeply than before. The three of them became afraid he would give their secret away by his recklessness. Richard must also have realised that, no matter how much extra money they were able to make, his brother's extravagance would more than keep up. Mountneigh said the three of them quickly agreed something would have to be done about Robert Laven.'

'By killing him?' Rose asked. 'Was there no other way?'

'None that was so certain to remove the threat he posed,' Adam replied. 'According to Sleeth and Mountneigh, it was Richard who argued the only way they would ever be fully protected was if his brother were killed. He even offered to do it, saying he could make it look like suicide. It would then be Sleeth's task, as coroner, to make certain that would also be the verdict of the inquest.'

'But to kill your own brother ...' Miss Matilda shuddered at the horror of what Adam was telling them.

'Robert stood in the way of what Richard wanted most dearly: to restore his family to the ranks of landed gentry. He was also throwing away the wealth Richard had worked so hard to amass. It wouldn't be surprising to find his dislike turning into hatred under such circumstances.'

'How did he manage it?' Peter asked. 'Wasn't the other Laven's body found in a locked room — with the key on the inside as well?'

'All I can tell you is how I believe it could have been accomplished,' Adam said. 'First you must imagine Richard hiding somewhere in his brother's dressing room, pistol in hand, waiting for Robert to come in. At that point, Robert himself might have locked the door behind him for some reason. If not, Richard must have done so before the noise of the shot attracted attention. Either way, Richard shot his brother in the head, perhaps from ten feet or more away, and quickly arranged the scene to look like a suicide. He would have escaped by darting through the connecting door into his brother's bedroom and locking that door behind him. When it was found there was no key in that door, people simply assumed Robert had locked it himself. Next, I imagine, Richard hid himself in the bedroom until he was certain everyone's attention was on his brother's body next door. At that point, he could slip out into the corridor and arrive at the dressing room as if he had only just come into the house.'

'Do we know how Surgeon Hawley worked out it wasn't suicide?' This from Dr Henshaw.

'The principal evidence came from the autopsy,' Adam explained.

'There were no signs of powder burns or smoke on the side of the skull and no wound where the ball had made its exit. He concluded, quite correctly in my opinion, the pistol ball had not gone right through. Now, if Richard had held the pistol in his hand, there would certainly have been powder burns. The muzzle could have been no more than twelve or eighteen inches from his head and probably closer. Since the shot came from a pistol that was lying next to the body, it was simple to judge the calibre. The most cursory look made it plain a large calibre ball was involved. In such a case, there should have been a massive wound on the opposite side of the skull through which the ball had made its exit.'

'No one else noticed this?' Dr Henshaw said.

'Few people are familiar with the terrible destruction a pistol fired from very close range must inflict on the skull. Mr Hawley had been in the navy and would have seen many examples of wounds from guns, some of them fired from close up. Members of boarding parties often fight hand-to-hand. He knew at once the damage to Robert Laven's head could not have been caused by a gun held in his own hand. There was also another sign the scene had been arranged after the man was dead. The pistol lay by the man's left hand, yet there is no evidence Robert Laven was left-handed or ambidextrous. I expect the only suitable place for Richard to hide himself happened to be on the left side of where his brother was standing. Rather than wait for his brother to turn around — and thus risk discovery — he pulled the trigger and hoped nobody would notice the oddity.'

'Richard's plan to dispose of his brother almost worked,' Peter said. 'It was simply bad luck that, first, Surgeon Hawley happened to be in the house at the time of the killing; second, that his naval experience meant he knew what manner of wounds there would have been, had it truly been suicide; and, third, that his conscience wouldn't allow him to leave the matter alone. Not even after he had been effectively silenced by Sleeth at the inquest.'

'Mr Sleeth should have known that from the start,' Rose said. 'The surgeon was a good man. He would never have kept silent when he knew that a crime had taken place.'

'I imagine Richard Laven didn't know anything of the surgeon,'

Adam said. 'In fact, Mr Hawley wouldn't have been involved at all, if the coroner's usual choice of medical examiner had been available. Had that been the case, the crime would never have been discovered. If there was any bad luck involved, it concerned Mr Hawley himself. Once he had decided it was his duty to explain all that he knew to the authorities, he naturally chose to begin with the local magistrate — Mr Mountneigh. Mountneigh probably promised to investigate, then told the other two what had happened. It would be obvious at once what a danger the surgeon had become to their safety.'

'But why kill him?' Rose asked. 'Couldn't the magistrate claim to be conducting an investigation, then say he could find no other evidence strong enough to overturn the finding of the inquest jury?'

'Hardly,' Peter said. 'What Bascom here has told us would be more than enough to re-open the inquest.'

'They were also afraid the surgeon wouldn't leave it there,' Adam added. 'The evidence he'd already presented would, as Lassimer here says, be more than enough to bring the verdict of the original inquest into question. They had to silence him. Sleeth was in the greatest danger, of course. Yet I am certain the others realised he'd probably try to save himself by turning King's evidence against them. They also guessed Sleeth was too much of a coward to make a good job of this second murder. Mountneigh would never dirty his hands in such a way, so that left Richard Laven. He'd killed already and so would face death in any case. No one can be hung more than once, however many they have killed. He was also the cleverest of the three. The way he carried out the murder was certainly ingenious, and he might well have pulled it off.'

'Only if you hadn't got involved, Bascom,' Peter said.

'They didn't know I was involved,' Adam said, 'until it was too late. They knew I'd talked with Miss Rose, of course. That raised their suspicions. When the gossips noticed we'd met again, more than once, and that I'd been to her house, the conspirators wondered what was going on. Yet even so, I don't think they were certain until a few days ago. Sleeth said they were convinced of an entirely different explanation.'

'That I was your mistress, I suppose,' Rose said. 'Perhaps I ought to be flattered.'

'You shouldn't be,' Peter said softly. 'Now if they thought that you were *my* mistress, that would be quite another matter.'

The look Rose directed at him made it abundantly clear he should forget any such notions there and then.

'Although Richard Laven eventually decided on taking you hostage, Miss Rose,' Adam said hastily, 'I don't think that was his original plan. He probably improvised when I burst into the room. I believe you're right when you said that he wanted to know how much the surgeon had told you. He must have been trying to make certain that no one could give evidence that would result in him being charged with his brother's murder. He even delayed any attempt at escape for that reason. It probably never occurred to him, as it did not to me, that the surgeon would have left detailed notes covering all he had seen at the time of the killing—'

'Seen? I know you said he was there, but I hadn't realised he'd actual *seen* the murder.' Dr Henshaw was flabbergasted.

'Not seen exactly. Just been close enough at hand to arrive on the scene within a few minutes of hearing the shot. Surgeon Hawley was in the house for a different reason but rushed up to the dressing room with everyone else on hearing the shot. I don't think he went far inside — not according to his notes — since it was not his place to involve himself without being asked to do so. However, he saw enough through the doorway to be able to describe the scene. It wasn't long after the others had arrived — the servants I mean — before Richard Laven also ran up, claiming he'd only just got back home. He took charge at once, naturally.'

'But Hawley was a medical man! He might have been able to help.'

'It was obvious to everyone that Robert Laven was beyond help, Henshaw. Besides, Mr Hawley was a lowly surgeon; a man who mostly treated artisans and the poor. Can you imagine Richard Laven turning to him for help?'

'I suppose not, stupid as that might be.'

'He wouldn't want anyone with medical knowledge looking over the scene too closely either, would he? He must only have had a few seconds to arrange his brother's body to look as if he had killed himself. His plan would be to declare it suicide and usher everyone away as quickly as he could. Sleeth would make sure the right verdict was reached by the inquest jury, and that would be an end of the matter.

'Sadly for them, Mr Hawley made a mess of their careful planning. Worse, he must have told Mr Mountneigh he could provide evidence pointing to murder. That's why he had to die. At the start, the conspirators would have assumed his death would end that possibility. I doubt they even thought of Miss Rose. She was just a servant. It was only later Richard Laven and the others began to worry about how much she might know and tell others.

'When I burst in, Laven had to change his plans on the spot. He rightly assumed I wouldn't stand there and allow him to kill you, Miss Rose. That's why he thought he could bargain with me to let him make his escape. Of course, he should have realised I had no means of guaranteeing he could get away, even if I had agreed. Mr Gwatkin and his men must be close at hand somewhere. Once they arrived, he would be cornered. At that point, he panicked. Despite his bravado, I believe he was genuinely reluctant to kill again, if he could avoid it. He also wanted to survive, if he could. The moment he killed again, his own life would be forfeited. He was one man against many. He therefore did the first thing that occurred to him: tried to use a threat to the life of an innocent person as a basis for bargaining his way out.

'There it is. My version of what may have happened. Unless Laven talks before he stands on the gallows, we'll not know whether or not it bears any actual resemblance to the truth.'

'I hope most sincerely that this really is the end of this business,' Dr Henshaw said earnestly. 'I'll be glad to forget about it. I have no taste for intrigue or the solving of crimes and much prefer to concentrate on my patients. Do you know what you are going to do now, Miss Rose?'

'Much the same as you, Dr Henshaw. Concentrate on my patients and try to establish my practice as a herbalist. My aunt is staying with me permanently, so I can leave the running of the household to her. My part will be to concentrate on my garden, drying and preserving the herbs I grow, and using them to try to bring relief from pain and illness. I shall also continue to set bones for any who wish me to do so. Mr Hawley taught me how to do it, so I must continue, if only to honour his memory. I imagine that, in time, another surgeon will come along and establish his practice in Millgate. It's an ideal place for any ex-navy man.'

'Don't you also have a wedding to attend?' Peter said to Adam, causing him to start with surprise. Could his secret have leaked out some way? 'Isn't your friend Charles Scudamore to wed the lovely Miss LaSalle?'

'Indeed so,' Adam replied, his heart resuming a more measured beat. 'The wedding is now set for Midsummer's Day. It was delayed a little by some problems Charles had with obtaining full possession of the house in Holt where they are to live. All is now concluded satisfactorily and they can proceed with the nuptials.'

'Midsummer's Day,' Rose said, her voice wistful. 'An excellent date for a wedding.'

'Won't Lady Alice's period of mourning for her late husband be concluded by then as well?' Peter asked. 'I imagine you'll have remembered that.'

Trust Peter to think of that, Adam told himself. He never misses any opportunity to tease me about Lady Alice.

'I believe it will be over by then,' he said aloud, schooling himself to reply in an off-hand manner. 'Lady Alice has been punctilious in giving Sir Daniel all the respect he deserved. From what I hear, her devotion has been both noted and commended widely.'

'Including by you?'

'Certainly. Sir Daniel became dear to me in his last days, as well as being my benefactor via his Will. I would not wish to lessen in any way the proper period of mourning that custom dictates.'

With that, the conversation moved on to other topics, until Miss Matilda advised her niece that it was getting very late and that they really should be home and getting ready for bed. Peter and Dr Henshaw both lived close enough to walk home, but Adam had already planned to send the two ladies home in his carriage. He therefore called for Hannah and sent her to tell William to bring the carriage round to the front door. He was feeling weary and was inwardly relieved the party was breaking up at a reasonable hour. Henshaw said he had no taste for solving crimes. Was that a hint to his mentor to stick to medicine in the future? If so, at that particular moment, Adam was prepared to give it serious consideration.

In the days that followed, Adam kept himself busy by attending to domestic affairs. He also spoke with his assistant, Dr Henshaw, and offered him the chance to take over the bulk of his practice in Aylsham. It had already become apparent Adam's duties in London and Norwich must preclude him from giving it the attention it deserved. To his delight, Henshaw expressed himself more than willing to step into Adam's shoes. In the relatively short time he had been in the area, he said, he had already begun to feel at home with both the locality and the people.

Naturally, Adam made several visits to Mossterton Hall. Lady Alice was eager to hear how the business of the death of the surgeon and the uncovering of the associated conspiracy had been resolved. Adam supplied a suitably edited version of events, hoping she would not press him too closely on his part in securing Richard Laven. Since she was, at least for the moment, rather preoccupied with arrangements for all the family members who had written to say they intended to see her nephew, Charles, married to Miss Sophia LaSalle, he felt he had been successful. Instead of probing further, as she would certainly have done under normal circumstances, Lady Alice was content to congratulate Adam on his cleverness in finding the murderer, praise the bravery of both the Thoday ladies, and leave things there.

Naturally, they also discussed where they might live after they were married and Mossterton Hall handed over to Sir Daniel's heir. Lady Alice had arranged, through her land agent, to visit the mansion and estate on the edge of Aylsham which Adam had identified earlier. She professed herself to be delighted with the building and its location — not to mention the obvious possibilities for improvement — and negotiations were put in hand at once to conclude the necessary purchase.

'What will you do with your present house?' she asked Adam. 'You have it on a long lease, do you not?'

'That's correct,' Adam replied. 'There is still nearly twenty years to run. Once we are able to make our plans public, I'll speak to Dr Henshaw and see if he would like to take it over. It's a good house and I have been happy there. It's also situated very conveniently. His current accommodation was only meant to be temporary, and I believe he already had it in mind to find somewhere better.'

With the wedding drawing ever closer, Lady Alice and Adam had far less time to be alone together than either would have liked. Even so, they managed to spend what time they had pleasantly enough. They walked in the grounds and the gardens at Mossterton, they had lengthy conversations in which they planned their future together, and they also managed to escape — so they believed — from the eyes of the servants for long enough to indulge in periods of kisses and caresses, all of which left them longing for more.

Two more weeks passed. Then another letter came from Sir Percival Wicken. This time it was not written in haste and the handwriting was clear and bold, better reflecting the character of the author.

*My Dear Bascom,*

*It will not surprise you to learn all three of the men whom you were involved in exposing as traitors and murderers were found guilty and sentenced to pay the ultimate penalty for their crimes. Pleas for mercy were made on behalf of Sleeth and Mountneigh, in consideration of their cooperation during the trial. I understand that the Lord Chancellor consulted His Majesty on the matter but found the king adamant in his belief that men who had betrayed their country for monetary gain deserved to suffer the full rigour of the law. All three were therefore hanged last Tuesday. Laven maintained his silence to the end.*

*I'm sure it will also gratify you to know that his Majesty went out of his way to praise your part in this affair. I believe he wishes to express his gratitude, together with that of the whole kingdom. Mr Pitt, our Prime Minister, and several members of his cabinet have also told me of their appreciation for your prompt action. Young Mr Gwatkin is going about telling everyone he meets of his unbounded admiration for you. For myself, I need only say that you have once again succeeded in placing me in your debt in the most admirable way. Mere thanks fall far short of what you deserve from me, but they are all I have to offer. That I do with a full heart.*

*I am, sir, even more than previously, your most devoted and appreciative servant,*

*Percival Wicken*

⚜

WHEN THE DAY AT LAST ARRIVED, THE WEDDING OF CHARLES Scudamore and Sophia LaSalle proved to be a splendid affair. The sun shone brightly, Lady Alice's cook had provided a gargantuan wedding breakfast, and the various friends and family who attended agreed that the bride and groom made a delightful couple and were obviously very much in love. Given Sophia's lack of family, the Bascom family did their best to step into their place. Not only were Adam's mother and his brother, Giles, prominent amongst the guests, Giles had brought his wife and children along.

Charles's parents and brothers had come from London, allowing Adam to meet them for the first time. All of Lady Alice's other brothers and their wives were also present. The sight of the diminutive Lady Alice, surrounded by her doting brothers, all of whom towered over her, caused several of the guests considerable amusement — at least until they noted how meekly the men deferred to their sister's every whim. Even Adam, who had heard about this phenomenon on several occasions, experienced some disquiet on seeing it before him. After a moment, however, he reflected that being managed by Lady Alice could not fail to be a most pleasant experience and would free him of many onerous domestic decisions. Fortunately, he did not yet realise just how many such decisions — and not just domestic ones either — this was going to involve.

At length, pursued by many good wishes, the newly-married couple departed for their new home in Holt, from where they intended to travel westwards to visit some of the more distant Scudamore relatives in Herefordshire over the next few weeks. On their return, Charles would establish his legal practice and Sophia would take up her role as mistress of his household.

A glance between Lady Alice and Adam was sufficient to convince them this was the ideal moment to make their own announcement, while so many of their friends and family were present. Somewhat nervously, therefore, Adam called for people's attention and announced that he and Lady Alice would very soon be beginning their own life together as man and wife. The many cries of approval and the loud clapping which followed finally convinced him that even Lady Alice's aristocratic family were prepared to welcome him amongst them. Adam's mother, of course, was ecstatic. Not only had her errant younger son finally done what she wanted and found a most acceptable wife, he had found one whose noble lineage would impress even the most snobbish of her friends in Norwich.

Even brother Giles expressed his pleasure at the news, though Adam had little doubt that, once he was back at home, he was likely to reflect more unhappily on the combined fortune his wealthy younger brother and his rich new bride would possess between them.

Adam's final act — or so he believed — was to write to Wicken to tell him the news of his forthcoming marriage. This he did on the next day, when he returned to his house in Aylsham, sending his groom, William, to Norwich to deliver the letter to the post office there. You may imagine his surprise, therefore, when Hannah came to him barely an hour later to say that a King's Messenger had arrived, bearing a package from London.

Inside, he found a letter from Wicken, expressing his warmest congratulations and very best wishes for Adam's and Lady Alice's future together.

'I felt sure,' Wicken wrote, 'that you and the lady would take the occasion of her nephew's wedding to announce your own betrothal. This time, you need not credit me with more than the usual common sense and observational skills I was born with. For several weeks now, it has been plain enough what was in the air. To say that I am delighted is to make a gross understatement. You may see the enclosed document as both an expression of the gratitude of your King and country for all that you have done, and a small gift to establish you and your lady in an appropriate position in society.'

The second document proved to be a copy of the Royal Proclamation by which the King now created Adam a baronet. It was as Sir Adam and Lady Alice Bascom that the couple would begin their married life.

All Adam could do at that moment was think about his mother and his brother. Mrs Bascom might very well faint from joy and pride; the good ladies of Norwich would become thoroughly tired of remarks beginning, 'My son, the baronet'; and his brother would probably never speak to him again!

8 22486

001003

Printed in Great Britain
by Amazon